THE CUSTOMERS

Talon Hawke Ellis

Talon Hawke Ellis

Copyright © 2025 Talon Hawke Ellis

All rights reserved

The characters and events portrayed in this book are used fictitiously. Any similarity to real persons, living or dead, is coincidental and not intended by the author.

No part of this book may be reproduced, or stored in a retrieval system, or transmitted in any form or by any means, electronic, mechanical, photocopying, recording, or otherwise, without express written permission of the publisher.

ISBN-Ebook 979-8-9927197-0-3

ISBN-Paperback 979-8-9927197-1-0

Cover design by: Elise Juvan

Library of Congress Control Number:2025903788

Printed in the United States of America

CONTENTS

Title Page
Copyright
The Customers
Chapter 1   1
Chapter 2   4
Chapter 3   9
Chapter 4   13
Chapter 5   19
Chapter 6   25
Chapter 7   35
Chapter 8   37
Chapter 9   39
Chapter 10   47
Chapter 11   50
Chapter 12   56
Chapter 13   59
Chapter 14   62
Chapter 15   64
Chapter 16   69
Chapter 17   75
Chapter 18   80

Chapter 19	87
Chapter 20	90
Chapter 21	92
Chapter 22	95
Chapter 23	100
Chapter 24	104
Chapter 25	111
Chapter 26	125
Chapter 27	128
Chapter 28	134
Chapter 29	140
Chapter 30	150
Chapter 31	155
Chapter 32	163
Chapter 33	167
Chapter 34	173
Chapter 35	176
Chapter 36	183
Chapter 37	190
Chapter 38	195
Chapter 39	198
Chapter 40	202
Chapter 41	210
Chapter 42	214
Chapter 43	219
Chapter 44	227
Chapter 45	231
Chapter 46	239

Chapter 47	241
Chapter 48	246
Chapter 49	249
Chapter 50	251
Chapter 51	255
Chapter 52	260
Chapter 53	265
Chapter 54	270
Chapter 55	272
Epilogue	275
The Customers	279
About The Author	281

THE CUSTOMERS

CHAPTER 1

6:20 AM

I look out the tall glass windows, eyes surveying the horizon. Soon, the night's brooding blue will dissolve into the warmth of a brilliant orange, washing away the remnants of last night's nightmares with the hopeful glow of a fresh day.

I begin to unlock the doors to the Lil' Cup coffee shop. *What a dumb name*, I think. *Where do you work?* someone will ask. *Oh, uh, the Lil' Cup.*

Welcome to the Lil' Cup.

I mean, who wants a little cup? Especially in a world where Ventis and Grandes rule. But the owners are in their seventies—older seventies—and they're not exactly asking for my opinion. Mr. Edwin Grant only hired me, their sole employee, as a favor to his wife. "We're even now," he had said to her.

He's as stubborn as the rusted backdoor lock that screeches and resists as I try to turn it. Even my most minor suggestions—like to put the cups closer to the register or to offer something other than the few items on the menu—get shot down. Now, I need to figure out what to do with the big bottle of caramel I bought last month.

Mrs. Grant is much more open-minded than her husband, and I've gotten to know her a little better.

One evening, as we were closing the shop together, she told me the story of her strange name—Margarine. During a bygone era, when butter was scarce and names were rarer, her parents thought, *Let's name our firstborn daughter after a butter alternative*. That's what she thinks, anyway.

From her stories, I've pieced together a picture of her early life: Margarine, the overlooked firstborn, standing in the shadow of her younger sister, Virginia—the dazzling "beautiful-eyed Virginia," as Mrs. Grant calls her. Virginia was the family's pride, destined to carry their legacy. But everything changed when Virginia vanished as a child, around twelve years of age.

After her disappearance, Virginia became more than just a memory; she became a revered ideal, the crown jewel in a string of shimmery stories, polished into perfection through years of retelling. I like to seek details about Virginia to pass the time, but Mrs. Grant inevitably gets sidetracked with stocking shelves or wiping smudges from the windows, leaving her sister's story suspended in the air, like an unfinished melody.

I haven't gotten very far. I tried searching for her online, only to find thousands of news articles about vanishing little girls. The closest match was an old story from the early eighties about a couple in Jacksonville, Florida, whose daughter was kidnapped from their front lawn, only to be found the next day. Mrs. Grant is as local to Slidell as they come, and the family from the internet story had just one daughter. There are too many differences in that case to be related to Virginia's story.

Mrs. Grant's other stories always center on Mr. Grant.

"Eddy hasn't always been so strict," she said once with a tone of nostalgia.

I don't know much else about Mrs. Grant. I don't think they have children; that topic has never come up. And I get the sense that she doesn't know who she is without her husband—I don't think she ever has. Still, there's something endearing about her. The way her soft, veiny, fragile hands wash coffee mugs while dancing to a song in her head is somehow reassuring. She seems so content.

I always enjoy opening the shop this time of year. The weather has cooled down following the intense summer heat of Slidell. The warm asphalt, heated by the sun, mixes with the cooler October air, creating a mesmerizing fog that rolls through historic downtown.

Almost five years in, I've memorized every car that's parked outside. Not that it's difficult. How hard is it to remember the obnoxious orange of the boxy car always parked across the street? Then there's the generic row of the same cars, always parked next to each other in various combinations on the opposite side of the street. It's almost as if they're in some exclusive club only that brand of car can join. I sometimes like to imagine that they are the cool kids in school and that ugly box car is the foreign exchange student who comes dressed in hideous clothes from his homeland. Come on square car, park on the other side. Just this once. Give my brain some new material to work with.

When I get lost in these ridiculous thoughts, I wish even more that Mr. Grant would let me listen to music while I open. I have a jazz playlist that would pair perfectly with the ambiance. The customers would love it too.

I know the first customer is always one of three.

CHAPTER 2

6:30 AM

The first possibility is Liz, a middle-aged woman who always smells like cheap vanilla air freshener. I imagine that in every outlet of her house, there's an automatic sprayer spitting a steady stream of toxic incense into the air. Maybe a desperate attempt to mask the stench of cigarettes—a semblance of a fresh start? I'm pretty sure she's divorced or unhappily married; all signs point to it. The way she fiddled with her bare ring finger last week while trying to decide which pastry to pair with her drip coffee. The bags under her eyes point to countless sleepless and teary nights. The nicotine under her pink, chipped nail polish makes me think she lives a life of struggle. Her brown hair is always in a bun. I imagine she throws it up haphazardly, the same way she sloppily slides into her slippers to walk out the door to her first and maybe only destination of the day: the Lil' Cup.

She's a decent tipper, though, especially if I pretend to be interested in listening to her go on about how men are inferior to women.

"Except for you, Mark," she once said. "You're a gentleman and a credit to your kind."

I feel sorry for her, but not in a condescending way. Rather, I'm genuinely sad that her life has fallen into such disarray. I doubt it was always like that. The contours of her face suggest she was once a natural beauty—maybe even that pretty girl in high school that everyone had a crush on. But now she seems to be withering on her path to old age, when she'll be filled with warning stories—not for grandchildren, though. Maybe she'll tell them to the women in the neighborhood or at the local bingo club.

She asked me out once. People do say I look a lot older than twenty-three. And what is a fifteen-year age gap, anyway? I had to make up a quick lie.

"Oh, I'm flattered," I started. "I wish the timing were better... but I'm in a semi-long-term relationship with the most beautiful girl. You would love her."

That seemed to do the trick. But now Liz has been begging me to meet her. I think she might be on to me.

"She's been gone all summer doing volunteer work for a church," I told her some time ago.

It's a pretty good lie, given Slidell's long history of women taking the lead in church activities. But I don't know whether Liz, a Seattle native, even knows that. My lie keeps getting harder to track. Now that summer has come and gone, I know she'll ask again about my made-up girlfriend.

I've enjoyed imagining this girlfriend. She has blonde, wavy hair and silky smooth, olive skin with the faintest freckles —splattered across her nose as if a painter had added them as one last touch.

I hope Liz doesn't come in today. Lying is exhausting, and I'm not up for it today.

The other regular who comes early is Gage, one of the quirkiest guys I know. Sometimes he's quiet and withdrawn, and other times he's bursting with energy. Once, he ranted in a panicked tone for about twenty minutes about our city's declining population. I politely nodded. It would be nice to have less traffic and keep our urban city quiet. Although, with just 28,000 residents, our city is hardly bustling over.

"It's the attitudes of the people here," Gage declared, his hands slicing the air for emphasis. "Not to mention the flooding issues."

This was by far the most uninteresting conversation I had engaged in all year, all for a fifty-cent tip.

Gage had been my very first customer on my first day of training with Mr. Grant. He had ordered his usual cappuccino—

dry with two percent milk. Gage always orders the same thing. It's easy to make—not that I have many options.

"I'm sorry, all we have is whole," I said, searching the mini fridge behind the bar.

"He knows," Mr. Grant said. "He's just testing you."

Gage let out a chuckle. "You got me," he said, clearly amused by his own humor.

I forced myself to join the laughter.

Gage is an intelligent, balding man, with a few strands of hair clinging to both sides of his head. "I'm hoping it's like a tsunami," he explained once. "It will recede to a certain point, and then, suddenly, when you least expect it—poof! A full head of hair with nothing to contain it."

I can't remember how his hair became the topic of conversation that day, but the image he painted stuck with me. So far, his tsunami theory hasn't materialized. He now wears an ivy newsboy cap.

I mostly like Gage. I just wish I could get him on a topic I want to discuss. But whenever I try to bring something up that I'm excited about—like the Saints or a planned vacation—his face gives away his boredom. Those conversations fizzle out, and he inevitably retreats to his usual spot by the front window, sipping his cappuccino while watching the joggers pass by in their sports bras and leggings. That's the only "sport" he likes to watch. Maybe I'll try talking to him about his taste in women next time. He might be interested in that conversation.

I do have to give him some credit. He's a knowledgeable man, and he did get me thinking about why the town's population is declining. I believe it has less to do with flooding and more to do with the sheer boredom of living here. Or maybe it's the supposed curse of the town everyone jokes about, an old Onionhead man.

Esther is the only other person I can expect first thing in the morning. She's the overworked, stressed-out assistant at Grimaldis' Justice for All, just a block away. She's been there for five years now, stuck working for two of the most awful men imaginable. They both have hairy chests visible through their half-buttoned shirts and matching gold chains with their initials—G—studded with diamonds. The G stands for Grimaldi, as in "Grimaldis' Justice for All—we fight for the little guy!" That's the locally televised commercial that plays during the nightly news, which airs during the midnight rerun. They're too cheap to buy a slot during the prime time 8 p.m. broadcast. Also, I imagine they target criminals who watch TV at that late hour, in desperate need of a lawyer to get them out of who knows what. And that's who Esther—sweet Esther—works for.

Esther and I shared most of the same classes in school after she moved here from New Orleans at the age of thirteen. She was shy and soft-spoken, with the gentlest voice that I had ever heard. But she had a way of making me laugh like no one else could. I knew I loved her the moment her hand shot up to answer a question our freshman history teacher asked: "During which war was the Christmas Truce called?"

She raised her hand sky-high without hesitation, although it was the first week of the new semester, and I'm pretty sure none of us had bothered with the winter break assignments.

"World War One," she said, her voice clear and confident.

At that moment, I saw another side of my timid friend. She was brilliant. She *is* brilliant. Her peaceful demeanor stood in contrast to my loud, outspoken mom and sister. I always thought she would make it out of this small town and go on to some prestigious college. Now that I think of it, my made-up girlfriend is kind of like Esther.

For years, Esther has been making coffee runs for the brothers, whose annoying motto and oversized, grotesque frames are posted on almost half of the billboards and bus stop benches in town. Every time I see them, I'm infuriated. They have turned my peaceful best friend into an anxious, overworked young woman who never seems to smile anymore. Invariably, she orders the same three drinks: two double-shot lattes for the Grimaldi brothers and an iced decaf latte for herself. I've been offering her some of the caramel I bought to switch things up. I think she enjoys it, but it's difficult to know what she's feeling these days.

She always looks professional, with vibrant red lipstick and dirty blonde hair that alternates between two styles—either perfectly straightened or pulled into a pristine ponytail. Her pencil skirts are always black or brown, and her varying blouses—those are the only hint of the fun girl I used to know. My favorite is the one with vertical black stripes. I tease her, calling her the referee from the football games we used to watch together on Friday nights. Come to think of it, I haven't seen that shirt in a while. I hope she's the first one to come in today. There's something I've been meaning to talk to her about—plans we've been discussing since senior year, plans that had taken an unexpected turn.

Bang! A car door slams, interrupting my thoughts.

CHAPTER 3

6:49 AM

I recognize the obnoxious sound of the back door swinging open.

"Kid, can I get some help over here?" Mr. Grant's strained voice demands.

Rounding the corner, I see him balancing the back door open with his foot stretched out while suspending three heavy boxes full of supplies for the week on his skinny, shriveling leg.

"I wish you would get a distributor to help with these deliveries," I say stepping to grab the top box. "Actually, one just came in the other day asking if we needed—"

"No, no!" Mr. Grant snaps, his tone sharp and final. "We have been doing things this way for the past twenty-five years, and if you change things now, the entire operation will come crashing down on us."

Like those boxes, I think, *ready to crash down on his fragile frame.*

"I understand, but at the very least, let me do these pickups for you. Where do you get the supplies from, anyway?" My words float in the air as he changes the topic.

"Have you counted the money yet in the drawer for the day?" he asks intently.

"Yep, all $325 is accounted for and ready to go," I say, still wondering why he insists on that specific amount.

"What about the drip? Is it brewing? I don't smell it."

"Yes, it is already brewing," I respond confidently. I continue before he can speak again, "The coffee is brewing, the grinder settings are set at 1.5 grams for the espresso, and the shots are pulling at twenty-six seconds."

"Twenty-six seconds?" he interrupts in a panic. "It's supposed to be twenty-five!"

"Yes, of course; that's what I meant; I just misspoke. It is twenty-five seconds. And the cups are where you like them, the tables are all sanitized clean, and the advertisement sign is out and ready to draw customers inside."

I rattle off ten more mundane details about what I did in the last half an hour, hoping he might overlook the twenty-six second mishap. No such luck.

"Excellent, Mark," he says at last, heading behind the bar. "I will pull myself an espresso shot while you open the door."

As I swing the front door open, I hear the grinder hum, filling the portafilter. Hot water pressures through the finely tamped grounds. I'm mesmerized as I watch the caramel-colored espresso drip effortlessly into the shot glass. A single shot represents endless possibilities. So much can be added to extract distinct notes from the coffee bean. That's why I bought the caramel. I knew it would pair nicely with the nutty, chocolate notes from the beans we had imported from Guatemala.

A few summers ago, during a trip to California with my family, I stumbled upon an ultra-modern coffee shop. The moment I stepped in, I was captivated by the design—an all-white bar with sleek tiles throughout, blending into the tiled floor beneath. Industrial-size ceiling fans humming overhead, an exposed brick wall to my right, and a rustic wooden plank wall behind the baristas complemented the modern aesthetic. Toward the back, a display featured coffee beans imported from around the world along with neatly arranged brand merchandise.

As I approached the menu and surveyed possibilities of creative drink options, a wave of pure envy washed over me. I wanted to work here. I wanted to say, "I work at High Tide Coffee."

With so many options, a flicker of doubt crept in. Maybe they are using an elaborate menu to mask the taste of horrible beans. So, I opted for a straight espresso shot.

When it arrived, served in a delicate glass with space at the bottom to give the illusion of the coffee floating, I knew I was in for a treat. One sip confirmed it: the shot perfectly balanced bitterness and acidity. The fruity notes burst through, vivid and refreshing, like drinking freshly squeezed juice. It was transformative—an espresso unlike anything I've ever tasted.

One thought consumed me as I savored the last drop: *How can I replicate this at the Lil' Cup?*

"Mark," Mr. Grant sighs, "my shot pulled at twenty-seven seconds. You need to get this adjusted before the first customer comes in. We can't be serving it this way."

"Ok, I'll get right on it, but I think it's because I opened the door," I say as I walk toward Mr. Grant. "I've noticed the cooler, humid mornings affect the espresso's pull."

I hear the door open behind me, and I wonder who the first customer will be today as I turn around.

Through the lingering morning fog emerges in a man I don't recognize. He's tall, 6'2" at least, with a lanky physique. Dark grey eyes, and deep, canyon-like wrinkles on his forehead give him a stern expression that instantly reminds me of my father. His stride is deliberate, purposeful, as he approaches.

"Are you Mr. Grant?" he asks.

Mr. Grant looks up from the grinder, pausing briefly. "Yes, and who are you?"

"Just someone looking for the famous coffee guru I've heard so much about," he says in a somewhat familiar tone.

"And who, may I ask, has been singing such high praises about me?" Mr. Grant asks, slipping into the false humility he's mastered over the years.

"The better question," the man says, "is who hasn't?"

I step forward. "What can I get started for you, sir?"

The man looks through me; his attention remains fixed on Mr. Grant. "I've been told you have many close connections with local businesses in town. I was wondering if you could help me learn a little more about your friends—the Grimaldis."

"The Grimaldis are open books; why don't you just walk on into their office and ask them your questions?" Mr. Grant says with a slightly dismissive tone.

"Oh, I suppose I will," the man replies. "In the meantime, can I get two shots of espresso over ice? And do you have any sparkling water?"

"I'll take this one, kid," Mr. Grant says, wedging his petite frame between me and the register. "How about you go in the back and grab the croissants out of the oven?"

Just when something interesting finally happens in this place, I'm excused. I do as I'm told and head to the back. I strain to catch snippets of their conversation. But it's hard to make out much of anything they say.

The front door chimes, and I figure that either the man has left, or one of the three regulars has stumbled into an uncomfortable scene.

When I return, the stern man is sitting in the far corner of the shop, espresso in hand and a laptop open before him. But where is Mr. Grant? He never leaves out the front door, especially without giving me some last-minute unnecessary advice. I glance at the man in the corner who seems far too amused with himself. The espresso shots can't be that good. What was all that about?

Before I can puzzle over it further, in walks a familiar face.

CHAPTER 4

7:25 AM

Gage steps through the door with an unusual pep in his step. His buoyance contrasts with the somber atmosphere still lingering in the air. Outside, the fog has grown so dense that even the bright orange of the square car is no longer visible.

"What can I get started for you?" I ask.

"Let me get a cappuccino. . .. And what kind of tea are you serving today?"

Tea? Since when does Gage ask about tea?

"Lemon ginger today," I reply.

That's about the only thing on the menu that ever changes. Mrs. Grant likes to match the tea selection to the weather. She missed the mark with this one, though. It's her first miss, now that I think of it.

"Ok, one of those, please," Gage says.

I wonder if he's meeting a woman today. He balances the two full drinks with care as he walks over, not to his usual spot, but to a table right in the middle of the room. Ironic. I'd been longing for a change from the normal routine, and yet, with Gage changing the most minor detail of his order and where he sits, Mr. Grant's sudden and unexplainable departure, and the mystery man lurking in the corner, I'm left feeling uneasy.

By the time 8:30 a.m. rolls around, my tip jar is up to $6, the shop is about sixty percent full, and the customers have been complimenting the coffee all morning. Far more than usual. The espresso machine is still pulling shots at twenty-seven seconds. That can't be the reason for the accolades, can it? At any rate, the hum of conversation fills the air, and for a moment, I feel a bit more content despite the unsettling shifts in the day. Now, more than ever, I deeply yearn for a feeling I once had.

I long for the way I felt with Esther.

Five years. That's all I needed. Five years to give back to the parents who gave me eighteen. My plan *is* going as expected. I wish Esther were here now. I want to tell her about the coffee truck I've been saving for—our dream from senior year. We had outgrown Slidell. Between her abusive father and brothers and my own family struggles, we needed to leave this place. Our goal was to drive until we found a new start somewhere—anywhere but here. But money was tight, and that dream disappeared, much like Virginia Rose. But unlike her, I may have found it again.

Debt has piled up to a point where all my dad can do is set up a payment plan, one he's concluded he'll need to pay off until he and mom are gone. I'm not expected to contribute, but the weight presses on me anyway.

If only I could talk to Esther like we used to. I've missed her so much. These days, I see her for maybe about five minutes, four days a week. When she orders her usual drinks, I always find ways to stall. I'll pretend the grinder isn't working or I'll put the steam wand in the milk without turning it on. I wonder if she notices.

She's so used to toxic relationships that I doubt she even realizes the impact those Grimaldi lawyers have had on her. I think I may be the only healthy human connection she's ever had. When I finally built up the courage to tell her I loved her years ago, her reaction said it all. She was a girl who had never experienced real love from anyone. Her mother left when she was still a baby to get away from their father, Brandon Foster. He turned to the bottle. Esther's brothers, Moab and Cain, both imposing figures at well over six feet and approximately 220 pounds each, became notorious around town for their racism and criminal activities.

I'll never forget my last encounter with Esther's family. I was picking her up for a movie, though I can't remember which one, probably something that would teleport her far from her reality.

When I pulled up to her house, a decent-sized structure badly in need of repairs, I heard muffled sounds from inside. As Esther opened the door to meet me, I could hear a very loud argument—the kind of angry shouting that still echoes in my mind.

"You need to leave now. Go!" she commanded.

At that moment, Moab's larger-than-life frame appeared and he barreled straight into me. I stumbled back, but anger surged in my chest. I stepped forward, ready to defend Esther.

Esther got between us, extending both of her arms to keep us apart. I noticed on her delicate hands the bracelet I had bought for her earlier that year, and on her arm—a dark bruise.

Moab flung her to the ground and came straight up to me. He cold-cocked me right across my jaw, and I fell flat on the opposite side of my face. Before I could rise, he stomped on my stomach, barely missing my sternum. For a horrifying moment, I couldn't breathe, my lungs gasping for oxygen.

"The girl said to leave," he growled before dragging Esther back inside.

Moments later, I crawled back to my car, every moment a painful struggle. I drove home, calling her nonstop. But she didn't answer.

She snuck out later that night and came to my house. Her body slid through effortlessly into my bedroom and straight into my arms. She spent the entire night tending to my wounds, even though she had her own. When I tried to check the bruises on her arm, she flinched.

"They should be arrested for this," I said.

"There's no point," she said quietly as she held an ice pack on my ribs. "You know who they are and the connections they have. I don't want you to risk your life any more than you already have."

She was right, of course. The G Brothers are her family's lawyers. It's some sort of trade-off, I assume. But Mr. Foster's job as a service technician should be enough for them to get by, I had figured.

She then noticed the bluish grey, swollen area where my eye was once visible.

She slid my hair that I had combed to cover the obscene mark and pressed her lips softly on the throbbing eyelid.

"We will be out of here soon, my love," she whispered.

But I could not make those dreams a reality for her.

The last conversation we had was on Friday.

"Hey, Esther, you look as lovely as ever this morning," I said. Where did that even come from? I must have heard too many stories from Mr. and Mrs. Grant's era.

I did want to fan a dormant spark in a relationship that was my entire world—and still is.

She looked down ever so slightly at what she was wearing, and a smile appeared for a second. In that moment, she looked eighteen again, untouched by time. My heart felt like it had stopped; I realized I had been holding my breath. Once again, I felt a slight burning in my lungs.

She stepped closer, rested her hands on the counter, and tilted her head slightly to look at me.

"I wish you wouldn't say things like that."

"Why not?" I asked, struggling to find my voice.

"You know why. I may be smarter than you, but I think you can figure this one out," she teased.

During the last five years, I 've been saving every penny for her—for us. But did I wait too long? Did her life move on without me while I was stuck in the limbo of this coffee shop? That day didn't seem like the right one to tell her about my plans. After waiting so long, I wanted it to be perfect.

This day is moving at a methodical pace now. At some point, Gage apparently left without me noticing. A break in the steady line of customers that has been inundating me for the last hour and a half allows me to collect some dishes. As I approach Gage's table, I'm struck with a pang of empathy. His smaller cappuccino cup is empty, but the other cup filled with our out-of-season tea, sits untouched.

Poor guy. He probably got stood up.

With all the chaos of the morning rush, I didn't even think to check in with him. I can relate to Gage because I've been waiting for a girl too. The only difference is, I know exactly who I'm waiting for. Gage probably doesn't. I wonder which is worse.

I notice the mysterious man with the stern face still sitting in the corner. I can feel his eyes on me. Every time I glance his way, he abruptly pretends to focus on his laptop.

"Excuse me, may I get another glass of water?" he asks.

"Sure thing."

I go to the fridge, grab the bottle of bubbly water, walk to his table, and twist off the lid. The effervescence bubbles up to the top of the bottle, which always satisfies me.

"Oh, so you do have sparkling water," he says with a smile.

Surprised, I look at the bottle. Why does Mr. Grant constantly put me in awkward situations?

"Oh uh, well, this was my personal—"

"It's ok; I'm kidding," he interrupts, his tone suddenly more genuine. "I know the owner doesn't like me."

He sounds different now—less guarded.

"I guess I came in a little strong. I need a lawyer, you see, because of a little legal trouble."

I take an unconscious step back with my left foot.

"Nothing like that," he says quickly, reading my unease. He takes a sip of the chilled soda water. "Never get married, kid."

Little does he know that's the entirety of my goal—the one thing I've been working towards for years. Maybe his relationship didn't work out, but I'm going to marry my best friend, the girl of my dreams, the one I should never have let go. This is nonsense, I tell myself. He's just a man down on his luck.

Still, the question lingers: Why didn't Mr. Grant give him any sparkling water? Of course, we have sparkling water. The Grants love to talk about how much better things are in Europe, where they traveled for their 25th wedding anniversary.

"They would offer still or sparkling water wherever we went" Mr. Grant always says.

The Lil' Cup has had sparkling water since he opened the shop. It helps cleanse the palate after drinking straight espresso. This mystery man clearly knows coffee, and I'm intrigued.

"I never caught your name," I say, trying to make up for any awkwardness in the conversation.

"Phillip, and yours?"

"I'm Mark."

"Mark what?" he asks, pulling out a pen from his jacket.

Nobody asks for last names in a coffee shop. It's always first names, except for Mr. and Mrs. Grant. Where is Mr. Grant? I wonder. He still needs to come for his noon check-in.

"Mark Stratford," I respond, instantly regretting it.

What could he possibly want with my last name?

"What is your last name?" I ask in kind.

He smiles, amused. "I like you, Mr. Stratford. A piece of advice: keep the coffee pulling at twenty-seven seconds like you have been. It allows time for the deeper notes of the bean to extract."

"Will do, sir," I say as I turn and walk toward the back.

When did he figure out how I time the shots?

What an interesting man! I've never been called Mr. before—was that deliberate? Was he somehow aware of my need for validation from older figures and used it to distract me from the fact that he never responded to my question?

He finally leaves around 1 o'clock.

CHAPTER 5

5:05 PM

"Hey, floss stick!" shouts my most annoying customer as she flings open the door and startles all the customers.

Everyone looks my way with amused smiles, trying to decipher the meaning of the nickname. They won't, of course—it's as nonsensical as the girl who said it.

"What would you like to drink?" I ask, my impatience clear as I lock eyes with my sister.

Dressed in black leggings, a sports bra, and a thin, white jacket zipped halfway up, she looks as if she just came from the gym.

We share lean builds with broad shoulders. At 5'9", she's taller than me by a centimeter, which has always irked me.

Her hair is dark like mine. And we both have sharp jawlines, only hers is a little softer. Her cheeks sit high and proud, and her face is longer than wide. My cheeks are much softer, and my face is more proportional with width and height —at least that's what I think.

"I'm looking, I'm looking," she replies under her breath as if she has never seen our menu before.

She scans the few items for about five minutes while I clean the dishes piled up in the kitchen.

"Hey, do you have any of those churro croissants in the back?" she asks.

"Churro?" I respond. "I don't know what you're talking about."

I do know what she's talking about. We started ordering them from the local bakery. I like to think they're better than the ones imported straight from Paris.

"Check behind the counter, far right," I say, glancing at my reflection in a glossy black mug. Has my hair really looked this disheveled all day? I've never liked the way my hairline curves like a helmet. I try to grow it out; that's the way Esther likes it. But now it's too long, and it's driving me crazy.

"Oh shoot, I forgot," I blurt out. "Hey, Meg, please call Dad. I'll be late for dinner tonight. I—"

"No, no, no," she interrupts, "I will not be the middleman for you two anymore. If you're bailing last minute, tell him yourself."

"Fine. I guess you'll have to watch me eat this," I say, grabbing the bag with the croissant out of her hand. "I wonder what life would be like if you thought about helping others for once."

"Ok, you win, I'll do it; I was kidding anyway. You know I would do anything for you, bro," she says in an exaggeratedly affectionate tone.

"Yeah, sure I do. Anyway, like I was saying, I'm going to check out the listing for that food truck I showed you over a week ago. The guy finally got back to me, and we'll discuss a price."

"That's great!" she exclaims, her mouth full of churro croissant, sugar dusting her face.

"What time?"

"8 o'clock," I respond, widening my eyes as I see she's already devoured the whole pastry.

"Where is the house?" she asks.

"On the other side of the tracks, by the graveyard."

Her expression becomes deadpan and worried as if she just spotted a ghost.

"Mark, do you think that's such a good idea to go to where —"

"Where the Onionhead roams?" I shrug. "I think I'll be fine."

She looks confused for a moment, takes a big swallow of her food, and forces a smile.

"Do you really believe that whole thing?" she asks.

"Hey, I'm not sure what I believe. But I do know some credible people who claimed to have seen a man with the most disgusting face roaming the area. Just last week, a customer came from Florida to write a paper on it."

"Yeah, have you ever seen *The Village*?" she asks, a smirk creeping onto her face.

"I have, and I know where you're going with this," I say, acting superior for not buying into her knockoff idea from an admittedly scary movie. "I don't believe that whole conspiracy that the mayor is dressing up like an Onionhead guy from the 1900s just to drive up tourism."

The story of the Onionhead was passed down by local families that lived in the 1920s, and each generation has added its own twist. To say that it might be embellished by now is an understatement. But it's a blast to tell. I like to refer to him as, Silas. It's a way to humanize him. The stories are either told firsthand or paraphrased from online articles. Meg told it to me years ago. I like the way the customer from Florida retold it. He even included the fake name I came up with. He thought it was an eerie touch.

Silas was born with a rare disease that made his head unusually large. For the mother's sake, I hope that deformity came after his birth.

Life was already difficult enough for fatherless children, let alone one with a gross looking medical condition. Usually, a couple of oddball kids will band together to help dilute some of the verbal abuse. Not so with Silas. He had to bear the full brunt of these vicious attacks alone.

Without a husband to protect and provide for the family, his mother did what she thought was best. She relocated with her son to an uninhabited part of Slidell far away from civilization.

The young boy became increasingly curious about the world around him and started roaming the woods near his home. It is said that he fell in love with climbing trees a way of escapism.

He started to push his luck, and his curiosity led him to spying on kids from the trees. He wanted to be one of them. He wanted to be accepted.

I'm sure he longed to understand their games and dreamed of joining their shenanigans. He was like the human essence of that cube shaped car—utterly out of place. And he was painfully aware of it.

Before long, his curiosity got the best of him.

Stories about the Onionhead spread quickly. Rumors that there was a monster who lurks beyond the tree line, ready to abduct innocent travelers and towns people.

As the years passed, the stories transformed the Onionhead from a boy suffering from deformity into a monster. He should have been the victim. This unjust world made him the villain. There are many variations of the story, but this is a constant feature. And this is how legends grow, by slowly distorting the truth.

He was soon blamed for atrocities committed by other criminals in the area. A girl was found murdered by the train tracks. Others say she went missing. Naturally, local legend and rumors lend to blaming the monster in the woods.

Determined to find the monster and bring justice, a mob traversed the harsh terrain of the swamp. They spotted Silas and began sprinting after him.

He ran through the familiar terrain. He knew every tree, every rock, every puddle, and sprinted toward the only refuge he had ever known: home.

But the angry mob was chasing close behind. And the Onionhead couldn't outrun the shots from their rifles.

They killed the boy, dismembered his body, and scattered his remains.

The mother screamed at the men, swearing revenge, as they quickly retreated without a word. Other renditions say it was the mother that was killed, and that Silas swore revenge.

The mother would have no doubt held a burial service for Silas.

I wonder if she buried his remnants without a tombstone, next to his father—whom he had never met. But if it was the mother who died, did Silas ever get to bury her? Would he have known about that simple tradition?

Regardless of who died, the legend of the Onionhead refused to.

Older brothers, or in my case, sister, like to scare younger siblings with the legend. Fathers share the spooky tale with their families as they roast s'mores by the campfire. Boys in my high school would take girls to the cemetery and tell them the story. Inevitably, the girls find themselves wrapped in the strong, protective arms of the boy. It worked perfectly every time.

I never took Esther. I always believed that I didn't need a foolish story to provide her with a sense of security. Instead, all she needed was a listening ear, to know that someone would be there for her unconditionally.

The streetlights flicker outside as the sun begins to set. A woman quietly writes in the corner. She's a semi-regular customer, though I can't even remember her name. A man is sitting in Gage's usual spot, sipping on a latte, while two teenage girls giggle as they share pictures from their social media and mindlessly scroll. And then there's Meg, sitting at the table closest to the bar. She had gone out back for an hour, and when she came back, she devoured the leftover pastries. I'm pretty sure she's high.

In my opinion, things at home have affected her more than they've affected me. It probably has to do with the timing. When I first found out, I was with Esther. As for Meg, she had a couple of non-exclusive flings, but nothing to distract her enough from the heartbreak we were both dealing with. It was around that time that she started experimenting with other non-human distractions. I've never asked her about it, and I'm too scared to implicate myself in any illegal things she might be involved in.

It looks like I'm going to have to drive tonight. I was hoping she would. She's the worst at giving directions. *Next right* means, *Not this one, but the next one*. She gives no warning but blurts out *left* or *right* immediately before a turn.

I, on the other hand, like to give precise and easy-to-follow directions.

"Ok, Meg, do you see that tree swing? Start slowing down; the right should be immediately after the speed limit sign."

How hard is that?

CHAPTER 6

6:01 PM

$67.30 is in the safe. (I got $18 in tips today.) The drawer is at double zeros, the coffee pot is cleaned with the timer set for Mrs. Grant's opening tomorrow, and the floor is swept—all in record time.

When I started sweeping by their table, the two girls who were lost in their phones left. Without fail, it works every time. I don't usually do this unless I work a double shift or I have plans. And today, both are true.

"Meg, you ready? Before we look at the truck, I want to swing by Mr. and Mrs. Grant's to check on them."

"Let me use the restroom first; it's about a twenty-five-minute drive to the address you sent me," she replies, her tone nonchalant and irritating.

"Well, in that case, hurry up. It's in the opposite direction of Mr. Grant's house, so we're looking at a minimum of an hour's drive."

"What's the rush? He told you 8:00," Meg barks back.

I ignore her snappy retort as she walks to the restroom next to the kitchen. I walk toward the front glass, checking for smudges.

"Sometimes you have to bend down and look at it from different angles," Mrs. Grant's sweet old voice echoes in my mind.

I hear the toilet flush, thankfully only after thirty seconds. I was hoping Meg wouldn't dirty my freshly cleaned restroom.

"Ok, I'm ready. Are we going out the back?" she asks.

I barely hear her as I try to comprehend what I'm seeing.

"Where is the orange car?" I mutter under my breath.

"What was that?" Meg asks, genuinely interested.

"Oh, it's nothing really. There's always an orange boxy car, that square car made over a decade ago, parked right across the street over there."

"And?"

"This is the first time I haven't seen it there—not since I started working here."

"You're not as observant as you like to think," she says scornfully.

"No, I know, but seriously, with my boring view, it's easy to memorize these things. You see the cookie cutter cars parked across the street, but the next block up?" I ask.

"Yeah, what about them?"

"Well, those three cars are always parked there, and right over here," I point back to the left where the vehicle is usually located, "is where this ugly burnt orange car is always parked."

"So, what do you think happened?" she asks with her usual attitude. "Do you think they left early to go rob a bank?"

"Ok, mock me; you don't understand how strange this is because you don't see it every day like I do."

"Yeah, you're right. I don't," she says, laughing. "Let's go already."

We walk out the back. Meg grabs the two bags of trash I had set out and throws them in the dumpster.

"What made you do that?" I ask.

"Just being helpful."

I guess there is a first time for anything, I think but don't say out loud. We head to my car, an older silver manual. It's more basic than the base model. Automatic locks did not come with my car. It's a pain in the butt, but it does get excellent gas mileage.

Meg tugs on the car's handle so aggressively that I swear she's going to pull it off.

"Chill out," I call out from inside the car.

As I lean over to unlock the door, she swings it open and almost sits on my head.

"Why don't you get that fixed?"

"Because it's not broken, and I won't spend that kind of money when the car's value isn't even worth that much," I say, thinking that will end the conversation.

"Maybe the car's value would rise if you invested something into it," she says. "Dad bought you this car to last, and at this rate, you will take public transportation by the end of the year."

She never used to talk like this. Our family's money problems must be clouding her thinking.

"Did you call Dad?" I ask.

"What do you think I was doing for so long outside?" she says, "He was devastated, of course, that his youngest was abandoning the family. After spending half an hour reassuring him, he accepted the fact that a food truck was more important than parental love."

Ignoring the over-rehearsed guilt trip, I shift the car into reverse, slowly backing up while balancing the clutch with my left foot and the brake with my right, then putting a little pressure on the gas. I'm more of a perfectionist than I'd like to admit. I don't want people riding in my car to be aware it's a manual, even though Meg already knows. Also, if she's been smoking, I need to be extra careful not to get pulled over—and definitely don't want her to get sick and puke in my car.

She spends the drive time heading to the Grant's house fiddling with the air conditioner and heater as if she can't decide whether she's hot or cold. She changes the radio stations and rolls her window up and down. She can't sit still.

I turn down Browns Village Road and notice the Old Rail Hiking Trail to my right. A wave of nostalgia hits me.

I remember the skeptical look on Esther's face the first time I took her there. You won't find the trailhead right off the main road; it was the type of place you'd expect someone to get murdered. The look on her face made me fall in love with her even more. But she trusted me.

We walked about three hundred feet to the tree with the

bright blue spray-painted arrow pointing the way.

"See, I told you it was an actual trail," I had said, relieved when I saw the blue marking on the water oak.

That was our first date. We were in 10th grade. I had offered to pick her up at her house, but she insisted she meet me at the library downtown. Now I know why. I waited almost two hours for her, and by the time she showed up, I could tell she had been crying. She looked beautiful, of course, in her beige turtleneck sweater, light blue jeans, and knee-high suede boots. Her hair was in a loose ponytail, with curtain bangs framing her gorgeous face.

She walked in, scanning the room for me, but I didn't call out to her immediately. I wanted to take in every detail of how she looked in that moment. Her blue eyes were perfectly spaced; her nose sat high on her face, upturned ever so slightly—you would think she had work done on it; her plump lips seemed to beg to be kissed. That night, I was determined to make that happen.

Finally, I called her over, and she walked toward me, squeezing a tissue in her right hand. That was the only sign that she had been crying. I didn't mention it. She'd done her makeup perfectly to conceal it, and I didn't want her to feel like her effort was wasted.

By now, it was dark, and I dropped my plans for an evening picnic at the end of the hike, with the lake as our backdrop.

"I'm sorry I'm late," she said softly, her voice so different from the flat, clipped way people talk around here. "I would have texted, but I don't have my phone. My dad forgot to charge his, and he needed to use mine for work."

"I've been catching up on some reading," I said, holding up her favorite book. She resembles the lead of the book. I know that's why it's her favorite.

"How far did you get?" she asked excitedly.

"Not far. I don't want to hear any spoilers." I said, watching her mind instantly transport to the various scenes in the book.

She was there now. Books were able to transport her from

her own life in a beautiful way.

"You ready for the best night of your life?" I asked, snapping her back to reality.

"I just thought we might go grab milkshakes," she responded.

"We can, or you can come with me on the romantic hike I had planned," I said.

"Hike? But it's dark," she said and gestured to her shoes, "and I'm not really dressed for it."

"Neither am I. Let's go."

The trail was a lot muddier than I thought it would be, but she grabbed my hand and led me right through it.

"Your shoes—" I said as she took that first step, submerging into the muck.

"I've already ruined your picnic; I will not ruin the hike."

"How did you—?"

"I saw it in the back of your car," she said before I could finish. "I'm so sorry. That must have cost a lot of money,"

$34 to be exact.

"No, not really. I wanted to make this special for you," I said.

We had trudged our way through about one-fourth of the trail before our feet were nothing more than muddy stumps.

"What was that?" she whispered abruptly. I turned and stiffened in anticipation.

The soft giggles of the girl to my right was all that followed. She wrapped her leg around mine and with her weight leaning into me, I lost my balance and fell hard on my tailbone. But I didn't even have time to process the pain before she was on top of me, her face inches from me. She leaned in and did the thing I had wanted for so long. Her lips tasted like the peach ChapStick she always kept in her back pocket.

She pulled away, looking at my face as I gazed at her, her hair falling to either side of my head. I reached up to caress her cheek but instantly pulled back as I realized a small trace of mud lingered on my hand. She opened her mouth with the most dramatic, appalled expression and then, smiling, leaned back in for another kiss.

As I drive past this memory with Meg beside me instead of my best friend, I feel a sharp emptiness settle in my stomach. It's been so long. I turn down August Road, where the Grants live, and as I do, the car thumps, causing Meg's feet to fly up off the dashboard and back down just as fast.

"What the heck?" she yells as she lifts back up from her reclined position.

"I'm sorry, I didn't see the pothole," I say, looking around vigilantly for more.

Serves me right for daydreaming about the road behind instead of keeping my eyes on the road in front. Maybe Meg was right; I need to take better care of this car.

I drive up the road, and to my right, I see Mr. and Mrs. Grant's house inset about twenty-five yards into their property. Tall, thin trees line the not-so-well-kept piece of land. I pull off the road into their rocky, private driveway.

"It'll only be a minute," I say as I get out of the car, pulling my hoodie over my head. I hadn't realized how fast the temperature had dropped in the last half hour.

As I walk up to the dark house, I sense an eerie presence. Thoughts of the Onionhead Man watching me from the trees in the back of the house leave me with a sense of being violated.

As I step onto the porch, the floor creaks beneath my feet. The faded white paint that once coated the entire deck is peeling. It must have been beautiful once, but like all good things, it needs maintenance. It's another thing the Grants have neglected on their endless to-do list. If Mr. Grant would let me have more responsibility at work, maybe he would have time to maintain his home.

I raise my fist and knock on the door—seven knocks, I count, then replay the rhythm in my head.

Utter silence. The only sound I hear is the birds high in the tall trees, where the Onionhead Man could be looking down on me. I ring the doorbell. It's old and crusted over because whoever painted it last didn't take time to mask it. Still nothing. The headlights flicker at me as my sister impatiently affirms that no one is home. Or maybe they are already in bed.

I walk down the steps, grabbing the old wooden rail for balance as I find the first step in the darkness. Jerking away quickly, I grab my hand, feeling a splinter lodged in my skin.

"Shoot," I mutter as I bring my hand to my mouth to yank out the stubborn, painful piece of wood.

I get back in the car and look at the small flesh wound left in the place of the splinter.

"Oh no, did you get a boo-boo?" Meg mocks.

"Just bring up my messages and get the address programmed in; it's under Mike Hill," I say.

I circle the driveway that wraps around the house. I can't stop my eyes from looking out into the deep darkness that lies on the other side of the ever-dense forest. As I do, out of my peripheral, I notice the warm glow of a light coming from what looks like a small attic window in the back of the otherwise dark house.

Someone must be home.

"Oil Well Road?" Meg asks.

"I don't think there are any houses out that direction."

"Well, there must be, because the address is right there: 5555 Oil Well Road," I say, pointing at my phone.

"I'm going to bring up an image search for this. Something doesn't feel right," she says, with a growing worry in her voice I'm not accustomed to.

"If you don't want to go, I can drop you back off at the shop," I say.

"No, I'll go; I just don't want to get murdered," she says. "Have you any idea about the number of people who disappear when purchasing items from unknown individuals online?"

I hop on Interstate 12, which eventually takes me to Interstate 59, where I remain for a dozen-plus miles until I hear a British-accented voice from my phone: "Take the exit onto Old Highway Eleven... In three-fourths of a mile, take a right onto

Oil Well Road."

It's extra dark tonight, with no visible moon. The old highway is not favorable for my little balding tires.

This is a road I haven't driven on before. The only thing out here that I know of is a wildlife reserve.

Just as I think about it, I see the sign, indicating a 20-mph speed limit, followed by the dreadful "Dead End" sign, which causes me to instinctively hit the brakes.

"What are you doing?" my sister asks, obviously not seeing the sign.

"It's a dead end. Are you sure you read the right directions?"

"Yeah, it's only another quarter mile and then we make a right onto Oil Well Road," she says with confidence.

"Take the next right onto Oil Well Road," repeats the British voice immediately after her.

The road is so obscure. It looks like it turns into a single lane, and there are absolutely no lights.

"What do all those signs say?" I ask while driving forward another few feet.

"Pull up closer so I can actually see them!" demands Meg.

As they come into view, I see one sign indicating that this is a wildlife management area. On the right-hand side are signs with numerous rules.

"What does that mean?" I ask, pointing to the yellow sign with instructions for those entering the area.

"That only applies to those who are going to be hunting," she says. "You need to check in, carry proper licenses, blah blah blah. Doesn't apply. Can you drive forward already so we can get out of here at a decent time?"

I slowly drive through, not breaking the 20-mph law.

"Dude, come on, the arrival time just went up by five minutes with how slow you're driving."

"Look, the last thing I need is a ticket to add to our list of expenses—not to mention the car insurance rates going up," I respond in a calmer voice.

I lean my head over the steering wheel, trying to find a semblance of the moon. My headlights are flickering now, the same as when I was standing outside. I thought Meg was doing that. *They resemble warning lights*, the thought emerges, cautioning me not to go any further. About twenty seconds later, the lights vanish.

"Well, that's great," Meg says, "That's it. I'm messaging this Mike guy. We can't make it tonight. Turn me around, and let's go home."

Maybe she's right. This is just too creepy. No! I need to go through with this. I've waited too long.

"I'm not giving up that easily," I say, turning on the high beams, "See, problem solved."

"Yeah, you're my hero. I hope a cop doesn't catch you driving with high beams on. Since you're already breaking the law, can you at least drive faster?"

More doubt floods into me. What am I doing out here? I won't buy the truck tonight, anyway.

At that moment, I spot the first house I've seen since turning down this road.

"Is that it?" I ask, gesturing to the house.

"No, I don't think so," Meg says, bringing the phone closer and then pinching to zoom in on the screen.

"I think it's the last house, but not even on the street. It looks like the street ends, but the dot shows another half mile after that."

"What?" I exclaim while grabbing the phone out of her hand.

I'm feeling major regret for being out here this far. Where in the world is this house?

We finally make it to the end of the pavement, and sure enough, there stands a *private property* sign at the start of a muddy, bumpy road. My car rolls to a stop.

"What do you think?" asks my sister.

Not responding, I open the messaging app where I've been corresponding with Mike. I take another look at the listing, trying to rekindle the excitement I had only hours earlier. I then look through his profile pictures. Nothing but pictures of him fishing and hunting. Great, so he has guns.

I type out a quick message asking, "Does tonight still work?"

"Is there a mailbox?" I ask as Meg rolls down her window, sticking her head out for a better view.

"I think I see one right over there. I'll get out and check."

Before I can even protest, she's out of the car and vanishes into the dark. "Meg, get back here," I demand through the passenger window. "Megan!"

She's so impulsive. One second, she doesn't want to come out here because she's scared to get murdered. The next, she hops out of the safety of the car into the unknown darkness.

Smack!

I jerk my neck instinctively toward my window.

CHAPTER 7

7:44 PM

"What in the freaking heck?"

A rush of embarrassment surges through me as I realize there's nothing there.

I expect to see something on the other side of my smeary glass window—a far cry from the spotless windows at the Lil' Cup. But there is only darkness.

I slowly turn the car in the direction Meg had walked toward. All I can see is the mailbox. No sign of Meg.

"Meg!" I call out, leaning out the window as my tires rotate on the muddy ground. "Meg! Where are you?"

I shift the car into park, my hands gripping the steering wheel so tightly my knuckles turn white. I take a deep breath.

"She's just messing with you," I say aloud. "Simply get out and check the mailbox."

I force myself to step out of the car. As I round the front, my high beams illuminate the dirt. As I approach the mailbox, my eye catches the address etched on its side: *5555 Oil Well Road* —a small relief.

I step to the other side of the mailbox when a sharp, jarring "Boo!" cuts through the stillness. Hands shove me backward. I try to catch myself but hit the mud with a splat.

Meg cackles as she follows me with her camera.

"That really hurt!" I snap, trying to decide what hurts more—my tailbone or my ego. The familiar sting on my butt sends me back to that first date with Esther—except this time there's no soft kiss from a beautiful girl to fade the pain.

"Let me give you a hand," Meg says, as she reaches out and yanks my arm with enough force to dislocate it from its socket.

I rise to my feet and brush off my backside as best I can. Then I head toward the mailbox to search for a name. Sure enough, there it is: Mike and Elizabeth Hill.

This is the spot, I think, as I turn toward Meg. She's grinning, still amused by her antics.

As we get into the car, I ask: "Was that *you* who smacked my window earlier?"

"What window?" she replies, with a dramatic tone.

"My window! I heard something smack—" I catch the mischievous look in her eyes.

Of course, it was her, you dummy.

"So," she says casually, "I take it you saw the address?"

"Yeah, and the name on the mailbox matches."

We speed down the road just fast enough to avoid getting stuck in the muck. In the distance, I spot a lit-up house. Sure enough, parked right where the online pictures had promised, is the food truck.

I glance at my phone while driving to check if Mike has responded to my last message. Nothing. Worse yet, the screen shows *No Service*.

As we near the reassuring glow of the house with white trim, the mud beneath us gives way to gravel, the crunch of the tires a welcome sound. I swear I could feel every pebble, divot, or insect I might drive over.

We approach a parked vehicle in the driveway—a sign that someone's home. But as soon as I catch a good look, I instinctively rub my eyes.

"What in the world!" I exclaim.

"What now?" Meg asks.

"We need to get out of here!"

CHAPTER 8

7:55 PM

There it sits, as clearly as I've seen it almost every day for the last half-decade. The object of my wandering mind. The inanimate vehicle that has taken up far too much of my time and mental energies: the orange square car.

"Do you see that?" I ask, pointing toward the vehicle.

"Oh, that's the car you were talking about," Meg says casually, not hearing the fear in my voice. "Ok, yeah, I know what you mean. It *is* ugly,"

"Yeah, it's the car! It's the car that's always there when I leave! It's the car that wasn't there today, and now it's here!"

"Oh my god! You're *so* dramatic."

"This is not a coincidence," I say with a calmer voice.

"Yes, it absolutely is," Meg says. "Do you know how often I see that car? If you don't want to buy this food truck, then don't —but stop trying to find excuses to leave."

Maybe she's right. Maybe I *am* afraid of finally moving on with my life after nearly five years of the same routine. This food truck means finally leaving Slidell. It means trying again with Esther. It means leaving my parents to deal with their debt alone. It means leaving Meg with Mom and Dad. It means leaving Mrs. Grant to deal with Mr. Grant on her own.

"Yeah, I think you're right," I say quietly. "Thanks, Meg."

"I wasn't trying to help, but you're welcome," she replies with a shrug.

I pull up right behind the cube shaped car, wishing I'd paid closer attention to the license plate. I shift the car into neutral, pull the emergency brake, and hand the keys to Meg.

"I'm going to go knock, and they'll probably come out

and show me the food truck. Would you come out when we're looking at it and let me know what you think?"

"Yeah, sure, just go already."

I walk by the familiar orange square, I try to glance discreetly through the tinted windows. But nothing is visible.

The house glows warmly, lit up by the lights from the porch and the downstairs windows. Then I spot a shadowy figure moving through the house. The upstairs, though, lies in darkness.

The front deck, made of resin, is uninspired. It's so pristine—especially compared to the one at the Grants' house. The structure looks to be no more than 2,000 square feet. As I climb the stairs leading to the door, I notice the front porch swing swaying faintly, eerily, in the evening breeze.

My gaze shifts toward the double-paned window, light spilling through closed blinds. To its left, another set of windows and a door remain as dark as the night. The porch wraps around the side of the house, disappearing into the shadows. I spot what looks like a video doorbell. Opting against it, I knock.

In that moment a horrifying realization flashes through my mind: *Mike and Elizabeth Hill.*

The pieces of this puzzle have come together—but a little too late. Before I can pull away, the sound of the door handle freezes me in place. Standing in the doorway is an all-too-familiar face.

CHAPTER 9

8:00 PM

"Mark!" Liz exclaims with a smile. "What are you doing here?"

Her hair falls loosely over her shoulders, a style I've never seen on her before. She's wearing a purple dress with matching lipstick, her makeup more vibrant than usual.

"Oh, hi," I reply. "I'm here because of the food truck." I gesture toward the vehicle behind me.

"Oh, *you're* the Mark from the ad?" she asks. "What a small city Slidell is. Things like this never happen in Seattle."

I'm not sure if I believe her.

"Come on in—we're friends!" she says with a warm smile. "Consider the food truck yours."

For a moment, I hesitate, considering Meg sitting in the car. But the promise of a free food truck is too good to pass up.

"Well, I was hoping to discuss the price before making any —"

"Oh please!" she says. "Like I said, it's yours. Free! It was my husband's, and I don't know what to do with it."

Can this be as good as it sounds? Can I really get a free food truck? No catches?

"I would love to take of look at it," I say, instantly wishing I sounded more appreciative.

I hear my father's voice in my head: *When something seems too good to be true, it's because it is.*

"Of course! But first, why don't you join me for a glass of wine?" she gestures toward the couch.

I head to the couch and spot two glasses and an open bottle of wine. The bottle is full, but the cork is sticking out. Did she open it when she saw me pull up?

This has been planned, I'm sure. Did she see Meg?

"I didn't see you in the shop today," I say, trying to steady my voice.

"I had some things I needed to take care of. Were you waiting for me?" she says with a flirtatious grin.

I don't know this woman or what she's capable of. I just know she's the owner of the orange car parked outside the coffee shop all day, every day. Does she just sit there, watching me through those illegally tinted windows? No, that's paranoid. Also, I've never seen her get in and out of that car. Could I somehow bring it up?

"I know my regulars, and when one doesn't show up, I can't help but notice," I say.

"Oh, I see. I thought you might have missed me," she says in a playfully dejected tone.

I need to get Meg in here. This woman is clearly into me. No imaginary church girl is going to bail me out of this.

"Mark," she says in a sultry voice. "I know you feel something for me too. Is it the age difference that holds you back? I'm only thirty-six. My husband was older—he is older—and people sometimes would lump me in with the forty-to-fifty-year age range, just by association."

This woman is precarious. Or am I being dramatic, like Meg always says? I have to play along for just a bit.

"Don't get me wrong, I have thought about it," I begin. "But like you said, you're married and—"

"Mike is no longer in the picture," she interrupts. "He was having an affair. When I confronted him, he gaslit me, making me feel like I was the one at fault."

Her voice becomes increasingly louder and more dramatic: "*I* was supposedly neglectful; *I* stopped spicing up the relationship. He even accused me of putting too much salt in my cooking to give him high blood pressure!"

She pauses, takes a long sip of her wine, and says with a lower voice, "There are easier ways to kill someone."

Easier ways to kill. I replay the words in my head. If I had any doubts before, I'm convinced now. *I need to get out of here.*

"You know, Mark," she continues, "last week I went to the mall to buy my husband the cutest little gift to surprise him. I planned it all out. I made his favorite meal, lit every candle we had, and wore this dress—and underneath, well, you can guess. But he never came home. I waited three hours, then finally drove to his office. I had to take that obnoxious van." She gestures with her glass toward the vehicle that has now become a distant memory.

"All to find him with that worthless assistant of his," she says with rage. "And this wasn't the first time—he cheated a year ago too."

So does the car that's always parked outside of the Lil' Cup belong to Mike? He must work at one of the office buildings downtown. Maybe he starts work before I do and leaves after I've gone. And the van she mentioned—is she referring to the food truck? Why did she call it a van?

Now that I think about it, she asked me out about a year ago. When I turned her down, she must have tried to make things work again with her husband. Until he cheated again.

"Now, it's my turn," she says with a child-like playfulness. "Want to see what I bought from the mall?"

"Oh, I, uh, would love to check out the food—" I start as she heads upstairs.

"I'll be right back!" she calls down.

I quickly get to my feet, trying to think of an escape plan. Forget the food truck—I need to leave. Who knows what she might do next? Is her husband dead? I slowly tiptoe my way toward the front door.

It's locked. Not just the deadbolt—the doorknob is flipped, locked from the outside. All I see is the keyhole staring back at me. I try the handle again but with no success.

I walk back to the couch, reach over to open the blinds behind it, and frantically wave my phone light to get Meg's attention. All I can see is the reflection of the light from her phone. She must have reclined back in her seat.

"Wi-Fi!" I whisper, creeping into the kitchen next to the living room, desperately searching for a password. I check the fridge and the junk drawers.

Nothing.

Then I spot a back door. I rush over and turn the doorknob, but it, too, is locked from the outside. There are other doors, but I don't know where they lead, and I probably don't have the time left to check them all.

I frantically look back at the front door, recalling my steps earlier. As soon as I walked in, Liz directed me to sit down on the couch. To the left, I passed the staircase and a darker part of the home—maybe an office or informal living room.

I march with deliberateness to the dark room. As soon as I turn on the flashlight on my phone, I notice the comforting green glow of a router and modem. I make my way toward the devices. On the side of the router is the password: *Silversocketwrench397*. Now, back out in the living room, I sit where Liz had left me and connect.

"Dang it!" I mutter.

Meg isn't connected, so even if I send her a message, it won't go through. Now, I can only hope that Meg will try to join a nearby network, and then I can share the password with her. Knowing her, she might. I just hope she hasn't tried to connect already. I grab my glass and swirl it in a panic, watching the wine legs run down the crystal.

"So, Mark," Liz's voice startles me, "what do you think?"

She gracefully strolls down the staircase, carefully gliding her hand down the wooden railing. She's wearing a nightgown with black lace and pinkish fabric that tries to sneak through. It's modest enough, thankfully.

But my stomach churns, and bile floods the back of my throat.

"Your husband is a very lucky man," I say with a smile, instantly wishing I could pull the words back and try again. I wish I could edit the sentences I utter like typed text.

I type a message to Meg while maintaining eye contact with Liz.

"No, he's not the lucky one," she says seductively.

"So, Liz," I say, ignoring her last statement, "Is that your husband's car outside?"

"It *was*," she says with finality.

This woman isn't even trying to hide the fact that he's dead. *If she can murder her husband so callously*, I think, *then what will happen if I reject her?*

Once I hear the swish of my message sent, I quickly lock the phone.

"Who are you texting?" she asks as she walks over, then grabs the phone out of my hand.

"Oh, is *this* your girl?" she asks, gesturing with my phone at the wallpaper that flashes an old high school photo of me and Esther.

"Sister," I say quickly before she can fixate on the notion.

"You must be close. And what happened to the girl you were dating?" she asks.

I don't think I can convince her with that lie anymore.

"Things didn't work out," I say, a tinge of sadness in my voice.

"So, would you say it's the right timing?" she asks.

"Not exactly. But I don't think this," I gesture to her and myself, "is entirely out of the realm of possibility. But I don't want to rush things. Let's just take tonight to get to know each other better."

At this point, I just want to get out of here alive.

"I already know you. You're the man I wish Mike was."

She walks over with one hand behind her back. As she tries to climb on top of me, I sense cold metal against my wrist. She has handcuffed herself to me.

"Uh, what are you doing?" I ask, unable to hide my panic.

I'm a fool. How did I let this happen?

She tries to kiss my neck as I move away from her. The smell of cigarettes masked by cheap perfume is overwhelming.

Out of the corner of my eye, I notice a request to join the network on my phone, which she has placed next to us on the couch. I flip her over so that I'm on top. And as I do, I click the share button.

"Oh, Mark," she says, imagining I'm making a move, but I quickly stand up, jerking both of our arms.

"Now listen, Liz," I say with an empathetic tone. "I won't do this. You're sad and confused and need to talk with someone."

She cries at these words, weeps, as a matter of fact. Instantly, I feel bad for thinking she killed her husband. He probably left Liz for his assistant, and she's all alone in this house.

"You're right," she continues. "I'm so sorry. I am so sorry! It's been unimaginably hard. I miss Mike so much."

"Where is he?" I ask, genuinely wanting to know.

"He's in town, staying at the Marriott."

That's a lie! His car is right outside.

"Follow me," she says, heading to the kitchen, still handcuffed to me.

"The key to these stupid things is in the drawer." The drawer she opens is not one I had gone through looking for the password. She rummages through it and grabs something.

She swings around with lightning speed, and I'm stunned by the feeling of my skin as it fillets open on my right uncuffed arm. I automatically try to reach for it with my handcuffed arm.

"What the—!" I exclaim.

"You're exactly like my husband," she hisses. "Just. Like. Him."

"No, no, I'm not!" I say grimacing despite the pain.

I inch away from her, but with every step back, I pull her closer. She has me pinned against a massive bookshelf and holds her knife pushed against my chest. The slightest movement and she could impale me—through my shirt, then my bare skin, and, eventually, my heart.

"Open the cabinet," she orders, nodding at the bookshelf.

Turning toward it slowly, I awkwardly open the cabinet

with my hand attached to my injured arm. It's shaking uncontrollably now. I feel the warmth of the blood dripping down my dark, long-sleeved shirt. The door of the cabinet slowly opens, and to my surprise, I catch the sparkling silver of a tiny key. Once again, the thought surfaces that she must have planned all of this, with every variation of how this evening might go.

"Take it slowly and unlock us," she commands with the knife still pressed against my body.

Despite my hand twitching, I slide the small key into the lock. The moment it clicks open, I want to pull away, to run—but there's no chance. I need to wait for a more opportune moment. Liz stands no more than 5'6", but she's strong. Maybe it's the kind of strength that comes from being unhinged, from having nothing to lose, and holding a chef's knife on someone's body.

"Take the cuffs and lock yourself around the wooden railing," Liz orders, this time pressing the blade on my back.

She forces me toward the staircase, the tip of the knife on my back. I carefully take the cuffs and wrap it around one of the pieces of vertical woodwork. But I choose a slender one. And she notices.

"No, not that part. The handrail," she commands.

Reluctantly, I latch both of my wrists around the handrail. She tugs, testing my restraint.

Without warning, Liz abruptly turns and races back up the stairs, as if struck by a sudden epiphany.

The second she's gone, I desperately start pulling at the staircase to break free. But the angle is terrible, the wood solid too. Even with both arms intact, it would be almost impossible to snap it. As it is, the slice on my arm spreads open with every pull and movement, causing unbearable pain.

Then I hear my phone chime on the couch just a few feet away. *Meg?*

I freeze as I hear Liz's footsteps pounding down the stairs. As she rounds the wall from the top of the staircase, I first only notice her changed clothes. Then my heart drops.

The knife is gone. In its place, Liz carries a shotgun—like the ones I recognize from her husband's hunting photos on his profile.

"Liz," I say, my voice a shaky mix of sincerity and terror, "what in the world are you thinking right now?"

"You don't want to be with me," she says, her wild eyes locking hypnotically onto mine, "just like Mike. I did all this for us, and just like Mike, you don't appreciate what I do."

She pauses. "And now, you know too much."

"Liz, I swear, the only thing I know is that Mike cheated on you and is staying at the Marriott. That's it!"

"No, you know, *you know*," she says, pacing back and forth.

Then she looks straight at me and her voice lowers to a whisper. "He's in the van with bullets in his head."

In that one chilling sentence, Liz has condemned me to the same fate as her cheating husband.

Now, I do know too much.

Meg, get out of here, I think. *Please get out of here.*

CHAPTER 10

8:42 PM

My arm shoots with pain, throbbing as blood gushes out. Liz stands inches ahead of the front door.

"Does anyone know you're here?" she asks.

I think of Meg, probably waiting outside in the car, oblivious to what's unfolding here. Then I think of my phone, left behind on the couch. Was that Meg who texted? Was it my father? Or maybe Esther? Every time my phone buzzes, I always hope it's Esther checking in, but she hasn't reached out in a long time.

No, no one, I think. *All my family knows is that I canceled dinner plans to meet someone about a truck.*

"There is Mrs. Grant," I blurt out. I feel bad for involving a poor woman who has no idea about any of this. But she's my last lifeline.

"*Who?*" she asks, raising the gun to my face.

I flinch, ready for the blow, and yell, "She's the owner of the coffee shop where I work!"

"What did you tell her?" Liz demands.

"I said I was finally going to look at the food truck I had been telling her about for months," I answer quickly. "I told her it was on the other side of the train tracks. I also told her I would call her after I bought it. She'll be expecting that call any minute now."

As the words leave my mouth, I'm struck with a cold realization: I mentioned to Liz months ago that I wanted to buy a food truck. I really need to be more careful about what I share and with whom.

Liz paces the room, muttering profanities under her

breath.

Crash!

The sound of shattering glass jolts us both.

"Who was that?" Liz whispers, ducking low.

"I don't know," I reply.

My thoughts race to Meg. *She must have seen me through the window and understood the danger.*

Liz heads to the darkened room with her finger on the trigger, and I strain my body, trying to see what's happening. She marches to the wall, her movements so military-like.

Run, Meg!

Liz flicks on the light switch with her elbow. As the room lights up, I exhale in relief. It's empty. But shards of broken glass are spread all over the hardwood floor.

Liz pivots back, sees me trying to peer toward the room, and storms in my direction.

"Do you know what that was?" she demands.

"I have no clue," I respond, and throwing caution to the wind, I add, "Maybe your dead husband?"

My chances of escaping alive must be dwindling by the millisecond. Just at that moment, she cocks the gun, raising it to my left temple. In that instant, I tell myself to picture Esther: her smile, her small dimples, the faint birthmark on the left side of her cheek that curves down towards her neck. I remember the perfume on the turtleneck sweater she wore on our first date. It smelled like honey and spices with a hint of fruit—maybe pineapple.

I wish I had spent these last five years with her. I hope she knows I was still in love with her when she finds out about my murder. I hope she knows that I never lost faith in us and our plan. I hope she finally leaves this town that has kept her trapped for so long. I hope she gets to grow old with a loving family.

Beads of sweat form on the back of my neck, and my heart races uncontrollably in expectation of how it might feel when the pellets enter my skull.

The gun fires. My whole body tenses up. Only, I'm still

conscious. My ears ring, but there's no pain. I finally force my eyes open, terrified of what I might see.

Drywall, dust, chunks of wood, and asbestos rain down. I keep coughing, as the dust settles to reveal the scene: Mere inches from me, Liz lies sprawled on the floor, her arms outstretched, the gun just beyond her reach.

My eyes spot an indentation at the back of her head. Dark, crimson matter oozes out, and the taste of metal fills my mouth.

CHAPTER 11

Unknown

I'm sitting at a desk, holding Esther's favorite book. It's open to Chapter Seventeen, The couple in the book are so good to eachother. They are a perfect match. In many ways, reading this book feels like reading about us. Except for what I am about to do.

Senior year is coming to an end. And I'm about to break her heart.

Most of the kids have already gone, eager to leave this place and never come back. I'm not sure if I, too, am ready to leave it all behind: structure, friends, romance.

I pass by stained lockers, each one displaying graffiti as unique as the student who used it. I stop in front of Esther's locker.

Tears press behind my eyes, begging for release, but I won't let them fall. Beyond the double doors, only twenty feet away, Esther is waiting for me. The knots in my stomach twist as I tighten my clutch on her beloved book. I had promised I would finish reading it before summer ended. But it's been two years, and now, that too will be a disappointment for Esther.

The perfect boyfriend in the book reminds me of everything I wish I could be. My mind drifts to just a week ago.

Meg and I were watching TV in the living room, eating the now-cold pizza we had picked up for dinner because Dad said he and Mom would be home late. The greasy pepperoni made me lose my appetite. Meg was scarfing down her pizza, laughing at whatever show was playing. *How does she stay in such good shape?* I wondered to myself as I observed my sister—who must have inherited our mother's good genes.

But that night took a sharp turn when Dad came home, wheeling Mom in her chair. Her leg was encased in a cast, and stitches lined a bruise under her eye.

"Mom," shouted Meg, rushing to her side. "What happened?"

"Your mother had a small fall at work," said my father. "I got the call that she was taken to the hospital."

"Why didn't you tell us? We could have come too!" I exclaimed with panic.

My mom, always a strong woman, quickly wiped away tears as soon as they appeared. Meg was still by her side, hugging her, probably too tightly. But mom wouldn't show it.

I looked at my dad, a steadfast man in his trusty flannel shirt and a dirty white T-shirt peeking out underneath. He smelled of car parts, metal, oil, and engine grease—a combination that's somehow comforting; the scent of someone who worked hard for his family. Dad was always the pillar in our family. But as I looked up at him then, all I saw was a man who looked like he had been gutted, stripped of all strength.

"Kids let's go over to the living room," he said, "so that Mom can be comfortable. Meg, would you grab her the blanket from our bed?"

"Dad," I said softly so only he could hear, "What is going on?"

Ignoring me, he moved to the living room, and we all sat down. Meg was back in her spot, Mom under her blanket with her leg elevated, and dad and I were on either corner of the couch.

"Megan, Mark. Mom and I love you both so much," my dad started in a strong voice. "Things are about to . . ." he paused as his voice cracked, "change in our lives."

He couldn't say more and broke down weeping. I moved next to him and put my arm around his shoulder.

"I'm sick," mom finally said.

"Sick?" asked Meg. "Like the flu?"

"No! Like cancer," I said, with little effort to be tactful.

"No, it's not cancer," my dad said in a muffled voice, his head still tilted between his legs.

"What is it then?" Meg asked, looking towards me.

"ALS!" Mom said.

At her words, my stomach nearly returned the pizza.

"Sign language?" asked my sister. "Are you going deaf?"

My sister's ignorance might have been hilarious under another circumstance. But not that moment. We spent that night discussing my Mom's diagnosis. Only twenty percent of people diagnosed with amyotrophic lateral sclerosis live longer than five years. We focused on how to best spend her last days. We would travel the world for the first year while her health was still manageable. We would go to California, where she could enjoy some sun. After hours of conversing about how to make Mom's remaining time special, the ache in my heart grew. Mom would take priority in my life. She had to. My promises to Esther would have to come after.

I've carried that night with me every second since, and now, as I walk toward Esther, its weight feels unbearable. To ask someone already so patient to be more patient felt heartless. But I could make it work. I must.

I walk outside through the double doors into the blinding sun. It's the brightest day of the year in Slidell—annoying because the weather never seems to match my mood.

"Mark!" Esther's chipper voice immediately makes my heart hurt.

Esther gestures with her hand to come sit next to her. She holds up her phone to show me a meme—an animated character looks out his window at two of his friends running joyfully. The caption above their heads reads, *Kids graduating high school with prospects*. Above the more cynical character's head reads, *Me, thinking about what I want for lunch*.

Me taking care of my mom with terminal illness, I think.

"So, where are we going tonight for our graduation dinner?" she asks, her voice light and hopeful, as she rests her head on my chest.

"Well, actually," I hesitate, as I realize the heaviness in my voice. "I was going to talk to you about that. I might need to cancel."

She pulls back slightly to look at me. "That's ok," she says, though I can sense a flickering of uncertainty. "We don't need to do anything."

"No, I want to do something. But my parents wanted me to come home for a special dinner they planned."

"Go, spend time with them," she says, "They deserve that. We will spend plenty of time together soon enough."

"Thanks for understanding." I take a long pause. "I also need to talk about the whole traveling thing that we have planned."

"Traveling thing? You mean moving?" she asks, defensively.

"Yeah, that. Well, I'm not sure we will go as soon as we thought."

She pulls away a little bit. "What changed?"

"It's just going to be a little longer than I thought," I say as I put my arm around her.

"If it's money, I have savings, plenty of savings. Enough to get us by until we find work."

This is not how I wanted it to be: her worrying about money.

"Well, it's not only the money, sweetie; my . . . uh . . . well . . ."

"You don't want to," she says flatly.

"No, I *want* to. I just need to become a little more grounded before I up and move."

"Mark, you were raised grounded but my entire life has been up in the air. You know this was my first real plan for myself? When you said that we would leave Slidell, it gave me . . . hope."

"Baby, I'm not saying we won't go; we only have to wait longer than I thought."

"How long?"

"Five years," I mutter under my breath.

"Five years? Why five years?"

Suddenly, using my dying mother as an excuse feels wrong. It would work, but I'd never know if Esther stayed with me because she wanted to—or forced out of pity.

"Esther, I can't just get up and leave my family right now."

She stands and walks away. *Have I lost her forever?* I could tell her about Mom. Tell her how I want to spend Mom's last days by her side. *No, I can't do that.* Maybe it doesn't make a lot of sense, but I can't base our relationship on guilt. I need to know she's going to stay with me for me and not because my mother is dying.

No, that's stupid. Her mom left her for different reasons, obviously, but I'm not with Esther out of guilt.

"Mark," she starts, "the one person I've been able to count on since I moved here, my best friend, you're telling me that you don't want to leave because you're not ready?"

"I didn't say that," I protest.

"I'm ready," she continues. "*I* don't have a family. You're my family. And I thought I was yours."

I'm losing her; I can see it now. Only two options remain: tell her about my mom and ask her to wait five years. She'd do it without hesitation, even in her awful circumstances. Or let her go. Maybe she'd leave this place with her savings and find another guy, someone who's more like the guy in her favorite book.

I walk over to her and pull her into my arms, ignoring her resistance.

"I love you; I love you so much. But I need to stay. I need time. Time to be the man you deserve."

"You already are the man I deserve. Where is this coming from?" she says, pulling away again.

"I wish I could tell you," I say, looking down.

"You wish you could tell me?" she snaps back. "You can tell me. But you're a coward. You're not sure that you want to make such an enormous commitment to be with me. You're such a coward!"

"No, please, that's not it. I want to be with you for the rest of my life. I love—"

"Don't finish that sentence if you don't plan on giving me a good explanation for all of this."

I stand there with probably the most pathetic expression on my face. Last chance. Do I tell her and sentence her to five years of misery before getting on with her life? And even then, can I really give her the life she deserves?

"You should still go," I say quietly. "Go have the adventure we dreamed of for both of us. I will be here, waiting for you when you get back."

"I won't be coming back," she says.

My vision blurs, as her silhouette disappears, walking away without turning back.

CHAPTER 12

9:00 PM

I once read about sleep paralysis. It's supposed to be one of the most terrifying experiences—you're fully aware of where you are, but you can't move. You struggle to wiggle an arm, a finger, anything, or to open an eyelid, but you can't.

That's how I feel right now: trapped. Trapped next to Liz's dead body; trapped in the memory of Esther walking away; trapped in a suffocating moment of unknowns. I want to turn my head to see where the blow came from. I want to move. But I'm frozen.

I begin to hear a faint sound of breathing. My arm shoots spikes of pain through my body again. I finally shift my weight to move away from the growing puddle of blood. My body jerks to life as I turn my head.

Meg is standing right over Liz's body, hyperventilating, her arms raised above her head. *What is she holding?*

I blink rapidly, trying to clear away the dust. A rock. She's holding a jagged-edged rock that looks like an enlarged kidney stone.

"Meg! Meg!" I cry.

No response.

"Megan, answer me!" I scream, the intensity of my emotion instantly scratching my throat.

"Oh my god, oh my god, oh my god!" she squeals, dropping the rock and waving her hands in front of her as if trying to air-dry them.

My sister is a murderer now. Self-defense, right? Well, in defense of her brother. What else could she have done? The woman had a gun pointed at me.

Meg runs over and tries to release me from the cuffs.

"What in the world were you thinking, you freakin' dumb moron?" she snaps, her voice shaking.

"I was thinking I was going to buy a food truck. How would I know the seller would be Liz?"

"Who is Liz?"

"The woman you just killed!"

I don't want to explain who she is at this moment. It's embarrassing.

"No, no, no, no, no," Meg mutters, rushing back to the body. She kneels beside her, checking for a pulse.

"Mark, what do we do, what—"

"Can you come get me out of these cuffs?"

"Mark, I think, I think she's dead."

"Can you just find the key and get me out of these cuffs," I plead.

"How did she get you in handcuffs?"

I don't want to answer that question. It's too humiliating. The truth is I'm a pushover. I don't have a backbone, no sense of control. I don't stand up to Mr. Grant. I let that mystery guy, Phillip, control our entire conversation. And now Liz. This kind of spinelessness nearly got me killed.

On the flip side, the only time I remember truly standing up for something was with Moab, and what did that get me? A black eye and broken ribs.

"Just find the key, Meg; I think it's in her pocket," I say.

"Oh, hell no, I'm not digging through a dead woman's pocket."

"Then take out your phone and call the police so they can," I command.

"The police?" she asks in a panic.

"Yes, the police! There is a dead body here—someone who tried to kill me. And I think her murdered husband is in the food truck. And I'm—"

Meg reaches her hand up to her mouth—a second too late—to stop the vomit that comes pouring out through her fingers onto the floor.

"Oh my god," I say, quickly averting my eyes and trying to ignore the disgusting sound emitting from my sister's mouth.

A sour, foul odor fills the room.

I wait a moment until the gagging stops.

"You ok, Meg?"

She takes a long, deep, concentrated breath. "Yes, I think so."

"Good. Now it's time to call the police."

Tears are streaming down her face. At first, I think it's from puking, but then the tears come uncontrollably, and her face squeezes up as she tries to hold back the sobs.

"I can't call the police!" she wails.

CHAPTER 13

9:05 PM

"What do you mean you can't call the police?" I ask. "That's what you do in a situation like this. They will come; we tell them we were meeting someone here to buy a food truck, and that they kidnapped me while you were waiting in the car. When you heard the commotion, you tried getting inside the house. When you looked through the window, you saw someone holding a gun to my head, and you threw a rock through the glass to get in and save me. You hit her in the head to stop her from shooting me, but you didn't mean for it to kill her. It's classic self-defense."

"You don't understand, I'm, I'm..."

"You're what? High? I already know."

"Not just pot," she interrupts.

"What then?" I ask.

"I've been experimenting with other things."

"*What* things, Meg?"

"Does it matter?" she snaps.

"Yeah, it matters! But either way, it should be out of your system by now."

"No, I don't think so. When I was waiting for you in the car, well, I got bored."

"You got bored?"

"Well, I didn't know you were going to get kidnapped by a woman half your size."

At this moment, I should be struck with panic. It looks like we murdered a woman, and the girl who did it is high on illegal narcotics. I should feel hopeless. But instead, sheer adrenaline is coursing through my body. I feel lucky to be alive. Just ten minutes ago, I was as good as dead.

"Just get the key out of her pocket so we can figure out what we're going to do," I demand.

"Ok, ok, just hang on!" Meg replies, as she flips Liz's body over and rifles through her pockets.

"Is this it?" she asks, holding up the miniature key.

"Yeah, yeah, that's it."

She hurries over and frantically unlocks the handcuffs. I pull my arms instantly from the awkward position, rubbing my wrists, and then reaching to check the cut on my arm.

"Oh my god, Mark, what happened?"

"Well, before our friend over there grabbed the gun, she used a knife to get me into the cuffs."

"See, I told you we shouldn't have come out this way. This was a huge mistake."

That is the last thing I need to hear right now! Without responding, I head to the couch to grab my phone.

"What are you doing?" Meg asks.

"What do you think I'm doing? I'm calling the cops."

"No, Mark, you can't!"

"Meg, no matter what you're on, I doubt they will even test you. And even if they do, it will be way better than if we *don't* call the cops. Our DNA is everywhere, and the proof that we were here will eventually come out when our phone records are searched."

"Mark, the product is in your car!" she blurts out fast.

"The *what* is in my *what*?"

"When I heard the fight break out, I was in the middle of . . . well, anyway, I spilled it all over your car. If the cops come, they will search the entire crime scene. How do you think that will look if they find you in possession of—"

"*Me* in possession of? No, no, no—it's *you. You're* the idiot who brought the drugs here!"

"They are not only here," she mutters, her voice barely audible. "I stashed the rest at the Lil' Cup, in the bathroom, above the toilet."

My mind races. My senseless sister might have just sentenced us both to possession charges. If the cops come here and link me to the Lil' Cup, they will want to search my workplace. The Grants will comply, and they will find the drugs in the most cliché hiding spot.

"How much is there, Meg?"

"Enough to sentence us for a long time. Mark, I can't go to prison when Mom—when Mom..." her voice breaks as she starts weeping.

I want to be furious. I *should* be furious. But as I look at her now, I see a little girl—the same little girl who cried when I drew all over her favorite Barbie with a Sharpie. The same girl who wept for weeks over her first heartbreak in middle school. The same girl whose muffled cries I heard throughout the countless sleepless nights over the past five years.

My sister has waited on our mother hand and foot, reading to her before bed, helping her take her meds three times a day, and feeding her breakfast, lunch, and dinner while Dad and I work to provide for us all.

She's a product of the chaos we've been living in, a reflection of our impossible circumstances. We are family. And if there's anything I've learned these last five years, it's that we need to have each other's backs.

CHAPTER 14

9:37 PM

When I was twelve, I had a collection of model cars. I loved the meticulously detailed process of assembling, painting, and displaying them. The hobby started as a way to avoid wasting my summers watching TV or getting into trouble with the other kids my age. I also wanted to be more like my dad, who liked cars. Seeing the rare smile of approval on his normally stern face as he saw me putting the pieces of those cars together was enough to keep me going.

One day, I went to the park with one of my favorites—a glossy black Rolls Royce. I can't remember the year of the car, but it was my pride and joy. I had begged my sister to take me, and she reluctantly agreed. She must have been fifteen. There were a million other things a popular girl at school could have been doing, but she came with me.

I staged the car on a park bench and started snapping photos to share with my dad later when he would get home from work. He had been working on a similar life-size version and would often tell me all about it. Of course, we could never afford one, but we could dream. I wanted these photos to look like they were of the real thing.

Out of nowhere, a tremendous gust of wind flew the car off the bench and destroyed it. For a moment, I stood frozen in disbelief, and then I burst into tears.

My sister didn't mock me. She sprang into action, gathering up the pieces together and consoling me for the entire walk back home. That evening, she helped me to organize the car parts, reassemble them, and repaint the scratched areas. When we were done, it looked even better than before.

As I look at the woman in front of me, I see someone whose life—once filled with family, friends, and prospects—is now in pieces. It's my turn to help her pick up the pieces and put them back together.

"Meg," I say gently as I head over to console her. "I won't call the police. This is my fault; this is my mess. You got dragged into it. Meg, you saved my life. You could have just left, but you saved my life."

She sniffles, wiping her eyes and nose. "No, Mark, call the police. It's not your fault."

"It's not yours either. You made some dumb choices, sure, but those choices were just a by-product of everything happening with Mom. If you promise, right here and now, that you're going to quit the drugs, I will figure out a way to get us out of this."

"I promise, I promise!"

"Meg, your side—it's bleeding?"

She looks at her shirt as if I'd pointed out her shoe is untied. Beneath her rib cage, a small tear oozes blood. It looks superficial. She touches it, and I expect to see her wince in pain, but she doesn't. She looks at the blood on her fingers, but her expression remains detached.

"It must have happened when I was climbing through the window," she says.

So *that's* how she got inside. I didn't even think to ask.

I steady myself before I speak: "We need to get this place cleaned of any signs we were ever here."

The words hang in the air for a couple of seconds, then hit me like a blow to the chest.

We're going to cover up a crime scene.

CHAPTER 15

10:00 PM

I unlock the deadbolt from the inside but quickly realize the door is still locked from the outside. Climbing out the window, I carefully avoid the shards of glass that had cut Meg. Once outside, I unlock the front door, and Meg and I walk down the steps to grab gloves from my car. Luckily, I have extras from work. Sliding them on, we ensure no more fingerprints could be added to the scene.

I also find some old rags and duct tape in the trunk of my car, which we use to bandage our wounds—not the most sanitary thing, but better than leaving more trails of blood.

We get back inside through the front door and start scrubbing. I search the garage and find exactly what I'm hoping for: an arsenal of cleaning supplies.

Meg takes charge of cleaning the vomit on the floor, a task I'm glad to avoid. She also searches for blood stains left from the cut on my arm. Liz's blood pooled near where her body was lying, but mine scattered throughout the house from Liz dragging me around at knifepoint.

Meg works systematically and meticulously, like when she had assembled the old Rolls-Royce.

My first order of business is to wipe down every surface: doorknobs, cabinets, wine glasses—anything I could think of that I had touched, and plenty more. I even wipe down areas Meg might have touched. Next, I tackle the window Meg had climbed through to see if I could find the glass shard that cut her. I wipe and disinfect *everything*.

As we wrap up the cleaning, a devastating realization sinks in: Mike and Liz's bodies are too far apart for our story to add up. The idea that a family quarrel turned into a double murder doesn't make sense. Besides, their deadly wounds are in the back of the head—clearly the work of a third party.

Surprisingly, the guilt of covering up for my sister isn't affecting me as much as I'd expected. Liz was a criminal—a murderer. After killing me, she would have hunted down Meg and killed her too.

"What if we drag his body inside and stage it like they killed each other at the same time?" Meg suggests.

"No, Meg, how could they both simultaneously strike each other in the back of the head?"

My sister can't be this dumb, I think. *No, that's not true; just because she can't think of how to cover up a murder doesn't make her stupid. It makes her innocent.*

"I have no clue, but we need to come up with something," she says with a panic back in her voice.

This is not going as I had so confidently planned. The cops would need to carry out a deep investigation to explain all of this. And there's no way to get into Liz's phone and delete the evidence that tie me to tonight's events.

"I think this is the end of the line. I'm out of ideas," I say, collapsing to the ground.

We sulk in the middle of the living room, defeated by our predicament.

"Meg," I say after a moment. "Maybe it's a good idea to clean out my car; clean up the mess you made."

She slowly stands, turning 360 degrees as if she's taking in every detail of the room. Her gaze turns up and lingers at the hole in the ceiling.

"Ok," she sighs, walking out the front door.

I commence weighing my options. If Meg thoroughly cleans my car, we can still call the cops. If they search my car, nothing will be out of place. But now that the house has been scrubbed clean, will they be suspicious? Worse, I've wiped away evidence that I was ever cuffed up. I should've had Meg clean up the drugs in the car right away before trying to clean the house.

Why didn't I think of that?

The only hope now is the body of her dead husband in the food truck, which proves Liz was a murderer. I need to make sure he's out there; otherwise, our story will fall apart.

I walk carefully toward the front door, trying not to screw anything up more than I already have. I see Meg with all the car doors open, desperately cleaning. She looks exhausted.

As the adrenaline fades, a headache begins to throb, and my vision feels off. Every turn of my head comes with a delay, as though my vision needs an extra millisecond to process.

As I head down the stairs, I spot the food truck parked on the side of the house, about twenty-five feet away. Familiar knots form in my stomach as I imagine what her husband's body looks like. How long ago did she kill him? Is the body starting to stink —or worse, rot? A spike of pain shoots through my arm, but not my sliced arm. Looking down, I find a thorn from the rose bushes has gone through my shirt and reached my skin.

"Shoot!" I mutter.

Any traces of fabric might tie me to a second crime. I carefully check for remnants of my shirt. Fortunately, there are none.

The gravel driveway shows no visible drag marks. I can't picture how she would've moved him without leaving any trace. They must have both been in the truck when she killed him.

As I make my way up to the food truck, I realize that it's a lot larger than I expected. It's painted with very low-quality black paint, almost like it was hastily spray-painted to conceal something. There are no visible markings, not even a clue to its model. It doesn't seem like it was ever meant to be a food truck. Come to think of it, it doesn't even look like the vehicle that was advertised. This looks more like a very large van—the kind used for shuttling tourists.

An uncomfortable feeling echoes through my body like sonar. Should I stop now? Cut my losses and walk away? But no —Liz said the body was here.

I stare at the passenger door trying to summon the

courage to pull the handle. It's probably locked, I tell myself. *If it doesn't open, I will walk away.*

As I slowly grip the handle, it gently opens towards me. I glance behind me to check the gravel for tracks I might have left. Thankfully, it's dry. I slip off my shoes and take one cautious step inside, leaning forward as far as I can to get a look.

All I need is a glimpse of the body. That's it. Just a confirmation, and then I'm out of here. But there's nothing. The windows are boarded up from the inside. If he's back here, there is no sign of it. I long for the rancid odor of decomposition. *What has my life become?*

I reach down for my phone, but my pockets are empty. I probably left it in the house.

Stepping fully in, I walk like a blind man navigating unfamiliar surroundings. The air is thick with the smell of mothballs, becoming stronger as I move deeper into the van. I hate it. It reminds me of death. Or maybe this is what a decomposing body smells like.

I can perceive what must be shelving lining both sides of the walls, filled with—I don't know what—maybe glass jars and canned goods? Was this some sort of camper van? I keep going, my hands bracing against either side as I carefully slide one foot in front of the other, waiting for the inevitable impact of a body.

Then my left foot catches on something sticky. This is it. This is the moment I will kick out and hit his flesh.

But nothing.

I'm now at the back of the truck, and there is no sign of a body. *What in the world was she talking about? Was she not a murderer? Was she insane?* The nausea comes back as I stifle the intensity of wanting to puke.

I race out of there as fast as I can and head over to Meg.

"What happened to you?" she asks.

"Just stop cleaning. We need a new plan."

There is no point in all that now. We have no way of explaining this, and we got rid of any evidence that Liz was ever trying to kill me. *We are so stupid. We are so absolutely, undeniably stupid.*

"So, what are we going to do, Mark? Don't tell me I just cleaned your disgusting car for nothing!"

"First, the only things that were disgusting about it were caused by you."

"Then explain all the used floss sticks I found on the ground."

Ok, those were mine, but it's my car after all. It's kind of nice to know that we can still bicker like siblings in times like this.

For a fleeting moment, I wish I could take on the mindset of some of the most infamous criminals in history. How would they cover this up?

But I'm just a lost, hopeless guy who is going to wind up a prison inmate without a mother. The Stratford legacy will be left to my father, who will live the rest of his days in grief and loneliness.

CHAPTER 16

11:40 PM

"What do you mean you didn't find a body?" Meg asks.

"I mean, I went to check if the husband was in the truck like Liz said, and there was nothing in there but preserved food."

Should I tell her about the sticky substance on the bottom of my foot? There's no point in keeping any secrets now—we're in this mess together.

I slide off my shoe. "Do you see anything?" I ask while lifting my foot and hopping on my right leg.

Meg leans in, grabbing my ankle to steady me. "Yeah, I do!"

"Well, what is it?"

"It looks like some sort of green slime, and I think I see a small alien fetus."

I pull away, catching my balance again on both feet as I'm reminded of why I didn't want to show her in the first place. I realize I'm alone—to an extent, at least. My sister isn't fully present; her mind is still fighting the drugs in her system.

"I just don't understand why she would tell you she killed him if she didn't," Meg says.

"I have no flipping clue! Probably because she's delusional!"

No logic could explain this. Trying to fix an irrational problem with rational solutions feels like a waste of time.

This entire night has effectively become one of those moral dilemmas—like the trolley problem. Do you save five people standing on a railway by pulling a lever that would kill another innocent person on a different track? And if you do nothing, you inadvertently kill five innocent people. Each choice feels worse than the last.

When I was handcuffed just hours ago, I was sure that calling the cops was the best decision. When I realized Meg was under the influence of illegal narcotics, I felt the best course of action was to protect my sister and cover up the crime scene. That decision, however, was met with the grim realization that my story wouldn't add up to the police: two people with blows to the back of their heads couldn't have killed each other. This led me back to calling the cops, but only if I could find Mike's body first. Now that Mike's body is nowhere to be found, calling the cops would be the worst possible decision.

My mind spins in endless loops, trying to find a way out. And morality is no longer a concern I can afford. My only goal is to get my sister and me out of any potential criminal sentences that would ruin the Stratford family legacy forever. I don't want people to tell our story a century from now, feeling pity for us as I do when I tell the story of the Onionhead.

"I think we need help from the Grimaldi brothers," I say with a low voice.

"You're joking, right?" replies Meg. "Those two defend the most notorious criminals in Slidell."

"Yeah, I know," I admit, "but right now, we *are* criminals. And I'm completely out of ideas."

"The body has to be around here somewhere," Meg suggests as she looks around frantically, trying to find a lead. "Did you check *all* the rooms in the house?"

She's right. Finding the body would be our ticket out of this mess. We could call the cops and easily explain everything, proving we're just innocent victims.

Entering the murder scene once again, we slip off our shoes and make our way up the staircase. My gloved hands are a protection, but everything I touch sends a jolt of pain through my head. As we round the top, a familiar layout greets us: a bathroom directly ahead and a spare bedroom to the left. That's the first place we will check.

We flip on the light, and the overhead light illuminates a room so generic it's almost eerie. A full bed, neatly made with crisp white sheets, is pushed against the wall in the middle of the room. A small desk with a solitary lamp sits on the left-hand side of the bed. Above the bed hangs a painting of a grassy meadow with a lone maple tree. It's a dull piece, yet so serene and soothing. I wonder what it would feel like to have peace like that again.

"Mark!" whispers Meg, pulling me out of my daydream. "What do you see?"

"Oh, uh" I stammer. "I'm just trying to be thorough and not miss any details."

Meg slowly opens a closet, revealing a single rod with empty hangers.

"Nothing," she sighs.

We step out into the adjacent bathroom. It's very nondescript, with no decorations or signs of use. The pristine, porcelain bathtub gleams.

Two more bedrooms to go. The next room is much like the first, but with different bedsheet colors and paintings. The closet holds neatly hung winter clothes. I wonder if Meg, too, notices the absence of any personal or family photos. This house is so clean, that it feels staged—like one of those model homes you tour to decide if you like the layout of the new housing development.

Finally, we enter the master bedroom. It's about triple the size of the other bedrooms and is dominated by a massive wooden armoire. Two nightstands sit on either side of the bed frame. A TV hangs opposite the bed, and in the corner, a small coffee table sits between two small chairs. The chairs face a sliding glass door that leads to a deck.

I allow myself another moment to daydream. This would be a perfect room for a couple in love. I imagine waking up before Esther, sneaking downstairs to make some coffee, and bringing it up on a tray along with waffles and maple syrup. I set it on the coffee table next to a slender vase that holds a single orange tulip—her favorite. I picture myself watching her sleep for a moment, feeling satisfied that I could finally give her a home where she could sleep so peacefully. I'd kiss her cheek gently, and she'd wake up with a soft smile, catching the aroma of coffee and syrup.

The sharp thud of something hitting the nightstand jolts my focus out of my perfect world and on Meg, whose clutching her shin.

"Meg, be careful!"

I step into the bathroom, once again tempted to daydream as I observe its gorgeous design with an exposed bathtub, separate vanity sinks on either side of the room, and a large tile shower with a waterfall showerhead. But I chase away an image in mind of Esther brushing her hair.

The lack of possessions in this house is unsettling. Maybe the Hills were not materialistic, but even the poorest have *some* things. A familiar memory surfaces: an unhoused man I used to see outside of the Lil' Cup pushing a cart overflowing with all his scavenged belongings. My surroundings fade as the image becomes more vivid.

I'm watching him through the glass door, as he waits for the shop to open on the cold, winter morning. His clothes are torn and utterly filthy; loose skin hangs low under his brown eyes; and his wrinkled face is covered in dirt and grease.

I try not to make eye contact as I carefully stack pastries in the glass display case, making them look as desirable as possible to the soon-to-be-hungry customers. But inevitably, our eyes meet. I can now make out the finer details of his face, etched out with decades of struggle and misfortune. But he doesn't wear a grumpy or angry expression, nor is he trying to seek pity with fake shivers or a feigned look of despair. He wears a content, humble expression—one of acceptance over his circumstances.

Against my initial apprehension, I walk over to welcome him inside the warm, cozy shop eight minutes early. I never do this—early arrivals are annoying, and I need that time to bring everything up to Mr. Grant's sky-high standards.

The old man sits by the front window. The delicious smell of the shop is not enough to mask the foul body odor clinging to him. I bring him some hot water, wanting to help him warm up faster. But when I hand it to him, the face looking at me is no longer the old man's.

It's Mr. Grant's. He smiles, exposing his rotten teeth. His eyes roll back, leaving only veiny whites. He lunges at me, tackling me to the floor and plunging a knife into my chest.

I run out of the bathroom, reality snapping back into place.

"What? What is it? Did you find the body?" Meg asks.

"No, let's just get out of here. This place gives me the creeps."

I don't know why my mind keeps drifting like this. I do have a vivid imagination, but I never lose touch with reality. Maybe it's the blood loss. At any rate, I need to stay present.

"Ok, we did our due diligence; there is truly no other option," I say with persistence. "We need to go to the brothers."

"I'm going to go look outside. The body has to be stashed somewhere," says Meg. "Did you see anything in the garage? Is there a shed?"

"Let's go check again," I sigh, feeling more distraught by the moment.

I don't want to keep looking. But I don't want to be left alone, where I might get sucked into another reality.

After turning off every light and double-checking to make sure we've left no traces, we make our way back downstairs.

"Do you think there is some sort of hidden room or basement where she might have stashed the body?" Meg asks.

Apparently, her mind has been doing some wandering too. I wouldn't put it past Liz to have some sort of secret bunker where she keeps her victims. But the longer we stay here, the more we risk getting ourselves into trouble. Who knows what kind of evidence could already implicate us? I think we've covered all our bases, but we urgently need help—professional help.

"I'm going to search the perimeter," Meg says, heading back outside.

"No, I don't think that's such a good idea. Who knows what evidence you could leave behind? We're lucky the driveway is gravel and we didn't leave any footprints, but wandering out in the woods would be foolish."

"You're just being a coward."

The words instantly take me back to that dreadful day when Esther called me the same thing. Maybe they're both right.

"Fine," I say. "Lead the way."

CHAPTER 17

12:00 AM

We make our way down the porch, and Meg looks to her left toward the van, then to the right. She ponders her next move for a moment, then confidently heads right. As we walk about thirty yards opposite the vehicle, a shadowy outline comes into view. A shed, I'm hoping.

We walk cautiously up the gravel path, afraid of leaving behind a trace. The rocks underneath our feet crunch in the silence, amplifying our paranoia. As we move farther away from the glowing home behind, Meg and I become enveloped in pitch-black darkness. I look left and right and even up, trying to adjust my eyes.

A sensation creeps over me, as if someone is watching us, tracking our every move. They say that when you feel eyes on you, you shouldn't ignore it—*they* being the women on a podcast Meg forced me to listen to. I recall the voices of the two women who skillfully dissected every small detail of a crime, evoking a sense of terror that I now feel trickling down my spine.

I need to focus on survival—for Meg, for myself, for Esther. Would Esther think of me as a criminal? Would she view me as a hypocrite for my actions, especially considering all the backhanded jokes I've made about her employers?

A sudden snap on the ground gives me pause. Meg stops too, looking around to see where the sound came from. Was it an animal? Did we step on a twig?

"It's nothing, Mark," Meg whispers in the faintest voice I've ever heard from the naturally loud girl. "Just keep going."

I know she's more nervous than she wants to let on. I'm nervous too. *But nervousness is not the same as cowardice.* That word bites, even in my thoughts.

We keep walking, but Meg shifts her focus solely to the right, where the dense forest lies just fifty feet from the carved-out piece of property. Meanwhile, I'm tasked with scanning the driveway that extends to the main road. It's so dark that my efforts feel futile. Anything could be lurking just five feet away, and I wouldn't be able to see it.

It's just like our city, not to bother lighting up the road. Probably some sort of deal the Grimaldi brothers brokered. I imagine they have a map that highlights all the spots in town without security cameras or lights. These would be prime areas for criminal activities.

Each step we take gives the illusion that the shadowed shed is getting smaller. Our phone flashlights feel useless. We only turn them on every ten yards for a quick burst of light. Our batteries are both dangerously low. Mine holds a ten percent charge, and Meg is at a measly six.

"The usual, babe?" the waitress's raspy voice cuts through my thoughts. Her name was Lyda, a middle-aged waitress at the diner that Esther and I frequented during senior year. Lyda explained that her voice wasn't strained because of smoking. Her husband had died from lung cancer, and she went on about it one slow and lonely afternoon.

The diner's food was disgusting, but the low prices kept a faithful crowd in the mornings and the evenings. The afternoons belonged to me and Esther. We had our usual booth in the back, a perfect hiding spot in case her brothers—or worst of all—her father ever showed up. That never happened, but the booth became our cherished tradition that year.

The deep maroon seat cushions had matching tears on either side, and the table was stained with water rings all over. I think it reminded Esther of herself: scarred but enduring.

"The beauty about the table is that it can be sanded down, stained, and coated for protection," Esther told me once as she rubbed the side of the table.

Her hand moved to the torn leather seats. "These could

easily be reupholstered. What color do you think?"

"Oh, you have a better eye for this than I do, love," I said.

The truth is, I didn't want to tamper with her vision. I was just enjoying her ideas and enthusiasm.

"What about navy blue?" she asked, her face lighting up.

"I love it!"

I pause suddenly. My heart aches once again. *Esther and I will be together again*, I tell myself, *and this time for good!*

"What is it?" Meg asks.

I have to come up with a believable excuse for the sudden change in my body language. Meg doesn't understand how difficult ending my relationship with Esther has been. In her mind, staying with Mom was an easy, moral choice. A son should choose his dying mother regardless over love. I never bothered trying to explain it—and I don't plan on doing it now. I don't even know if she knows about Esther's horrible life—something Esther had only shared with me.

"I thought I heard something," is the best I can come up with.

"Like the snapping sound again?"

"No, more like a whistle," I lie.

"Like from someone?"

"No, no, it must be the wind blowing through the trees."

As we walk ahead, the shed finally comes into view. It's an ancient-looking structure about the size of a two-car garage, with its foundation set far higher than the house.

"Jackson was so stubborn when he found out about the cancer," Lyda's voice starts again in my head. "He refused to put down the damn cigarettes. I told him that's why he got it in the first place—the cancer, that is—but he told me to leave him alone for his last dying days. That's why I'll never touch the damn things. They are poison and should be illegal."

This went on for another twenty minutes. I just wanted to converse with Esther, but didn't want to be rude.

"Anyway, I'll leave you two lovebirds alone. Can I get you a sundae? My treat?"

We accepted, not wanting to be unappreciative. The only thing we trusted on the menu was their freshly baked pie—a different option every day: blackberry, raspberry, boysenberry, blueberry, strawberry, all the berries.

"How bad can the ice cream be?" I had whispered to Esther as she contemplated taking the first bite of the fudge sundae that sat between us.

"You would be surprised at the videos I've seen online. Businesses like this rarely clean their machines."

My upper lip rose in disgust as I imagined the mold.

"What if it was freshly made? Or scooped from a carton?" I asked, optimistically.

She raised the spoon as the processed ice cream didn't melt off, but kind of oozed off, like slime.

We decided to dump the sundae in the bathroom toilet like co-conspirators. Esther distracted Lyda with more conversation about her late husband. And I took the full glass cup with me to the bathroom. I dumped the whole thing, watching it swirl in circles as it slowly disappeared down the bowl.

"We would make pretty good criminals," she joked afterward. "I could distract bank tellers while you sneak behind and snatch the money."

Now, standing twenty feet in front of the shed, I'm filled with terror. If there is a corpse around, it would definitely be here. The siding up the exterior walls is warped from humidity, and so is the paint—long strips of teal paint peels expose the timeworn and rotting wood underneath.

"Just you, hon?" asked Lyda in her sweet voice.

"Yeah, yeah, just me," I responded.

I traced my hands over the table and found the spot where our initials were engraved: M for Mark and E for Esther, along with a slightly crooked heart. An image of Esther, filled with hope, filled my mind as I touched the carving.

"There!" Esther had said, "Now, if we ever come back to this place, we can remember how it all started. Maybe we can come visit it on our fiftieth."

"Anniversary," I finished leaning over to kiss her.

"Your girlfriend was in here just last week," Lyda had told me. "She was sitting in a different spot from your usual, but with the Grimaldi brothers."

I didn't feel like telling her that was no longer an accurate statement. She leaned in, like she was about to dish some tea.

"I think she was getting interviewed for a job," she said excitedly. "You know, I've always liked those two. They get a bad rap, but when Jackson was sick and the bills piled up, they got us out of some hospital bills that insurance wouldn't cover."

I barely paid attention to her defense of the G brothers, more consumed by what Esther could have been thinking. We had gone on and on about how they were the lowest of the low —worthless criminals. If what her brothers were doing was bad, we were sure that the G brothers were in a league of their own. And now she wanted to work for them? Why wasn't she leaving this place?

"How did you know it was an interview?" I asked.

"Sweety, when you've been doing this as long as I have, you pick up on body language. Trust me—it was an interview."

Meg and I are just steps from the shed now, and we flash our lights toward the entrance. As the light hits, we both gasp.

"I think I'm going to be sick!" Meg says, bringing her hand to her mouth, this time stopping herself from ruining our attempts at discretion.

The rancid smell of decomposing animal corpses—at least a dozen—is trapped in the stale, humid air.

CHAPTER 18

12:08 AM

This must be another hallucination. The animals are hung on a giant clothesline, their bodies in various stages of decomposition. But as I look over at Meg, her face tells me it's all too real.

Lifting my shirt to cover my nose and mouth, I examine the assortment in front of me: the skin of what appears to be a bobcat, half a dozen rabbits with their skins neatly sliced from their bodies; and a lot of dead squirrels.

I'm instantly reminded of Meg's podcast. The word "decomposition" had once made her turn it off; the word is so vividly descriptive that you can almost smell it when it's spoken.

The only episode of the podcast I can remember was about a missing person. It covered the story of a young girl who vanished from her home in the middle of the night. I was intrigued. It was a long shot, but I had hoped that it was related to Mrs. Grant's sister, Virginia.

Ever since Mrs. Grant told me about her sister, I've spent countless hours thinking about her. Thoughts of Virginia have even crept into my dreams. In one, I saw her walking alone down a dark street late at night, a bright, pink backpack over her shoulders. She looked back panicked, as if someone was following her. Then a shadowy figure ran past me and chased after her. I sprinted after them, but I couldn't catch up. He picked her up and disappeared into the woods. I jolted awake, drenched in sweat.

The podcast episode about the missing girl started with a request: "If you have any information about the case we're about to discuss, please contact your local authorities."

As the story unfolded, I realized the details were similar to what little I knew about Virginia Rose, but the timeline was off by about three decades. I wanted to share the episode with Mrs. Grant, but I hesitated for fear of triggering her. She always had so many stories to tell, but so little of the ones I really wanted to hear—the ones that would help me understand her life better.

I don't know why I'm so fixated on Mrs. Grant. Maybe it's a way for me to escape my life, which has been feeling so out of control. I can't stop my mother's mortality and Esther has grown distant. She barely comes into the shop anymore, and when she does, she clearly doesn't want to talk. She's never responded to my many texts over the years, though she once claimed she didn't receive them, which I don't believe. What I don't understand is why she comes into the coffee shop at all with so many other options around. It must be because she wants to see me. I've romanticized it, convinced myself that she comes in first thing in the morning so we could spend those few moments alone before other customers arrive. I really hope that's the reason.

Should I call her? Should I make more effort, especially since I plan on—

"What in the heck is this freak show?" Meg's voice breaks through my thoughts.

"I'm guessing this is where Liz's husband did the dirty work after bringing home the game he hunted," I reply.

"Should we still go inside?" asks Meg. "I can't imagine Liz being so heartless that she would store his body with all these dead animals."

"You should have heard her," I protest. "I think she really hated the guy. But I also don't know how Liz could have dragged his body up this road."

"There are plenty of ways," Meg says. "She could have stuffed him in the car, or she could have killed him in the shed."

"Well, I was the one who had to check the van. Now it's your turn to lead, Meg."

With some hesitation, Meg finally steps through the

entrance lined with animal corpses. She approaches the wide double doors, secured with a wooden latch. We keep turning our lights on and off, just long enough to figure out how to open it. There is no lock, so it seems simple enough.

Meg slowly lifts the wooden latch, and the doors come flying open, slamming into us. Meg and I stumble backward onto our butts. I quickly shine my light into the shed, expecting to see a corpse. But nothing. Just the swinging doors banging against the outside wall.

We exchange a glance and then check our hands for any fresh cuts. All we find are a few pieces of gravel that we brush off.

I stand and extend my hand to Meg.

"That was..."

"Alarming?" I offer.

"More like haunting."

Just like my sister to put a paranormal thought in my head on an already terrifying night. As we walk in, the logical reason for the doors flying open becomes apparent. The window in the back is opening and slamming shut.

"Just a cross breeze," I say.

"Yeah, sure it is."

We flash our lights to the left of us first. The burning smell of strong bleach fills my nose and makes my eyes water. Old license plates hang on the walls along with generic tools, pitchforks, rakes of various shapes and sizes, saws, brooms, and drills. This has got to be one of the most well-organized sheds I've ever seen—not like what I'd expect from the appearance on the outside.

"Lights, there have to be lights somewhere," I say scanning the walls behind us, where a light switch would normally be.

I touch the wall with my hands, trying to preserve my phone battery, which is now only at seven percent charge. But all I feel are wood panels and some dust and cobwebs.

I quickly pull away.

"What?" Meg asks, as she shines her light on me.

"Nothing, just some..."

"Mark," she says. "Don't move, don't move."

I roll my eyes as I start walking toward her.

"Mark, stop! What are you doing? Stop."

"Meg, you aren't going to get me this time!" I say, and at those words, I feel something sharp sink into the back of my neck.

I instinctively slap at my neck where the fangs sunk in, squirming away from the spot and shining my phone toward the ground where it would have fallen.

Meg approaches, shining her phone at the back of my neck.

"Well, is there something there?"

"Yeah, there's a bite," Meg says with concern in her voice.

"Is it swelling?" I ask, feeling the spot grow warmer and warmer to the touch.

"Move your hand so I can see."

Just as I do, her light instantly turns off.

"Son of a—well, now you made me waste my light checking your stupid bite."

"If you didn't constantly joke around, maybe I would have listened to you."

"My tone was so obviously serious. I swear you should know me better than that."

Is she for real right now?

"Well, help me find it so we can at least see if it was a poisonous one," I say as I scan the ground with my phone.

"Stop, right there, go back. I think I saw it," Meg whispers, pointing in the direction opposite the tools.

There it is—a creepy little thing. An eight-legged arachnid with freakishly long limbs and yellow streaks that contrast against its black body. I must have injured it when I slapped the spot on my neck because it's limping now, trying to find refuge in the corner. I fight feelings of guilt as I look at the pathetic thing. It bit me, but probably out of self-defense. It's amazing how a simple misunderstanding can lead to sour consequences. I'm sure it felt like a venomous sting when I told Esther I couldn't leave with her.

"Hurry, squish it, step on it or something."

"Hang on a second."

I observe with curiosity as it limps its way to safety. What now? Moments ago, it was fighting for its life, and now it's escaped. What will it do next?

The little guy slowly makes its way to a table and crawls up the leg.

It's stupid, but I want to see where this spider goes. I feel a little itching now on the back of my neck where the spider might have injected venom into my bloodstream. My phone battery is at five percent.

"I don't know why you do this, Mark. You get lost in preposterous daydreams all the time, and now you're intently looking at this bug that just bit you for who knows what? A sign?"

I ignore my sister. I'm going to see this through.

The spider is now at the top of the table, which is covered in sawdust and red stains—probably from Mike skinning his prey. The little spider makes its way to a cord and follows it. It's moving like it's done this its whole life—probably born and raised in this old dinky shed. It has the whole thing mapped out and is fully aware of its location and where it's heading.

I follow the cord with my light a lot faster than it crawls. Right when it reaches the drywall, my light flicks off.

"Well, did you find what you were looking for?"

"It's a Brown Widow, I think."

"Is it poisonous?"

"Yeah, to a certain extent, but I know some who've been bitten with no side effects."

"Well, did you kill it?"

"No point; it was just defending its home."

"No point? It bit you; that's what you do when something bites you; you bite harder."

"I'm not a murderer!" I say, raising my voice.

I didn't mean it the way it came out.

"Screw you!" she yells.

She starts storming out, and I reach over to her arm. She pulls away and walks through the door.

"Meg, I didn't..."

"Do you even have a clue what it's been like having to take care of Mom while you and Dad are off at work all day?" she snaps. "Do you know what it's like to deal with you as you emotionally detach from everything and get lost in these wild imaginations of yours? Your mind is always somewhere else. It's been exhausting!"

The drugs must be wearing off, and the real Meg is resurfacing, along with the emotions she's tried to suppress.

"What do you mean, my imagination?"

"I mean, you're never present. You haven't been for years."

Not present? What is she talking about?

"Why did you even come out here for this stupid truck?" she asks angrily. "What's the plan? Are you going to leave your widowed father and only sister?"

"Meg, you know this has been my plan for years," I respond gently.

"Your plans changed, I thought. When . . ." She pauses, contemplating her next words carefully.

"When what? When mom got sick? What is it? Are you really going to make me feel guilty for wanting to leave?"

"Mark, listen to me—"

"No, I will not let you put me through another guilt trip about not doing enough! I know I've been processing this whole situation differently from you, but I don't make you feel bad for whatever the heck you do. So let me have this."

"Tell me exactly what your plan was, Mark."

"Just go! Leave! I mean it! Leave! I will not take another second of this. I've put my plans with Esther on hold for long enough!" I blurt out.

"Esther?" she replies, disbelief in her voice.

"Yes, Esther! The girl I dated in high school, my best friend since seventh grade. The girl I'm in love with."

Come to think of it, Meg didn't hang out with us, and since she was three years ahead in school, we never interacted. She didn't converse much with Esther beyond just generic greetings.

Meg doesn't know that I never moved on. I've kept these feelings to myself. With our family's circumstances, I feared that if I mentioned anything about leaving with a girl, it might have blown up into a quarrel.

Esther was just a girl to my family, no different from the guys Meg would date at school. My parents weren't too strict about who we dated.

"I can still have a life after all this," I say quietly. "That's what Mom would want; that's what she wants."

"And have you told Mom and Dad about these plans with Esther . . . well . . . Dad?"

Mom hasn't been able to speak for the last six months.

"Leave me alone, Meg; I'm going to figure the rest of this out on my own."

She quietly pulls out her phone. Then seeing the battery is dead, she curses.

CHAPTER 19

12:20 AM

As I watch my sister walking back down the way we came, I'm gripped with more memories.

"Do you know if they hired her?" I ask Lyda, as she serves me a delicious slice of strawberry pie and a glass of water.

"I couldn't tell, sweetie, but I did hear her say something about thinking it over. Why don't you ask her? I'm sure she'll talk to you about it. You two are just the cutest couple I've ever seen."

The words bite.

I poke at the pie. "Yeah, I'm sure it will come up soon."

My voice is tinged with too much sadness, especially for a woman who prides herself in reading body language.

"Honey, what happened? Are you guys fighting?"

"No, we, um . . ."

"Hold that thought."

The door chimes, and someone walks through. *Good timing*, I think. I regain my composure so that I don't humiliate myself.

"Sorry about that, hon. Ok, so you were saying."

"My, uh, mom, well, she's sick, and . . . Esther and I were planning on going away together." I sniff a little, taking a bite of the pie, trying to hide the sound.

Should I really confide in this woman about Esther's private matters and why I had to make the decision I made? But I do need to talk; the burden is too heavy.

She takes a seat in front of me. I go on about the first time I met Esther, our first date, getting punched by her brother, our plans to leave town, my mom getting sick, and not wanting to make Esther wait.

"That's heavy, kid. I'm sorry."

"Yeah, it is," I say, taking the last bite of the pie.

"I don't mean to tell you what to do or how to act, but I'm gonna. I think you're being sweet. But I think you're being a sweet nitwit."

The words catch me completely off guard, and I start choking on the pie's crust. I reach out for the glass of water in front of me and chug it down.

"Kid, a love like the one you described, and the one I witnessed this last year, comes along once in a lifetime. I didn't even have that with Jackson. I swear he loved his damn cigarettes more than me. But you know what, Mark? I stuck by him through thick and thin. And ask me if I regret it. Go on, ask me. Don't be shy."

"Do you regret it?"

"You're damn right I do."

What exactly is the point of this whole story?

"I ruined my prime years. I wasn't lucky, kid. And I live with regret. I don't want *you* living with regret."

"But what about my mom? I can't leave her."

"Now, who said you gotta go and leave your dying mother?"

"Well, it seems like you have a plan in mind, and I've been at my lowest this week, so if you want to enlighten me, I would love it," I say, with a little more attitude than an older woman deserves.

"I'm sorry, Lyda. I'm just feeling really down." I sigh, looking dejectedly at the leftover crumbs on my porcelain white plate. "Really down."

"I ain't gonna fault you for that, sweetheart. Lord knows you've put up with my ramblings. If you think I've never gotten backlash from a teenager, then you have another thing coming. You know, there was this one night a bunch of 12th graders came in just ten minutes before closing."

As she goes on with the story, I find myself fiddling with

the slightly sharpened edge of the chip on the plate, almost wanting it to draw a little blood just to see the sharp crimson contrast against the white of the plate.

"Anyway, baby, I digress. You want to know what I think you should do about this little heartache dilemma of yours?"

She leans in, arms crossed on the table. A big smile breaks across her face, showing her white teeth that shine against her darker complexion. Then the smile fades and she looks out the window in contemplation.

The shed door slams open again with the wind. *For once, I'm going to finish what I started.*

I walk into the shed, and the sound of a slow, deliberate, unfamiliar voice fills the air.

"Hello, my friend."

The doors behind me slam shut.

CHAPTER 20

Unknown

Terror pulses through me, not just in my stomach or heart or lungs. But it crawls down the back of my neck, snakes down my spine, shakes my knees, and slithers all the way down into my toes.

I turn back to run toward the door, a faint crack outlining its frame. I push against it, but it won't budge. I throw my weight into it, slam my shoulder, and even kick it. My voice breaks as I shout for Meg.

"No need to be afraid, Mark," the voice says. "I won't hurt you."

Blood rushes to my head, and ringing fills my ears once again. *How does he know my name? Why didn't he say anything when Meg was here? Was he waiting for me to be alone?*

"Shhhh . . ." the sound emanates from the shadows, the darkest corner of the room.

I squint but there is nothing visible.

"Who?" I start. "Who . . . how do you know my name?"

"I've been watching you for a long, long, long time."

"Dude, you need to shut up with that creepy nonsense and tell me right now who you are."

I can now see the faintest outline of someone rising from the shadows.

"Don't come any closer, you freak!" I shout.

"Mark, I remember you. I remember you playing with your model cars many summers ago, right on the edge of the tree line—where was that again?"

He's fishing for information, like some phony psychic who throws out a few bits of random details that happen to be true until you fill in the blanks. Then he takes all the credit.

"If you know so much about me, then tell me—what's the name of the park?"

"Salmen . . . Salmen something."

My stomach falls, like the first drop on a rollercoaster.

"Salmen Nature Park," I whisper.

"I told you," the voice says with an eerie calm. "I've been watching you since you were a little boy."

He starts approaching me, but the darkness is too deep to reveal his face. And I don't recognize the voice.

"Let me out of here!" I shout.

"That's not up to me," he replies. "That's up to your sister. She left you in here, didn't she?"

"No, we had a . . . No, shut up and let me out!"

"Mark, why are you here?"

Why am I here? My mind races.

I'm here to move on with my life; to make the dreams of the girl I love come true; to free her from her nightmare; and to give her a better life. I'm here to escape home. I'm here because I refuse to let my final memories of my mom be of her struggling —unable to move her arms, feed herself, change the TV channel, or even tell her family that she loves them.

"I'm here so I can escape!" I cry out, falling to my knees as the tears stream down.

A hand rests on my shoulder. I don't flinch. I'm not scared anymore—just numb, like a callus hardened from repetition, the kind that forms on the tips of your fingers when you're learning to play guitar.

I look up slowly to finally see the face behind the voice looking right at me.

CHAPTER 21

Unknown

I gasp as my eyes study his head—easily double the size of anyone I've ever seen. But it's not just the size that's unsettling; it's the shape. One side bulges unnaturally, like a massive tumor, while the other appears sunken, as if caving in. The back of his head is lumpy with stretch marks. His eyes sit far apart, stretched to the edges of his face as though they had been forcibly repositioned. His nose is repulsive, pulled up toward his forehead, exposing the cartilage inside. His scalp is sickly pale, like a white onion.

"Silas?" I whisper.

At the sound of his name, a smile appears on his face, revealing just a few teeth, dingey and crooked.

"How, how are you even alive still?" I tremble.

"That's a question for another time. We need to talk about why you're here."

"I already told you," I say, as he moves closer to me.

I instinctively pull back, and for a moment, his expression shifts to sadness.

"I'm not going to hurt you," he says gently. "I've never hurt anyone."

"How long have you been watching me?" I ask.

"I've been watching you your whole life," he says. "When you looked up at the trees, I was looking back. When you would drive at night, staring off into the forests, I would see you. When you were at the Grants' house earlier, you looked into the attic and then back at me. I even saw you and Esther on your first night together, madly in love. I was so happy for you when you got that first kiss."

"Why have I never met you before?"

"You didn't know you needed me."

I don't need him, I think. *This can't be real. I'm not here; he's not here. I'm imagining the Onionhead the same way I imagined Mr. Grant attacking me.*

"I know you're not real."

"Of course, I'm real, Mark," Silas says. "Just not to anyone else. But I am real to you, and I can help you."

"Help me? Help me with what?"

"I can help you figure out what's wrong with you."

"Nothing's wrong with me!"

"I guess you weren't ready to see me," Silas replies, circling me.

On the second round, he stops halfway in front of the barn doors. *Is he examining me? Sizing me up?*

As I look up at his repugnant face, my vision blurs. Then the double doors swing open. As a bright light flashes into the shed, the Onionhead vanishes.

"Oh my God, Mark!" Meg says, running over to hug me.

Her warm embrace is comforting.

"Do you, do you see him, Meg?"

"Who? *Mike*?"

"No, no, not Mike. Forget Mike. Do you see the Onionhead?"

"The Onion? Mark, what are you talking about? There is no one in here."

She shines a powerful flashlight all around the room. There is nothing but tools, the back window, and several tables with equipment.

"Mark, you need to get some water. You're probably dehydrated."

"No, no. There was . . . there *had* to be. I did not imagine this."

"Well," I brush tears, feeling shame for crying, "do you see a body anywhere?"

"No, no one is in here, but let me check the perimeter, to

see if there are any hidden trap doors or anything."

She starts at the right side of the room where the spider had bitten me. Shining the light up and down the walls, she takes her time making a thorough examination.

"There is no sign of a body anywhere," she sighs.

I'm still in shock. *What is happening to me?*

"Meg, I'm so sorry for what I said; I didn't mean it."

"It's not a big deal. We've been through a lot tonight, and we both just snapped—in different ways, but that's all it was."

She's right—I must have imagined the Onionhead. I'm dehydrated, with a cut and a spider bite. Also, just a few hours ago, I thought I was going to die.

"We need to get out of here, Meg."

"Yeah, I agree."

It's time to turn to our last resort—the Grimaldi brothers.

CHAPTER 22

Unknown

"So, where did you get the flashlight from?" I ask.

"From the garage," Meg says. "I wish we had the brain cells to think of these things before wasting our phone batteries."

This night has been filled with one mistake after another. Now, I need to get my hands on some ice-cold, refreshing water; maybe that will cure my hallucinations.

"Were you able to get a hold of Dad?" I ask, realizing it's a stupid question. Her phone died before mine.

"No, I was hoping to call him on yours."

"That's not gonna happen now," I say, with despair in my voice. "Thanks for coming back for me."

"I didn't come back for you," she says. "I wanted to finish the..."

My sadness must be apparent because she rethinks her response. It's too late, of course. But I appreciate Meg not being easy on me. I don't want her sympathy. I already feel like a pathetic, emotional loser. Why did I imagine the Onionhead? At least, I *think* I imagined him. If he were real, Meg wouldn't have missed him. Why was he so insistent that something was wrong with me? Were my thoughts playing tricks on me? Does the venom from the Brown Widow cause delirium?

"I wasn't going to leave you; I just wasn't expecting to find you locked in there," she giggles for a moment. "What would you do without me?"

"Shut up," I say, nudging her as we approach my car.

"Mark, do you think you're up for seeing the Grimaldi's? I don't want you spacing out again," Meg says, her tone unfamiliar—not mocking or protective, but the way a parent would speak to a young child who's scared of the dark, convinced there's a monster in the closet.

"Meg, I'm not crazy! I know what I saw. But I also know it wasn't real. Stop acting like I've spaced out like this my entire life. This is all new. Like you said, I need to get some water and I'll be fine."

"I know, but it's still something that you need to get a hold of. I'm not gonna sugarcoat it; I'm a little worried about you."

Worried about me? *How dare she.* If anything, I should be worried about *her*. I'm not the one doing illegal drugs and then hiding them at my brother's workplace.

"If . . . if . . . I'm going crazy, it's because of you."

"Did you know I went to a class once for my addiction?" she says.

I'm taken aback at her honesty.

"You're lying."

"It was about eight months ago. I saw an ad stapled to a post downtown. They met on Thursdays, and I knew you and Dad would be off work and Mom would be taken care of. So, I went."

How did I not know about this? How could I be so wrapped up in my own plans, that I didn't even notice my sister needed help? We, her family, should have been her support, not some random self-help group.

"Meg . . ." I start but then realize I don't have the words.

"Just let me finish, Mark. Otherwise, I'll never get this out. When I went, I noticed the group was filled with some of the most down-on-their-luck people I had ever seen. I didn't feel like I fit in. I almost walked out, but they were so welcoming. I didn't want to admit that I was like them. Of course, some of their addictions were much more extreme. This one guy was literally rocking back and forth the entire time. Another woman was constantly moving her head in every direction as if she was being chased from every which way."

"Meg, I know where you're going with this. But I'm not an addict."

"Mark, just let me finish! When they started the meeting, everyone was asked to share what brought them there that day. I was the newest person and had the displeasure of going first. I simply said, 'I'm here because my mom is about to die, and my life only seems good when I'm completely and utterly unaware that I'm living it.'"

My sister's raw honesty feels almost as surreal as everything else that has happened today.

"At the end of the session, the leader of the group complimented everyone for their honesty and said, 'The first step to healing is to admit that there's a wound. Your body has the natural capabilities to heal on its own. But sometimes, when the wound is deep enough, you'll need stitches. By being here, you're letting the doctor stitch you up.' Cheesy illustration, I know. But the point, Mark, is that I think it would be good for you to—"

"I don't need to see a therapist!" I burst out. "I'm fine, I promise. I mean, for freaking heck, I was just cuffed to a railing hours ago with a slice in my arm. I had a gun pointed at my head and then I saw a dead person. I can't call the cops because I want to protect my sister. As if this nightmare couldn't get worse, a spider bites me. Even the sanest person on the planet would act a little crazy! So I dealt with it by having a few delusions. I think that's perfectly acceptable!"

"Mark—"

"No, I let you talk; now it's my turn. Here is what we're going to do. We're going to take my piece-of-sh—" I stop myself, "*crap* car, and go to Esther's house. I'm going to talk to her and ask for her employers to help us come up with a defense."

"When was the last time you even talked with her? How do you even know she'll help us?" Meg asks.

"Because she loves me!"

Meg looks concerned. Of course Esther loves me. But now, hearing it out loud, I can see why it might sound ludicrous.

"Fine, let's go along with that plan," Meg says. "You seem to have it figured out."

I feel good about the way I handled this. I'm not crazy, and I don't need a therapist. The only thing she was right about was the need for stitches—not for my emotions, but for my sliced-up arm.

"Do you think there's anything else we should do before we leave?" I ask, after Meg gets back from returning the flashlight, "I feel like we are forgetting something."

"Are you kidding?" Meg asks. "If anything, we've been here too long. Let's go see Esther."

Despite my decisiveness, I feel some unease. I wish we would have found Mike's body. Before tonight, I had never seen a dead body. I just assumed the first one I would see would be that of my mom. That thought had kept me up late into the night. How would we find her? Would she slowly drift off as we waited by her bedside? Or would I wake up to screams and panic from my father?

The first few years still held a sense of hope. There were no major signs that ALS was progressing. It kind of felt like being in an airplane. Logically, you know that you're moving through the air at an insane velocity. Yet, you can't feel it. If you close your eyes, you could almost trick yourself into thinking that you're completely still. We all tricked ourselves into thinking that my mom's disease wasn't moving at a vicious rate.

But an airplane experiences sudden drops in altitude as the pilot adjusts, searching for the most comfortable invisible airways through which to fly. In those moments, you're reminded that you're thousands of miles in the air, traveling at hundreds of miles per hour.

The first "drop" for Mom came when we returned from California. The last suitcase was in the back of Dad's SUV. I told him I would get it since he had driven the whole way back. I was whistling, feeling content that night as I looked up at the crescent moon illuminating our otherwise dark street. I even had a little hop in my step, kind of like how Gage did this morning. But all that changed when I stepped inside.

My mother lay curled up in a fetal position on the ground.

Meg and Dad were on either side of her. Mom's legs and arms shook and twitched uncontrollably. She was laughing, so for a split second, I thought my dad had told a funny joke and she was laughing so hard, she fell on the floor. Then came uncontrollable wailing, followed by violent dry heaving.

That night felt endless. Meg and I stayed by Mom's bedside, our heads resting on her legs. Dad sat in the small, uncomfortable hospital chair beside us. In the sterile, fluorescent room that smelled like death, the only pop of color was the bright red Jello.

The altitude hadn't just dropped—it had plummeted.

CHAPTER 23

12:49 AM

I take a long sip of water from the who-knows-how-old, scrunched-up bottle Meg found in the backseat. It tastes stale and plasticky, but I don't care.

"Want a sip?" I ask as Meg takes the bottle and drinks the last bit down.

I flick on the headlights, and the car ahead reflects the beams back at me. I've almost forgotten how it all began. Did an innocent errand really spiral like this?

The dashboard comes alive as the gauges shoot up and then settle back down. I have about a quarter of tank of gas. The clock reads 12:49 a.m. The lights on the dashboard alert me to check the engine, change the oil, examine the tire pressure. Nothing's wrong with the car—I just haven't fully twisted the key to start the ignition.

These cautionary signals amuse me. If only life were so simple, and humans had warning lights that could help them identify exactly what they need to fix about themselves. I imagine a dozen plus lights would appear on me: the "depression light," the "anxiety" light, the "check for despair" light, and maybe a "you're going crazy" light. I glance over at Meg, half-expecting to see her "lights."

"Why are you looking at me like that?" she asks, her eyes scanning me as if to say I'm giving her the creeps.

I don't respond.

Focusing ahead, I step on the clutch and start the engine.

Esther's house isn't far, maybe ten minutes away. But as I pull from the gravel back onto the muddy road, my eyes grow heavier. And the mud feels thicker.

"Step on it, Mark, or you're going to get us stuck."

"It's in second gear," I mutter, frustrated. "I don't know why it's not accelerating."

The shifting feels off.

My dad taught me how to drive this car. He bought it for me as a belated graduation gift. I'm not even sure how he was able to afford it with Mom's bills flooding in.

One Saturday afternoon, my dad wheeled my mom into my bedroom. I was wearing headphones, staring up at the ceiling, looking at the few old glow-in-the-dark star stickers that remained.

As a kid, before I developed my love for model cars, I spent hours stargazing through the telescope in our backyard. On clear Slidell nights, my parents would lift me up so that I could catch a glimpse of distant stars and planets.

When I was in first grade, one day I came home from school, and my parents made sure to keep me away from my bedroom until it was completely dark. I can't remember the excuse they used, but I remember sitting on the couch, overflowing with curiosity and excitement. My dad sneaked up behind me and blindfolded me with a kitchen rag. They guided me into my bedroom, excitedly whispering to one another. They stationed me in the middle of the room, and I heard the door shut.

"Ok bud, you can take off the blindfold," my dad said with a warm smile in his voice.

I lifted the blindfold and immediately felt engulfed by the universe. A little globe projector on my nightstand lit up the walls with stars and planets, which accompanied 3D stickers of stars throughout the walls and ceiling. My jaw dropped, and I spun in circles, trying to take it all in.

"So, what do you think baby boy?" Mom's sweet voice asked.

I didn't respond, too busy traveling through the solar system.

Years later, a large bright lamp replaced the faint glow of

the stars.

"Mark, follow us outside," said my father.

Outside, I found an ugly car with a big red bow on it.

Now, as Meg and I hop out, the car is even uglier, its front tires mired in deep mud.

"You've got to be kidding me," shouts Meg.

"Dude, keep your voice down. Did you forget where we are?"

"How could I? I'm in Hell, or purgatory, or some other sadistic place," she rants. "Because this can't be real. Am I in one of your god-awful hallucinations or something?"

I don't blame her for this moment. I had mine in the shed.

"Hop in the driver's seat, and I'll push," I suggest.

"Just call a tow truck!" she yells.

"Ok, yeah, I'll get right on that. Oh, could I use your phone? It must have magically charged itself, right?" I ask, delighting in my sarcasm.

But the look of despair on my sister's face instantly fills me with regret. I guess we *do* have warning lights.

She struggles through the concentrated muck, moving like a toddler trying to walk for the first time.

It hasn't rained, so the presence of this mud is peculiar. I move off the road to investigate. Tall grass surrounds me, leading to a rickety wooden fence barely two feet high. It's as modest a fence as they come. Two wooden cross beams lay horizontally between two vertical posts that are spaced apart about every four feet.

As I near it, I hear a hissing sound that becomes more distinguishable the closer I get to the overgrowth. Following the fence line out towards Oil Well Road, I find a broken sprinkler head, spitting water into the crushed grass.

The trampled grass leads me back to the muddy driveway, where car tracks are visible. *A car must have swerved off the road and crushed the sprinkler, causing the leak.*

I examine the fence, and it too shows some damage—a clear indentation near the sprinkler. It couldn't have been Mike's car, unless it had happened some time ago and they had repaired the vehicle. I don't recall seeing any damage on the van, though it had been spray-painted.

Liz must have run it over when she drove off in a rage to catch her husband red-handed.

I start towards my car but the flashing lights tell me Meg is running out of patience. *At least she didn't honk.* Just as I think it, the horn blares.

Keep it down! I think, jogging toward the car.

"You want the whole town to know we're here?" I whisper through the driver's side window.

"The only people dumb enough to be here this late on a Tuesday night are you and me."

"Wednesday morning," I interrupt smugly.

"Zip it and push!" she says in a matter-of-fact tone.

The wheels spin uselessly, slinging mud back in my direction. I push with all my strength, but the only thing that moves is the light frame.

"I just want to get the hell away from this godforsaken place," Meg says.

"Then get out, we will walk."

"Walk?" She repeats the word, clearly repulsed by the notion.

"I'm tired of dragging things out," I say decisively. "The car is stuck, so we'll worry about it later. We need to get to Esther's house, then find the Grimaldis. So get out and follow me."

CHAPTER 24

1:04 AM

I grab the keys from the ignition and switch off the headlights. Shaking the empty water bottle, I hope for a single drop—but there is none.

My shoes are no longer visible in the mud. Without the high beams from my car helping us see ahead, there's no way to avoid the worst of the muck.

"Shoot!" whispers Meg as she steps into a deep section of watery dirt.

"Ok, let's think about something other than the disgusting ground. So, how did you know I was in trouble with Liz? Was it my text message?"

"No, I didn't get a text; there was no service, remember?" Meg replies. "I had finished, well, you know, and wondered what was taking so long. So, I sat up and saw shadows moving through the blinds."

"Wait, you didn't text me?"

"How could I?" she asks, as if the answer is obvious.

How have we not talked about this? I'd just assumed I shared the network with Meg and that she had texted.

"Wait, so you didn't request to join the Wi-Fi network?" I ask persistently.

"No, why?"

I pause for a second, and Meg walks into me. She had been shadowing my footsteps trying to avoid more mud puddles.

"Whoa, keep moving," she says, nudging me forward.

"Sorry, sorry. I'm just trying to figure something out."

"Of course you are. Well, what is it now?"

"I got a notification that someone had attempted to join

the Wi-Fi, and I just figured it was you. So, I shared the password. About ten minutes later, I got a text. Then you arrived moments after. I just assumed it was all you."

"Hmmm . . . that is odd, but why did you assume it was me?"

"Because I had sent you a text asking you to come inside and get me out."

Meg's pace slows, and she asks the question I've been dreading: "What exactly happened in there, Mark? Walk me through it and don't miss a detail."

For the next several minutes, I recount every excruciating detail: who Liz was, how she had asked me out, and the fake girlfriend I invented to ward off the advances. I tell her that it was no coincidence that I went to her house. I tell Meg about the nightgown Liz put on, how she cuffed me and then manipulated me into feeling sorry for her.

"She started going on about her husband and how she caught him cheating," I say.

"So, what did she want with you?" she asks eagerly.

"She wanted . . . me," I respond, realizing how gross that must sound to my sister.

"Ewwww, oh my gosh. Forget I asked—ewwwww . . . !" Meg's reaction is as dramatic as it is prolonged.

I decide to lean into the humor. After everything we've been through, it's a welcome change in mood.

"What can I say? I'm pretty desirable."

"Ok, I've seen some pretty gross things tonight, but *this* tops it all."

The mud is starting to dry and fall off my jeans, its original light blue color no longer visible. The mud doesn't stick as heavily to Meg's black leggings. Her shoes, on the other hand, must have absorbed an extra five pounds of mud. She stomps her feet, trying to get the clumps off.

"How is your side feeling? I ask. "Does the cut still hurt?"

"It stings, and I'm trying not to think about the infection I'll probably get since you wrapped it with that disgusting rag from your car."

"Yeah, we need to get antibiotic ointment on it; I'm sure Esther has some."

The words are thrown out, but they fall flat. I hate it when you say something that warrants a reply, but the other person doesn't respond. The awkwardness always leaves the back of my neck feeling exposed. Not with Meg, I don't feel awkward with her. Only annoyed. Annoyed because her manners should be better than this.

How's your arm feeling, Mark? Would that be too hard to ask?

"I'm going to catch the bus or something," she finally says. "I'm not going to wherever it is you're headed."

Wherever it is I'm headed? I'm heading to the run-down house I've been to multiple times. It's not that far of a walk.

"There's not even a bus stop nearby. Esther's house is this way—"

"Mark, stop, just stop. You can go there, but it's a waste of time. This is why I worried about you coming out this direction. I thought you might get this way."

"*What* way?"

"That you would start thinking about Esther again."

Again? I've never stopped thinking about Esther.

"Why didn't you like her?" I ask.

Meg stops abruptly. I can tell she's looking at me, even though it's dark.

"Mark, we all loved Esther; she was wonderful for you. She was a great girl. Why would you say that?"

"Then why didn't you ever talk to her or ask her questions?"

"I did," she insists. "I always asked her about school and stuff, but I wasn't the one dating her. What did you want me to do, bombard her like Mom and Dad did the first time you brought her over?"

The first time I had Esther over was for dinner. We were in the 11th grade. And Mom was making her famous jambalaya.

"I hope Esther likes spicy food," she said with a smile as she added more Cajun seasoning to the simmering pot of shrimp, rice, and sausage.

"She's from New Orleans, Mom; I'm sure she can handle it better than me."

My parents were a little concerned, to put it mildly, that I was dating a girl from the Foster family.

Moab, Cain, and Brandon were notorious around the school. Brandon once showed up drunk to pick up Esther, and the news spread like wildfire amongst the parents. He drove right up onto the school lawn in his old beat-up Chevy truck with dice hanging on the mirror.

We were in the 8th grade and hadn't started dating yet. But we were best friends. When we walked out after school, my mom and dad were waiting outside.

"Mark, do you want us to give your friend a ride home too?" my mom asked.

"Yeah, come on, Esther, we can go get ice cream first and then take you home," I said excitedly.

"Oh, thanks, Mrs. Stratford, my dad should be here soon, and I think he's going to take me to the arcade," she replied, her face filled with hope and excitement.

Choosing to hang with my parents over my friends at that age seemed so taboo.

About two hours later, she texted, asking if the offer for ice cream still stood.

When I called her, she had tears in her voice. She said her dad never showed up and wasn't answering his phone.

"That poor girl, she's been waiting all this time?" my mom asked as she drove back to the school to pick her up.

As we pulled up, we saw Brandon Foster's truck parked on the school grass instead of the parking lot. He dragged Esther by her hair and threw her into the truck.

My mom hopped out of the car, yelling at him.

"You cannot treat that child like that!"

Brandon flipped off my mom, staggered into the driver's

seat, and drove off over the curb.

"I'm going to follow him and call the cops, what an intolerable man. He's going to get arrested for this," my mom said as she tailed behind him.

"Mom, you're just going to make it worse."

"Now, Mark, you listen here. You always go to the proper authorities with things like this. Always. He's a horrible, abusive father, and he needs to be punished."

The cops did go to the house, and we watched from a distance as they handcuffed Brandon and escorted him to the back of the white police car with horizontal blue stripes. Esther just watched from the window of her house.

It was nothing more than a slap on the wrist. The G brothers got him out of jail that same night. He was put on probation and in a public service program.

I tried calling Esther that whole night but never heard back.

The next day at school, she acted like nothing had happened.

The doorbell rang, and I ran to the door but a second too late. Mom and Dad welcomed her in.

"So, you're the famous Esther we've heard so much about?" my father recited the cheesy line.

My mom immediately brought her in for a hug, and Esther flinched slightly, which only I noticed. My mom squeezed her tightly, rocking her back and forth as if doing so would cure her from the years of abuse.

I expected Esther to look at me for help. Instead, she soaked up the warm embrace.

"So, Esther, tell us a little bit about yourself," my dad said as he brought a bite of food to his mouth.

"Oh, ooh, that's hot!" he said as he dramatically breathed, trying to cool his mouth.

Esther's genuine laugh filled the room.

"Not much to tell, Mr. Stratford—" she started.

"Call me Patrick," my father said, food still in his mouth.

Esther smiled and looked down ever so slightly, avoiding the display of masticated food.

"Dad!" I said, gesturing for him to cover his mouth.

"I come from a small family. My mother left when I was a baby, so I never knew her. I knew my grandparents, but . . . I'm pretty sure they've passed. At least that's what my dad told me. My brothers work for the Grimaldis, and my dad is the service manager at the For the Love of Cars mechanic shop."

My parents shared a concerned look at the way Esther brushed over the loss of her mother and grandparents.

"So, what do you see in my brother?" Meg chimed in.

Normally, I would have been offended by the question, but it was better than the pity that now covered my parents' faces.

"Oh, well, let me think . . ." Esther started, tucking her hair behind her ears. It wasn't up like usual but fell on her shoulders in loose waves. And she wore a charming, floral summer dress—I could tell she had put special effort into getting ready.

"You don't have to answer that question," I interrupted, putting my hand on her lap so she could hold it for support. She did and gave it a tight squeeze.

"Your brother is just the nicest guy I've ever met, and he's my best friend."

"Friend-zoned," my sister muttered, raising her drink to her lips.

The rest of the evening was spent playing games and eating my mom's delicious double chocolate cake paired with scoops of vanilla ice cream.

When it was time to leave, I walked Esther out as my parents waved from the doorway.

"It was so nice meeting you, sweetie!" my mom called as I hurriedly walked Esther to her car.

I hugged Esther goodbye, then gently closed the car door. She immediately rolled down her window and gazed into my eyes.

"You're so much more to me than what I told your sister. I could have spent the rest of the night telling them what you mean to me and how much I adore you. But I figured I would save the mushy stuff just for you," she grinned, pulling me in by my buttoned-up shirt for a kiss.

Meg now leans in for a hug, pulling me out of the past.

"I understand if you need to go there for some closure," she says. "But I'm going to head to a gas station and call Dad to pick me up."

"Call Dad? Are you going to tell him about—?"

"Tonight? The murder? I don't know yet. Maybe. I've got about a mile to walk and think about it."

I don't need closure, I think. Closure is about putting an end to something. But my life with Esther isn't ending, it's about to begin—as soon as I can figure out how to make this night vanish or at least fade into a distant memory.

CHAPTER 25

Unknown

It's a strange thing to walk the streets I've only ever driven. On foot, I appreciate the speed of driving just twenty miles an hour. The road seems endless. The marsh's pungent scent hangs in the air, especially unbearable with long exposure. The contrast of hot days and cooler nights intensifies the odor, making it even more oppressive.

Bugs incessantly zap at my face, and after a while, I stop trying to swat them away. The spider bite on my neck swells, growing rapidly. My arm aches and throbs as the rags covering my wound grow heavier with moisture. The duct tape securing the rags is so tight, that the area pulses with my heartbeat.

I hear a zap from Meg's direction as she swats away another mosquito.

"Ugh, why on earth did God create these creatures?" she asks. "What purpose could they serve?"

It's nice to hear her talking about a higher power again. Believing in something greater than oneself is grounding, especially when everything around us seems so random and disorganized.

"I have no flippin' clue," I reply. "Maybe they're here to confirm that our senses are intact. The moment we stop feeling annoyed at the mosquitos is a red flag, a sign we need help."

"Wow, so deep. So are you going to come with me or still go to . . ." she trails off.

Is she not even going to say her name now?

"Esther's?" I ask, annoyed.

"Don't go there, Mark; it's not healthy."

"Meg, Esther and I have been seeing each other regularly.

She comes into the Lil' Cup to get drinks for the Grimaldis."

Once again, my words float up and evaporate into the atmosphere. She probably assumes I'm a hopeless romantic clinging to a long-gone love from high school.

"When did you start talking again?"

"I don't know. We never really lost contact. It's not like how it used to be, of course. The breakup was rough, but I've been trying to get things back to the way they used to be."

"Mark, I don't think that's possible."

"Well, with your skepticism, I'm not surprised that none of your relationships lasted longer than—"

"Why are you such a jerk?" she cuts in.

"I'm the jerk? You're the one making me seem like a creepy stalker who's hung up on some girl from high school."

"Don't you see I'm trying to protect you? You really don't remember how things ended?"

"Of course I do! You weren't even there when I had to break her heart outside of school."

"I was there to pick you up, remember? You ungrateful little prick," she mutters that last part.

"If you do nothing for me ever again, fine, but stay with me and don't go to her house. Not tonight. I'll take you any other day but stay with me and let's go to the Grimaldis. Please, if it's the last thing you ever do for me, please. I'm begging you!"

I've never heard her talk like this before. What in the world does she think is going to happen if I go to her house? Is she really that scared of me moving on with my life?

"Whoa, calm down, Meg. Fine, I'll stay with you. Let's go," I say. "Why does it matter so much to you what order we do things in? Esther will be there when we go to the Grimaldis anyway."

"Yeah, yeah, sure she will. But what if we go to some decent attorneys for help instead of the Grimaldis?"

"No! We're going to them. I have a feeling they will be the best choice for our situation. Any other lawyer will make us go to the cops and, at most, get us off with a self-defense claim. But even then, there'd probably still be some prison time. I can't leave

Esth—." I stop, realizing this is probably why Meg hates Esther—she resents the idea of us together.

"Mom, for that long," I correct myself.

We continue along Old Highway 11, now back out of the wildlife management area. The sound of late-night travelers on the main highway is soothing, a reassuring sign that civilization is once again within our reach.

The soreness in my calves is distracting slightly from the constant throbbing in my arm.

"Oh no!" Meg exclaims suddenly.

"What? Are you ok?" I say wishing I could sound a little less concerned.

"I just realized that there's no way to get across the river. The highway is the only path."

I didn't even think about that. We were walking like we could conquer the world on foot, confident we could make it all the way back to Slidell without a problem.

"Is there a gas station off this exit?" I ask.

"I don't remember seeing one. Do you?"

I sigh, "No."

That's just how it goes in life. For a fleeting moment, I felt relief at the sound of traffic. But that meager semblance of happiness vanished only seconds later.

We follow the road, walking in the damp grass that follows the flow of traffic.

"Hey, look!" says Meg as she crosses the street.

Two trucks are parked in the grass. Meg runs up and cups her hands around her eyes, trying to look in the windows.

"Nothing," she says in a dejected voice.

"Do you think it's possible to walk on the highway?" she asks.

"Possible? Yes. Illegal? Also yes. Safe? Absolutely not!"

"Well, do you have any other ideas?"

"We could try to find a home on the other side of the highway. There has to be someone that would help us."

"Mark, if I saw how crazy we looked, I wouldn't help us,"

she says, laughing to herself.

She's not wrong. I've seen too many online videos of a seemingly innocent stranger begging for help at a door. Some claim they got a flat tire and need to use a phone to call a tow truck. Sometimes young girls will say they've been running from a creepy man who's stalking them. The goal is always the same: to lure the unsuspecting homeowner into some kind of trap. Usually, someone is waiting around the corner ready to abduct or rob the victim.

"I don't have any other suggestions. My plan is to keep following this road and see where it leads," I say.

"Remember the *river*, dummy! The highway is the only thing that crosses the river."

She's referring to the Old Pearl River, a murky, wide expanse teeming with alligators. It would be a death trap. Hitchhiking might be our only alternative, though that feels less promising than knocking on someone's door and asking to use the phone to call for help.

I ignore her insult and keep walking.

We've failed at successfully solving even one dilemma. Calling the cops would have solved everything. I was stupid and didn't think to have Meg clean the car of the drugs before we tampered with all the evidence in the house. Finding Mike's body to prove Liz's guilt was another dead end. We couldn't find a phone charger to at least call our dad for help. We couldn't get our car out of the mud. Now we can't find a gas station. We can't even get close to Slidell.

If we could at least solve one problem, even a minor one, maybe the rest would follow, like dominoes falling over one another.

Walking under the highway bridge makes me feel so unimportant. The occasional car races over the top, making me envious as I imagine how insignificant their troubles must be compared to mine.

This road stretches endlessly. My feet feel numb as they shuffle forward, one after the other. My mind has switched to autopilot.

My eyes have adapted nicely to the darkness. I can see things far more clearly now than when I first switched off my car's high beams.

"How much farther are you planning on walking?" Meg asks. "This road will eventually dead-end into the river—I'm sure of it."

"I don't know, but I can't think of any other options. I'm not going to walk on the highway."

"What if we just stay all the way to the right and walk single file? I haven't seen many cars driving by," she insists.

The highway has now leveled with the road we've been walking down. I glance over in its direction, which sits about fifty yards away, across a grassy ditch. We could just follow on the grass, but it will eventually rise again as it forms into the bridge that crosses the river.

"Give me another twenty minutes, and if a better solution doesn't present itself, we will go with your plan."

There is no way to process time, and I'm far too exhausted for my internal clock to be working properly. I know Meg will start complaining again far quicker than the actual twenty minutes, so I start counting in my head.

Fifty-five Mississippi, fifty-six Mississippi, fifty-seven Mississippi, fifty-eight Mississippi, fifty-nine Mississippi. Fourteen.

A few seconds later, right on cue, Meg says, "Mark, it's been twenty minutes. Come on, you agreed."

"No, it just reached fourteen."

"How do you know?" she sighs.

"I've been counting in my head. There's nothing better to do."

"At least it kept you from noticing the strange man that was looking at us back there?"

I hurriedly head back, seeing that she's fallen about ten feet behind.

"What?" I ask.

I know it's a joke, but the visual her words conjure spooks me more than I would like to admit.

The image of the Onionhead is fresh in my mind—along with his chilling words: "I've been watching you your entire life."

I decide to wait for Meg to catch up. She's moving sluggishly, her shoes scraping against the asphalt with every other step.

It's been nineteen minutes now, and I pick up the pace, knowing that one minute is all I have before we'll have to cross the highway. Meg has probably started counting too.

"Yes, I knew it!" I exclaim as I spot the railroad crossing sign ahead.

"This is it, Meg!" I say, my voice filled with relief. "We'll follow these tracks back into town."

"There is no way I'm walking down those tracks," she protests. "This is too creepy. How are you fine with this? I'd much rather the danger of the highway. At least there are headlights instead of the darkness and the forest. All I can picture is the Onionhead watching us from behind the trees."

"Would you shut up about that nonsense," I demand, more so because I don't want to think about that possibility.

I know her pride isn't allowing her to admit that my plan is the better one after all.

"I'm going this way," I insist. "If you don't want to get abducted by a serial killer truck driver on the highway, I suggest you do the same."

I know this will put fear in her mind. It's only fair that I return the favor. I don't know why she loves listening to those podcasts that cover stories of missing girls. The one she made me listen to still bothers me. And not knowing what happened to Virginia Rose bothers me. I can't handle knowing how many missing people there are in the world.

I wonder how people stay missing for so long. Especially the children. It's sad to think that so many of them are victims of senseless murder. But what about the ones who aren't? Are they just trapped somewhere in a basement? What happens when they become adults? Is there really no way for them to escape? I can't help but wonder about Virginia Rose. What if she's stuck in some horrible cellar? Most likely, though, she's dead—probably preferable to being imprisoned by some lunatic.

"I hate you," Meg mutters. "Why did you have to say that? Fine, after you, little bro." She gestures toward the dark path of the train tracks.

This walk feels even more monotonous than the old highway. There's nothing to keep my mind from picturing what might be lurking beyond the endless line of trees stretching endlessly on either side. The rocks under our feet crunch with every step, the uneven terrain adding more pressure on my right leg.

It's impossible to know how far we've traveled now. The river must be nearby, but there's no sign of it yet.

This endless walk feels like a perfect metaphor for how I used to feel waiting for Esther. Until recently, I felt like I was aimlessly wandering in the dark, unable to gauge how far I had gone or how much was left.

Who was it that had requested to join the Wi-Fi network? If it wasn't Meg, who could it have been? There was no one else in the house. There were no signs that anyone had been in the shed recently. Chills run up my spine as I picture someone watching us from the trees as Meg and I scrambled, trying to cover up the crime and find Mike's body. Was it Mike who tried to connect? No, it couldn't have been. He would have already been connected to his own network.

A shadow of a sign that I can't read appears on my right. Meg's footsteps become slower and she drags her feet. I wish we kept that flashlight.

"How are you doing?" I ask, empathizing with her for tagging along on this meaningless errand.

"I am super!" she says in an over-the-top jovial voice.

Yet again, she doesn't ask how *I'm* doing.

"Why did you ask about the last time I spoke to Esther?"

"No reason," she says dismissively.

"I know it may sound like our relationship is one-sided. But I swear she still loves me. You only saw the superficial side, but we're in love. I promise I wouldn't leave you and Dad for just anybody."

"Mark, I can't deal with this right now. We will talk about it later with Dad. I can't do this by myself."

"Ok stop! I'm trying to be real with you now and you act like I'm doing something terrible. Why do you need to drag Dad into this? I'm going to tell him when the timing is better."

"Oh my God, please! I can't do this with you right now. I don't know how."

An image of Esther thanking Meg for picking us up late one night when we were trapped in New Orleans keeps me from snapping back.

"Oh my gosh, I can't tell you enough how grateful we are for picking us up, Megan," Esther said while we hopped into Meg's disgusting backseat.

Esther had surprised me with round-trip tickets to New Orleans to show me where she had grown up.

"You're going to love it. I have our whole itinerary planned. We leave at 7:00 a.m."

I remember the tapping on my window—the sound blended into my dream until I woke up to Esther standing over my bed, gently shaking me awake. It was 6:00 a.m. My mind was in a daze, and I quickly wiped away the drool on my face, feeling absolutely embarrassed.

"You must have been dreaming about food," Esther said, laughing.

"How? How did you get in here?" I asked, rushing to the mirror, dreading how I must look. My hair was a little messy but other than that, I didn't look too bad.

"The window was open. You look fine, babe. But you need to hurry. The train leaves at 7:00, remember? And my phone says it's a thirty-minute walk from here." she said, pulling out clothes from my closet.

It was winter break, and we had spent that Wednesday

visiting her favorite childhood memories in town. It made me sad that she could easily fit all those happy memories in one half-day.

"Ok, lemme just shower really quick. Just be quiet. My parents don't know that we're going. They would hate me visiting the big city alone. You know how they are."

Esther was busy laying out my flannel shirt and holding up two pairs of pants to match it.

"You really need some new clothes. Maybe we can add that to our list of activities for the day."

She was in the cutest outfit, and the realization hit me: I did need to step up my game. She's already out of my league. I mean I'm ok looking, but she's drop-dead gorgeous with the kind of undeniable beauty that could attract anyone.

I'm still curious about what Esther's mom looks like because she doesn't take after her father or brothers. Brandon has a bigger forehead with a nose that sits a little too prominently on his face. Moab and Cain have smaller noses, probably taking after their mom. But their faces are distinct. Moab—the one who punched me—has a scar under his right eye, eyes too close together, and a mouth that's permanently curled into a sneer. Cain has a crooked nose that I'm pretty sure isn't genetic. Both have strong jaws covered with beards. Cain's beard is more maintained, while Moab's is patchy and gives the impression that he doesn't care about his looks. Tattoos line both of their arms and run up their necks.

Esther was wearing a tan sweater layered with a black vest, a gold crescent moon necklace, and pearl earrings. She always puts care into the details of creating the perfect outfit—maybe another form of escapism. Meg has always been careless with fashion. Guys drool over her anyway, which probably made her assume she could wear anything—baggy PJs, sweatpants, or leggings paired with a basic shirt.

Esther and I climbed out through the window, and I gently closed it behind us. We ducked under my parents' bedroom window so they couldn't see. She took my hand, and we sprinted down my street towards the bus station.

She was wearing boots with fuzzy little ball shoestrings that bounced in the air as we ran.

"Now boarding the 7:00 a.m. Amtrak departing for New Orleans," announced the intercom as we sprinted through the train station, navigating the crowd of commuters rushing to make their trains.

I entered the train and grabbed the railing to stop my momentum. And my body stopped Esther's as she fell into me. We made it just seconds before the doors closed.

She looked up at me and she closed her eyes while leaning into my chest.

The train ride takes about an hour and a half, and normally, standing that long would have been a dreadful experience. But being with Esther, I hardly noticed the time as it flew by.

She showed me Yelp reviews of where she was taking me for breakfast.

The name of the diner didn't sound too appetizing, but when they set a plate of blueberry pancakes in front of me—topped with scooped butter, powdered sugar, fresh blueberries, and a side of steaming hot maple syrup—any doubts disappeared.

"So . . . what do you think?" asked Esther as I took my second bite, closing my eyes while savoring every delicious flavor.

"Amazing!" I said, still chewing, then quickly covered my mouth, realizing how gross that must have looked.

"Better than the diner in town, huh?" she asked.

"Well, to be fair, we've only tried the pie there," I said laughing.

"True. And you can't beat the service we get from Lyda."

After breakfast, she took me to the Museum of Art, nestled in a gorgeous park. Walking with my girl while surrounded by beautiful scenery, I felt an extraordinary sense of peace and contentment.

As we approached the museum, I was struck by the grandeur of the massive pillars that line the exterior. Even while we climbed the staircase leading to the entrance, my eyes remained fixed on the pillars—their intricate craftsmanship evoking thoughts of the Roman Empire and the magnificence of the Roman Forum.

I reached for my wallet, glad that Louisiana locals get a five-dollar discount. Meanwhile, Esther pulled two tickets from her pocket and presented them to the teller.

"Ok, you two, have a great time now," the friendly woman said as she marked our tickets with a sharpie and handed us a brochure for the self-guided tour.
But I had a feeling Esther had plans of her own. She had thought of everything.

"When did you get those tickets?" I asked.

"Doesn't matter, I got them," she replied with a smile. "Now come on, let's start upstairs."

The building's interior was breathtaking. Large white pillars held up the structure, supporting a ceiling made entirely of glass, allowing sunlight to flood in. A grand marble staircase rose ahead of us, splitting midway, then branching off to the right and left to reach the top. But what *really* stole my attention was a sculpture.

As Esther walked up to it, tears welled up in her eyes. The brown sculpture, seemingly made of clay, was a slightly abstract depiction of a woman holding a child close to her face, as though she were whispering in the child's ears. Its beauty lay in the palpable reassurance conveyed by the whisper—perhaps a gentle "shhh . . . it's okay."

I wondered if Esther pictured herself as the child, receiving the consolation and comfort she so desperately needed.

To my surprise, Esther didn't picture herself as the child, but rather, as the mother.

"I want to make my children feel as safe as this mother does for her child," she said, her eyes still gazing at the sculpture.

"I don't ever want them to know the kind of evil that exists in the world. Ever!"

The hairs on my arms shot straight up. I knew in that moment that I would never genuinely understand the horrors that Esther had experienced.

As always, her selflessness was evident. Esther embraced the role of the giver, rather than the taker, her focus on what she could offer others.

We spent the next couple of hours looking at ancient artifacts in glass cases. I tried to unearth deeper meaning in each of the objects we observed but didn't experience anything like Esther's feelings for the first sculpture.

Masks, in various styles and shapes, lined one of the displays. Some had teeth, some were growling, and still others smiled.

"I feel that all people wear masks," I said. "Some are silly, others scary and intimidating. But at our core, we're the same. We put on different masks but for the same goal. We're all just trying to navigate this brutal life."

Mrs. Grant wears a smiling mask. But underneath it, she's utterly lost. And Mr. Grant wears a growling mask, but he's just a scared old man.

"And what mask are you wearing, Mark?"

Esther had asked me the question. But now all I can see is Silas' face in my memories.

I guess you weren't ready to see me, I recall Silas' words. Before the terror could freeze me over completely, Meg's voice yanks me back to reality.

"So, what in the hell are we going to do now?"

The Amtrak River bridge looms ahead, rising about twenty feet above the water on massive cement beams. Thick metal railings encase the structure, rising higher than the elevation.

"Ok, time to go back," Meg says, turning around to head back in the direction we came from.

"Walk all the way back?" I yell. "No way! I'm going to cross here."

"You can't be serious. What if a train comes?"

"What are the odds of that? I haven't heard one this entire time that we've been walking," I counter, feeling good about my argument.

"Exactly! That means we're overdue! How can you be so calm about all of this anyway?"

It's a better point than I would like to admit. But I'm not even sure that the trains run this late.

"Do you really want to walk all the way back only to cross the dangerous highway?" I ask. "We've been walking these tracks for at least thirty minutes now."

Meg's shadowy figure paces as she contemplates what to do next. She chews on her fingernails, a telltale sign of her growing anxiety.

"God, I hate the things you make me do," she finally says.

Before I can reply, she sprints across the bridge.

"Meg! Wait!" I yell. Her figure shrinks as she makes it through the first quarter of the bridge. I expect her to turn around and at least check to see if I'm following. But she doesn't look back.

I count under my breath: "One, two, three—" and sprint, the dread of an oncoming train propelling my feet forward faster than they've ever moved before.

The bridge begins to rattle.

I'm about halfway across, and I can see the glow of green trees from train lights.

"Shoot! Shoot!"

Meg is nowhere in sight, though I assume she made it safely to the other side.

The train's blinding lights burst through the darkness, and its deafening howl engulfs me.

I'm going to die. Images flash through my mind: my body crushed, contorted, or smeared all over this bridge. I glance at the river below, but the thought of the gators lurking beneath outweighs the fear of being hit by the train.

I picture Esther. She stands on the other side of the bridge, wearing a red dress—one I've never seen before. The train runs through her and straight at me.

I drop, curling into a ball, waiting for the impact.

CHAPTER 26

Unknown

"Dude, what in the world are you doing?" Meg asks, chuckling.

"The train—where did the train go?" I ask, still curled up like an infant.

"There is no train."

My sanity is slipping away, just like my mother. I'm losing my grip on it, just like I lost Esther. The weight of these parallels sinks my weight further into the cold ground. I'm immobilized.

"You aren't joking! See, I knew we shouldn't have gone to these stupid tracks." Meg says, running over to comfort me the best she can.

After only a moment, I stand up and dismiss her, feeling ashamed once again.

"Let's keep going," I say. "I think there is another bridge we will need to cross."

"Are you sure you're ready to continue?"

I move passed without acknowledging her.

My hunch was right. This next bridge is only a quarter the size of the first as it crosses a smaller branch of the river.

After another hour or so of walking in awkward silence, we begin to see the streetlights in the distance.

"You want to talk about it, Mark?"

"No, and you said you can't handle it anyway."

"Well, I didn't know how bad it's gotten. That sucks. I'm sorry."

I let her words hang in the air, unable to think of a response—my mind blank with humiliation I'd never felt so deeply. How can I even begin to think about leaving Slidell with

Esther when I'm going insane? Maybe worse than a prison cell would be an asylum.

Finally, a gas station appears.

The station's fluorescent lights blind us as we near it. The sensation reminds me of the time my eyes were dilated. We must look crazy as we walk toward the payphone in the front of the store. As we step into the harsh light, I look at Meg. Her blue eyes are squinted shut, her eyelids puffy from crying, with dark circles etched underneath. Her dark hair is a frizzled mess. Blood stains her jacket, having seeped through her makeshift bandage of rags. She walks with deliberateness, hunched as she hugs her arms around herself.

"Dang it!" she says. "I can't remember Dad's number since he changed it. I've always had him in favorites on my phone," she says, with her hand on her temple as if the gesture will help her remember.

"It's 504—" I begin, the familiar area code springing to mind.

"Shoot!" I can't seem to remember the rest. "Is it 431-6060?"

"Yeah, yeah, that sounds right," she says as she slips in the quarters and dials.

She holds the phone up to her ear, and I lean closer so I can hear too.

"Where did you get the quarters from?" I whisper.

"Your disgusting floss sticks weren't the only thing I found under the seats."

The dial tone makes us both flinch, followed by a robotic female voice: "We're sorry, the number you have dialed has been disconnected."

"Well, that wasn't right," I say. "How many more quarters do you have left?"

"Only enough for one more call," Meg says with panic in her voice.

"Can I help you with something?" a voice interrupts.

We look up to see the gas station attendant, a young

Latino man.

"No . . . no, we're good," I say, trying to hide my face and traces of blood.

"You sure? You guys look like you've had one hell of a night."

"No, it's been chill," Meg says in the most casual voice she can muster. "We just got lost and took the wrong exit,"

"Ok, well, if you need anything, feel free to come inside and ask," he says in a friendly voice.

"Actually, do you have any quarters to spare?" I ask.

"Claro que sí, I'll be right back!"

"What did he say?" Meg asks.

"Well, *sí* means yes, so I think he's going to grab some for us."

A few minutes later, he comes back out.

"Sorry, I thought we had some in the register, but we're all out."

What kind of gas station doesn't carry change? If he didn't want to give us money, he didn't have to offer in the first place. What a strange kid.

"Anyways, I hope you guys can find your way. Have a good night," he says quickly as he rushes back inside before we can respond.

"What the heck was that about?" Meg asks.

"He probably saw the blood on your jacket. Let's get out of here before we attract more attention."

"Do you know *any* numbers?" she asks.

"Only Esther's," I say, bracing for Meg's look of disapproval. "Hang on a second—I do know one other number, but it's a long shot."

"Well, what are you waiting for? Go on then," she says, holding out the phone.

I dial the numbers and hold the phone up to my ear as Meg now leans in to listen. It rings once, twice . . . ten times before finally, to my relief, we hear, "Hello, who is this?"

CHAPTER 27

Unknown

"Mrs. Grant!" I say with unbridled relief. "Oh, my god. Thanks so much for answering."

"Who is this calling so late?" she asks, in a skeptical tone that's still as kind as ever.

"It's me, Mrs. Grant, Mark."

"Mark, oh my dearest boy, what on earth are you doing calling me at this hour?"

"I know, I'm sorry. It has been one of the worst nights of my life. My sister and I got ourselves . . . " I start but then see Meg's eyes widen.

How can I phrase this so that we don't incriminate ourselves?

"My car broke down when we were driving and, well, our phones died. So, we walked to the nearest gas station, and yours was the only number I could remember since I call the house all the time from the work landline."

Mr. Grant requires me to call him at his house to check in if by some chance he cannot make it into the Lil' Cup that day.

"Oh, that is terrible, Mark. I am sorry, but I'm unable to pick you up. Eddy has the car, and I haven't seen him since yesterday morning when he went to drop off supplies at the shop."

"I'm so sorry. I didn't know. Have you heard from him?" I ask.

"No, and I didn't want to worry you about this last night, but if he didn't show up by the morning, I was going to ask you if anything happened yesterday that you were aware of?" she asks, her voice laced more so with curiosity than concern.

Should I tell her about Phillip, the mystery customer? And how Mr. Grant just left out the front without saying a word? I don't want to worry her unnecessarily. My memory is probably an embellished version of events, anyway. But if I don't tell her, and Mr. Grant is in trouble, then I would be responsible. I couldn't live with that kind of guilt.

"Well, now that you mention it, I came by your house after work last night to check on you both. Something . . ." I pause, trying to think of the right word, "*peculiar* had happened."

"You did? Around what time? I didn't hear you?"

"It was around 6:30."

"Oh my! I was upstairs looking through some old photos and must not have heard you. I'm sorry. So, what happened that was so *peculiar*?" she says the word as if she was using it for the first time.

"A customer—a man I've never seen before—showed up first thing and started asking Mr. Grant questions."

"What kinds of questions?" she interrupts with more interest in her voice.

"He was asking if Mr. Grant was the famous coffee guru he had heard about. Then he wanted to know more about the Grimaldi brothers, you know, the defense attorneys."

"Yeah, I know who they are. What did he want to know?"

"Well, that's just it. Mr. Grant had me go grab the pastries from the back. I was gone for only two minutes, at most, and when I came back out, Mr. Grant was gone."

"And what about Phillip?"

The air stills around me.

How did she know his name? Did I mention it already? No, I hadn't.

"Phillip?" I repeat, intentionally sounding ignorant.

"Mark, there are some things you need to know, but I can't say them over the phone. Where are you right now?"

Meg must see the sudden panic on my face.

"What is it?" Meg asks.

I hear the question but don't respond.

Do I tell Mrs. Grant where we are? Can I trust her? How does she know who Phillip is? What is she up to?

"I'm at a gas station."

"Yes, dear, you already said that. Which gas station?" insists Mrs. Grant.

My heart is racing now, and I don't know what to say. Why does she want to know if she can't pick us up anyway?

"Mark, are you still there?" asks Mrs. Grant.

"Answer her Mark, tell her where we are," demands Meg.

I keep staring straight ahead at the grease-stained gas station wall. What has happened to Mr. Grant? Did Mrs. Grant do something to him? Is Phillip some sort of hit man? Were my impressions of Mrs. Grant as far off as the ones I had about Liz?

Meg yanks the phone from my hand. "Yes, yes, hi, hello, this is Mark's sister. We're at the Gas station off Highway—"

"We're sorry, your call has expired. If you would like to continue, please deposit fifty cents."

"Shoot, shoot, shoot. Mark, what in the hell are you thinking?"

I don't know how to respond. Am I thinking that Mrs. Grant might send Phillip to get rid of us now because we know too much?

Meg pushes into my chest with her hands.

"You've really screwed us," she says, angrily. "What are we going to do now, huh? We can't call anyone, and our car is still stuck in the mud at the crime scene."

I hear her but all I can think about is Mrs. Grant.

"The trick, Mark, is to spread the butter on the outside of the croissant before putting it into the oven. This will prevent it from getting too burnt on the top and it will heat more evenly." Mrs. Grant said this on my second day at the Lil' Cup.

I was nervous. It was my first job, and I had already burnt the pastries. The shop filled with smoke and most of the customers left because it was unbearable.

"Mark, what were you thinking? What on God's green earth were you thinking?" shouted Mr. Grant as he tyrannically waved his arms at me while I pulled out the trays with burnt, smoking pastries. I was frantic. My hands were shaking, and the sound of my skin smoldering as the pain hit my forearm didn't even phase me. The burning was preferable to the yelling.

"Eddy, he's trying," Mrs. Grant said in my defense. "Leave him be. Let me show him how we do things."

I was desperate to find work to help my family financially. Meg could never hold down a steady job, so I had to step up. Also, I needed to distract myself from my misery. I hadn't seen Esther in six months. Not even once—not at the diner, not at the grocery store, nowhere.

I had applied to grocery stores, warehouses, and even fast-food places. The interviews seemed to go well, but I always seemed to get the same, crushing response: 'We think you need a little more experience.' But I didn't give up.

One day, I was picking up my mom's medication at the pharmacy, and the sweetest old lady was standing behind me in the line. I must have looked nervous, clutching the paper for the prescription drug Rilutek. I'd never had to pick up medication before.

"What's a healthy young man like you doing here?" the voice behind me asked.

I turned around, shocked by the question.

"Oh . . . um . . . I'm picking up this." I said, holding up the paper so that she could see.

I wasn't going to try to pronounce the word.

"Oh my. This isn't for you, is it?" she asked with concern in her voice.

"No, it's for my mom."

She instinctively reached out and gave my arm a gentle squeeze.

"I'm so sorry to hear that. How are you coping?"

I told her about my mom, the mounting bills, and the difficulty of getting her the best care without proof of income.

"What are you doing for work now?" she asked.

Embarrassed, I looked down. "I'm . . . in between jobs right now."

"I see. Well, it just so happens that my husband and I could use some help."

"Really? With what?" I asked, thinking it might just involve chores around their house or odd jobs.

At that point, I would have done anything.

"Have you ever heard of the Lil' Cup? It's right in the middle of downtown Slidell."

"No, I haven't. What do you do there?"

She smiled, but not with a condescending smile. I didn't know what she was thinking but as I remember the encounter now, I think she might have been happy that I had never heard of Mr. Grant's famous coffee.

"It's a coffee shop. My husband and I have owned it for the last twenty years. We have never hired anyone, but my arthritis is getting so bad that I could really use some help. What do you say? Would you be interested in being a barista?"

My heart flipped. This was far better than any of the other jobs I'd been applying for.

"Yes! Absolutely, I would! Thank you so much! When can I start? I think I can come in this afternoon, or first thing tomorrow."

"Hold on a second, before we even get started with that, let's have you come by the shop. How about you check it out this Friday? Get a feel for things. See if you even like the environment," she said. "I'm Margarine Grant, by the way. And you are?"

"I'm Mark, Mark Stratford."

"It looks like you're up, Mark. Wait for me before you leave, and I'll give you my home phone number."

I picked up my mom's meds and waited for Mrs. Grant by the front entrance.

"Oh, there you are, my dear. So do you even like coffee?" she asked, writing down the number.

It's impossible to forget: *504-777-0000*. How did they even get that phone number?

THE CUSTOMERS

I called later that week, my hands were sweaty as I nervously typed the digits on my phone.

"Edwin Grant speaking," a stern older voice came from the other end.

"Hi, I'm calling to speak with . . . your wife, I think. Is Margarine Grant there?"

"Who, may I ask, is calling? And for what purpose? She didn't accidentally sign up for one of those *Insider Magazine* subscriptions again, did she?"

"No, nothing like that. I met her at the pharmacy the other day and we spoke about . . ." I clear my throat, "a barista position in your shop."

"Hey, get over here!" shouted the man on the other end.

I flinched, as it sounded extra loud through the phone.

"Did you tell someone that we were hiring?" he asked in an intimidating voice.

"Yes, Eddy, I . . . I've been in so much pain, and I could really use some help. I didn't want you to find out this way, of course." she said, her voice almost fearful.

"Is this it? Would this make us even?" he asked, almost as if I wasn't on the other line.

"Oh, Edwin, are you seriously going to talk about this now with that poor child on the other end? Let him at least give it a try. You might enjoy the extra help."

"No, this is it. We're even now!" he said with the finality in his voice.

"Hello, are you still there, kid?"

"Yeah, I'm here," I responded.

"Come in tomorrow, 6 a.m. sharp. Don't be late. If you're so much as a minute late, you won't be working here."

As the years passed since that first encounter, Mr. Grant softened—though only slightly. He remained a harsh man, yet he had a surprising capacity for thoughtful remarks. I don't know what he was like behind closed doors. Had Mrs. Grant finally had enough and decided it was time to get rid of him?

CHAPTER 28

3:47 AM

"What is your problem? Answer me floss stick!" Meg yells.

"You don't have a clue what you're talking about," I respond.

"I have a clue! You're insane! You've lost touch with reality!"

"Do we have a problem here?" asks the young man from the convenience store.

We don't acknowledge him as I look at Meg in disbelief.

Her hands have landed on her hips, and without breaking eye contact with me, she says: "No problem. Is there, little bro?"

"No problem," I reply.

"If you two are done with the phone, I'm going to have to ask you to leave. My manager doesn't like having people here..." His voice trails off as he thinks about how to phrase his sentence more politely.

I don't blame them. With the way we look, I wouldn't want us here either.

"Well, people who aren't buying customers," he finishes.

"Ok, I'll buy something," I say, remembering the $18 in tips that's in my back pocket.

"Oh, ok. Then I'm sorry for the misunderstanding. Take your time and come in whenever you're ready," he says and walks back awkwardly.

"How are you going to buy something? We don't have any money," Meg says.

"*You* don't have any money. *I do,*" I say, pulling a wad of cash from my pocket.

"Where did you get that?"

"Where do you think? Some of us *work*."

I want the words to hurt. I want them to hurt as much as the last hurtful thing she said to me.

"Mark, I'm sorry..."

"No, don't." I interrupt. "You meant what you said."

"Well, I wasn't going to say I didn't mean it. I'm just sorry for saying it the way I did. Seriously though, why did you not tell your boss where we are?"

"You have no idea what happened this morning before you came in. And I'm not going to tell you because you will only assume that I'm 'insane'," I say with air quotes.

"I promise I won't!"

I pause for a moment, weighing the pros and cons of telling her.

"A man I never have seen before came into the shop today and was interrogating Mr. Grant. And then Mr. Grant left without saying something first, which he never does. The man stayed for a couple more hours, just observing things. I spoke with him, and he told me his name was Phillip, and he asked for my name—my full name. When I told him, he took out a pen, and I think he wrote it down."

"He wrote it down?" Meg asks, and I'm relieved she thinks it is strange too.

"Yeah, he then told me something about the way I was pulling the espresso that he couldn't have known."

"What do you mean?"

"I pull shots at twenty-five seconds like Mr. Grant taught me," I see Meg struggling to process the unfamiliar terms. "Anyway, he knew how the shot was pulling at twenty-seven seconds. No customer could know that because the timer is only on my side of the bar."

"Well, maybe he looked when you went to do dishes or something."

"Maybe, but he would have had to pull the shot to start the time, and I think I would have heard that," I respond, trying not to excuse her theory.

"Did anything else happen?"

"Not with him. But after Mrs. Grant told me that Mr. Grant never came home, she asked if anything happened at the shop. And . . . this is the strange part—I told her about the man who came in and how Mr. Grant left when I was in the back, and she asked, 'What about Phillip?'" I say pausing afterward, expecting to see the shock on Meg's face.

"And? Go on!" she says, just wanting to know more.

"And? That's it. How did she know about Phillip and use his name? I never told her."

"Are you sure?" persists Meg.

"Meg, I'm positive," I say, realizing of course that my words probably mean little right now. I was also positive I saw the Onionhead and that a train was going to run me over.

"That is odd, I guess. So what do you think happened? You think the old lady on the phone had something to do with what's-his-name's disappearance?" she asks.

"I think that after what we just went through with Liz, anything is possible. I believe Phillip may have done something to Mr. Grant."

I decide to go inside so the attendant doesn't have to come outside for another awkward encounter.

I make my way straight to the waters that line the fridge at the back corner of the store. Meg goes in the opposite direction towards the snacks and chips. I'm hungry too, but my thirst is overpowering.

I look over the options and see a two-for-five deal for a higher end water brand that I never buy, preferring the cheaper options. I reach into the fridge and grab the bottles, one for myself and one for my sister. They are ice cold to the touch, and my warm hand frosts up the plastic.

I take a moment for myself as I twist off the lid. I bring it up to my mouth and the cool, crisp water invigorates the back of my throat. My head is instantly refreshed.

I stretch my arm against the glass and lean my body into it for relief. I allow myself to close my eyes.

"Come on in, son. I'm glad you found the place okay," Mr. Grant said on my first day of work. "So, what do you think of our little shop?"

I took a moment to look around, mostly taken by the exposed fireplace in the back-left corner of the room. Its vent stretched up through the ceiling. In front of it, sat a pair of couches and a coffee table. Straight ahead from the glass door entrance stood the mod bar, its shelves lined with bags of coffee with names like *Grant's Special House Blend*, *Lil' Taste of Guatemala*, and *Marge's Merry Blend*.

Outside, two circular white coffee tables paired with matching metal chairs stood against the winter backdrop. I was surprised by how many customers enjoyed sitting there, sipping hot drinks in the chilly air.

One regular, Leland, would come in with a short-sleeve shirt and workout shorts, order two extra hot lattes, and take them outside, settling onto a chair that was way too small for his body.

"I like to finish my workouts by sitting on the ice-cold metal. It's my version of an ice bath," he once told me with a chuckle.

Leland was a cool dude, literally. His clean fade haircut stood in stark contrast to the thick bushy beard extending down to his chest. Every time I served him drinks, he'd shake my hand, his enormous hands making mine feel childlike. He did this at least three times a week. But like so many of the Lil' Cup's customers, he eventually left Slidell.

The rest of the Lil' Cup's interior was filled with wooden tables and stackable chairs, functional for cleanup.

The walls were adorned with local art, much of it created by artists who had moved to Slidell hoping the marshlands would inspire enigmatic undertones in their work. And they did often capture Slidell's mystique with foggy landscapes and dense foliage. One piece featured a solo girl holding a book that had slipped to her side as she stared at the vastness of a forest. Another depicted an old rundown cottage in the middle of a marsh, with a trail of smoke curling from its chimney and vanishing into the top of the canvas.

"Where did you get these, Mr. Grant?" I had asked.

He was banging on the jammed grinder, cursing under his breath. He looked up, almost embarrassed. "Oh, those? Crazy people come in here thinking they have some special gift. They believe they can see the world in a unique way. So, they try to capture it in their work. Take this one, for instance."

He led me to a painting over by the fireplace, a piece by an unknown artist. It was grim and full of depth—shades of black, grey, and charcoal formed the impression of being in a dark cave. As I gazed at it, I became engulfed by darkness, but a faint glimmer of light emerged from a faraway distance, creating perspective. The longer I looked, the closer and brighter the light grew.

"Ah, so you like this one?" asked Mr. Grant, pulling me out of the painting. "What do you see?"

I looked back at the canvas and the light was smaller again. It was as if I had gone backward into the cave.

"I see . . . Well, I think that the artist was in a dark place when they painted this. And even in the darkest moment, they saw light. The light grew as they focused on it. I guess the light was their hope . . ."

My words trailed off as I found myself, once again, closer to the light. I coughed and put my hand behind my head, a nervous habit I've acquired over the years.

"Wow, I didn't know my wife had hired someone that saw the world so deeply." Mr. Grant said.

"Oh, I'm not sure that I do."

"You do, Mark," he insisted. "I bet you have the most depth out of anyone else in your family."

The validation I received from Mr. Grant in that moment was enough to endure his more intolerable nature—like the following day when he yelled, "You've got to be the most useless employee!" as I frantically pulled out overcooked pastries from the oven. My arm burned from pain, and I looked down to find the outline of the pan responsible for my wound,

"Eddy, if you yell at him, you won't be able to train him properly. He will freeze up." Mrs. Grant said in my defense as I ran my arms under cold water. It didn't help.

"Use lukewarm water," Mrs. Grant said. "After you suffer from the extreme temperature of the hot pan, you shouldn't shock the skin with the other extreme. You have to let your skin gently ease back by running lukewarm water on it."

The life lessons I learned from her over the years, her cautionary tales and thoughtful insights, have helped me time and time again.

The next morning, Mr. Grant approached me as I was counting the cash register.

"Listen, kid, about the other day. It's just that I have high expectations for you because I see what you're capable of. You have so much potential. Do you know that? I bet your parents have never told you that."

The constant shift between Mr. Grant's kind praise and his harsh outbursts became the new normal.

I open my eyes, the empty water bottle in my hand a visible reminder of Mrs. Grant's warning against shocking the body with extremes. My stomach churns, and nausea rises through my esophagus. I run to the bathroom.

CHAPTER 29

Unknown

Loud gagging echoes through the bathroom, its condition typical for a gas station. Seeing the filth in the toilet only intensifies the violent convulsions through my body.

For several minutes, I'm caught in a cycle: puking, pausing, thinking it's over, then starting again. My ribs ache. Finally, I gather myself and look at my reflection in the scratched-up mirror. A pale, tortured face stares back. My hair sticks in every direction, and the duct tape wrapped around my arm looks ridiculous. With a trembling hand, I scoop water into my mouth to rinse out the rancid taste of bile.

As I open the bathroom door, the young worker is waiting outside with concern painted on his face.

"Are you ok, amigo?"

"Yeah, I just drank the water a little too fast. I'll come pay for it now."

"No problem, bro, take your time. I'm again sorry about earlier."

"Don't worry, man. I know you're just doing your job."

A customer walks in. "Like I said, take your time," the young man says as he walks back to his post.

"When a customer walks through that door, what do you say?" Mr. Grant had asked.

"Welcome to the Lil' Cup. What can I get started for you?"

"Good!"

"Why don't we use one of those tablets that lets you click on the drink the customer orders, and it automatically brings up the total?" I asked, instantly regretting the question upon seeing Mr. Grant's face.

THE CUSTOMERS

"We have so few options, Mark. A cap costs $4.50, a latte is $5.50, a straight shot is $3.00, and so is a drip. What's so hard to remember about that?" he asked scornfully.

"Yeah, I remember all that. But what about the tea? And how much do the extras cost? What do the different milk options cost? Oh, and what if the customer asks for more shots in a latte? Are they $3.00 for each one?"

He sighed, looking down.

I made valid points, but I also saw things from his perspective. He had all this information memorized because he had been doing it for decades.

"Never mind," I replied. "I can make a list of everything for now until I can memorize it like you have."

"Good evening, sir . . . I mean, morning," greets the young employee behind the register.

I can't see who he's talking to behind the tall shelving.

"Good morning. How are you doing?" replies the customer.

"I'm doing alright. If you need anything, just let me know."

"I actually need some assistance. I'm looking for a brother and sister pair, probably a couple of years older than you. Have you seen them?"

Now, I recognize the voice. It's *Phillip*—the mystery customer. I duck my head as I navigate the aisles, trying to get a glimpse of the man to confirm my suspicions.

"Oh, may I ask why?" inquires the young man.

I'm thankful for his caution. It probably seems strange to him that a man of Phillip's stature would be looking for two young people.

"They are in trouble. I got a call from them asking me to pick them up," he says as I feel the anger inside me rise.

He's not only lying, but once again, he knows more than he should.

I look through the bags of chips that line the shelves on an aisle, trying to get a peek at him. Sure enough, a tall, lean man—definitely Phillip—is standing at the front register. I duck back down, falling to a crouching position. Where in the world is Meg?

"Oh, yeah, I saw them calling you about twenty minutes ago. They are here. Pretty shaken up about something. The guy is right back there . . ."

"Oh perfect, I'll go check in on them. Thank you, sir."

I hear the man now methodically making his way down the front aisle. He's tall, but he can't quite see over the shelving. I'm trying to guess which way he will check first. If it were me, I'd go to the back wall that's full of the various refrigerated items and follow it to the bathroom as I look down each aisle that flows horizontally in the store. If he does that, I will need to go to the opposite end.

I get lucky. That is exactly what he's doing. I awkwardly walk while squatting down and make my way to the end cap of the aisle. I sit squatted in a catcher's position. How am I going to get out of here?

I wait until I think Phillip is near the bathroom. Now is my only chance. I sprint to the front register.

"Here, thanks!" I say quickly, leaving an unknown amount of cash on the counter.

I race out the door as the kid yells, "Wait, that's too much! What about your change?"

I desperately scan the area outside, hoping to spot Meg. My eyes are not yet readjusted to the darkness. I race around the building, still holding the other bottle of water.

"Meg! Where are you?"

I run out now to the main road.

"Mr. Stratford. Wait up!" Phillip calls out. "I'm trying to help you."

I run down the street in full panic, ignoring the man. It's a straight road with a chain-link fence on the left and a marsh on the right.

I need to go to Esther's! It would have been better if I had gone there from the beginning. I'm running as fast as I can. Burning from the acidity of my vomit aches in my chest.

Do I hop the fence and sprint through the field inland? Or should I dive in the marsh?

I won't be able to jump the fence with the condition of my arm. The marsh will cause an infection, or worse, an alligator will attack me.

Why would Phillip say he's trying to help me? What could he possibly do to assist me?

"Hurry, Mark! You're so slow sometimes," Esther had said as we were trying to make it to her all-time favorite seafood restaurant in New Orleans.

"I've been running for the last mile. Why couldn't we just get an Uber?"

"We would walk a lot more than this when we lived here. I've actually taken it easy on you. You're from a small city," she said as if New Orleans was so superior to Slidell.

Of course, it was, but I had to stay faithful to my little city.

"Watch it! Slidell is your home now too," I said pretending to be offended.

"Not for long, babe, not for long!"

"What kind of restaurant closes at 6:00 p.m., anyway?" I asked.

"The best kind! They always use the freshest caught seafood. When they run out, that's it—the shop closes."

"Why don't . . . they just . . . catch more?" I asked, running out of breath.

"You're so silly. Have you ever fished a day in your life?"

I hadn't and still haven't. The idea sounds so ludicrously boring and there are so many other things I would rather do with my time.

"Esther, the lights are red! What are you doing?" I shouted as she ran through the busy street.

"Come on, people jaywalk here all the time. We only have fifteen minutes."

She waited across the intersection and when I caught up, I thought I was in for a brief breather. She grabbed my hand and yanked me as we started sprinting another six blocks to the restaurant.

"Oh, my goodness! There it is. You're going to love it. You're going to absolutely love it!"

This part of town felt more business-residential than the downtown with its charming hotels and restaurants. This must have been near where she used to live.

"How are you not tired?" I asked.

"Because we haven't done anything tiring yet," she said, laughing.

This city opened my eyes to a side of Esther I had never seen before.

We slowed down as we crossed the final block, reaching a lone red building with a white base, definitely in need of a paint job. An old AC unit hung haphazardly from a window. We passed electrical boxes, and then Esther opened the dirty glass door.

"This is it?" I asked, less than impressed.

"Yeah, this is it. Come on, you know better than to judge a book by its cover."

I walked in and my senses were instantly enveloped by the smell of various sea creatures that had been deep-fried throughout the day. There was no dining area—just a register in front of me.

"Where are we going to eat?" I asked.

"You're so spoiled, babe. You eat standing up or you take it outside. Stop complaining," she smiled playfully.

"No, I'm not complaining. I was just expecting something different. That's all! I'm super excited!" I said, mustering up fake enthusiasm.

She rolled her eyes and approached the register.

"Oh my gosh! Art?" she asked.

"Yes, and . . . I know you, sweetie?"

"Oh yeah, I must look totally different. It's little Esth."

The man squinted as he studied her intently. His thick curly hair and dark beard were laced with coiled strands of grey. His dark skin was nearly wrinkle-free and his brown eyes looked wise, like they carried the weight of countless stories. He had

THE CUSTOMERS

one of those faces that instantly drew me in. I felt like I knew him, even though I didn't. Esther did, but I wasn't sure if he would remember her. My heart was beginning to hurt for my girl as I could tell this might have been a one-sided relationship. *Come on, at least fake remembering her.*

His eyes suddenly lit up. "You're Brandon's kid, right?" he asked to my relief.

"Yup, that's me," Esther responded with pride, far more than I would have felt being associated with such a harsh man.

"Oh, baby girl, where have you been? How are your brothers? Still a handful, I bet."

"You have no idea. I'm sorry we never got to say goodbye. My dad had some problems come up and his lawyers helped relocate him to Slidell."

"Well now, last time I checked that's only an hour away. You could've made a trip if you really wanted to see your ole nonc."

The sadness that painted Esther's face made the older gentleman step out from behind the glass fridge that displayed fresh seafood items.

"Oh, baby girl, I was only kidding," he said, pulling her into a big bear hug.

"I wanted to," Esther said softly, "but Dad's condition has been impossible to deal with. I'm so sorry, nonc."

That was the first time I heard about Brandon's financial situation.

"And who might this young man be?" Arthur asked, still holding Esther but glancing up at me.

"I'm Mark. Esther's boy—"

"Oh my gosh, I'm so rude," Esther interrupted. "Art, this is Mark. Mark Stratford."

She introduced me as if she were presenting me to the Queen of England. I could see how important this man was to her. I even wondered if he would be the one to walk her down the aisle on our wedding day.

"I see . . ." Art said, stroking his chin and examining me

carefully.

"I still have my nephew, Liam, if this doesn't work out," he said with no indication that he was joking.

"Oh no, that won't be necessary. Mark is the best guy I've ever met, well, besides you, maybe. You'll love him."

He walked up to me with a blank face and looked me in the eyes with an intensity that froze me.

"You hurt her, and I'll kill ya!"

I gulped and stepped back.

"I . . . I would never—"

Arthur burst out laughing. "I'm just messing with you boy. Get in here," he said, pulling me in for giant embrace.

Walking back around the counter, Arthur asked, "What can I get started for you two?"

"Oh, I was thinking about getting . . ."

"You know what, I'm gonna bring you the works. My treat. Hang tight and I'll be right back," he said.

I was relieved because I couldn't decide between the lobster claws or the oysters.

About ten minutes later, he returned, balancing plates and baskets of food on his arms, and set them down in front of us. One basket was filled with his house Cajun-seasoned crawdads. The others included various shrimps with different marinades, lobster tails, fish sandwiches, fries, and deep-fried oysters. He also brought out garlic bread and coleslaw. The variety of dipping sauces was astonishing.

"I'm in heaven!" I said, after taking the second bite of a crawdad.

"See, and you didn't want to come." Esther said.

"You didn't want to come? Now why on earth not?" Art responded, sounding very offended.

"Oh . . . no . . . I was just shocked when I saw . . ." I started.

"Boy, I'm just teasing ya! I know my shop isn't pretty. But she sure gets the job done," he said, grabbing my shoulder.

During the remaining time, Art shared stories from Esther's childhood.

"There was this one time, this little girl came in here, about this high," he said holding his hand about three feet from the ground, "and she held up one dolla bill. 'What can I buy with this?' she had asked in her quiet little voice."

I wished I could have experienced this memory firsthand, but this was the next best thing.

"I told her, 'You see those drinks in there? I'll pour you half a glass, and I'll have the other half.' Her little eyes widened, and she looked so thrilled with the offer. My heart melted, and I ended up bringing her some of the food you now see in front of you."

As he shared the story, Esther covered her face with her hand, glancing over at me.

After a while, Esther and Art exchanged phone numbers, promising to keep in touch.

Art boxed up all the leftovers and saw us out.

"It was nice meeting you, son. You take good care of my baby now, ya hear," were his last words as we waddled out, our stomachs full of delectable food.

"Wasn't that the best meal you have ever had?" Esther asked.

"You once again exceeded my wildest expectations."

I stopped her mid-step, gently taking both of her hands in mine. I absorbed every detail of that moment: the cool breeze in her hair, the honking of irate drivers behind us, the bashfulness that grew on her face as I gazed at her, my eyes full of love and admiration.

"I'm in love with you, Esther Leanne Foster."

I had never said the words like that before. The depth behind the simple sentence reflected in her expression.

She touched the side of my head and leaned in, but instead of a kiss, she pressed her forehead to mine. We stood there like that, I don't know for how long.

"I want to kiss you so bad, but I wouldn't give this breath to my worst enemy," she said, breaking the silence.

"I don't give a damn," I said, pulling her in for a kiss.

She pulled away with panic.

"Oh no!" she said, looking at her phone for the time.

"Mark, the train! We missed it!"

"Worth it. We'll find another way," I said, not feeling the least bit stressed. Wandering along the streets of New Orleans all night sounded like a dream. The history, the culture—it was all breathtaking. The stories that could be told by each street corner would fill a library.

We walked for the next couple of hours, then waited for Meg to pick us up—after I begged and pleaded with her.

Esther and I snuggled in the back of Meg's gross car.

"You two make me sick," she said, looking at us through the rear-view mirror.

I glance behind me now, expecting to see Phillip's headlights. I had made multiple lefts and rights in an attempt to lose him, but now, I'm lost.

I jog onward. Poor Meg. Where could she have gone? She'll never find me now.

I make my way toward a water tower in the distance, for no particular reason—I have no purpose or destination at this point. A playground appears, and I'm filled with nostalgia, a brief reprieve from my panic. I remember my parents pushing me on the swings.

I take sips of Meg's water, each swallow weighted with guilt. Is Meg ok? Did Phillip find her? Where did she go? Was she in the store still?

Dog barks echo in the distance accompanied by the rattling of animals scavenging through trash cans. Exhaustion and pain pull at my body as my legs drag more and more. I finally collapse on a bus stop bench. At this point, I don't even care if Phillip finds me. Bring it on, old man.

What am I going to do? I'm nowhere close to the Grimaldis' office. I can't even tell where Esther's house is from this direction. Even if I could, my body is far too exhausted to make the trek.

I recline back and look up at the stars, trying to find

constellations. No moon means the stars are abundant tonight. Ursa minor comes into focus first. Then Jupiter. It's amazing how small Jupiter appears, even though it's the largest planet in the solar system.

Time and distance. Time and distance. The distance between our planet and the gas giant is 411 million miles. It would take about 2,000 days to travel into the planet's orbit. That's about five-and-a-half years. Recalling these facts helps me keep my mind off Silas. Shoot, there goes that plan.

I've been waiting for Esther for almost the same length of time it would have taken me to reach another planet. And my mom's life expectancy, after her diagnosis, was about the length of time it takes to travel to Jupiter.

It's amazing what you can accomplish in a short amount of time compared to what little I've accomplished in the last five years. Sure, I can pour rosetta art into a coffee cup. But I can't free my girl from her nightmare of a life.

I wish I could accomplish something tonight—get Meg and I off the hook for what happened with Liz. For once, I wish I could do what I set out to do. I just need a sign.

Justice for the little guy. How will the G brothers get me out of this bind?

I lean back further into the bench. My eyes grow heavy, and I close them, wrapping my arms tightly around myself for a little extra warmth.

Esther appears, wearing that red dress. How did I see the dress so clearly by the train tracks—a dress she'd never worn? Its delicate straps rested on her shoulders, the fabric flowing just above her knees, swaying in the breeze. She stood before me, so graceful against the backdrop of an oncoming train.

Her smile gleams brighter than the lights from the convoy. Clinging to the warmth of this image, I drift off into sleep.

CHAPTER 30

Unknown

I wipe down a black ceramic mug as the sun shines on my face, its light reflecting from a car mirror straight into my eyes. The door chimes.

A woman wearing a sweater and a pencil skirt walks in, clutching her purse. She surveys the shop—the way I must have on my first day.

"Welcome to the Lil' Cup. What can I get started for you?"

She takes off her sunglasses and smiles at me. Her hair is pulled up in a bun.

"Hi, give me a second," she says, holding up a finger and looking intently at the small menu.

Her nails are long and painted with black and white nail polish.

She's a striking woman with large, dark, melancholy eyes and long eyelashes. Her smile, even as she looks at the menu, is comforting, even familiar.

"What do *you* like?" she asks me.

"I'm simple. I drink either the drip or a cap."

"Ah, I see . . . a little advice, never tell girls you're simple. Say 'I appreciate the beauty in simple things.'"

Warmth rushes into my cheeks. This woman is charming.

"I like that," is all I can think to say.

"What kind of tea do you have . . . um?" she asks looking at my shirt for a nametag, which I don't wear.

"Oh, my name is Mark. We have a cinnamon nutmeg that pairs nicely with the falling leaves outside," I say, feeling embarrassed at repeating the line Mrs. Grant came up with when she was brewing the mixture last night.

"Sounds lovely. I will take one of those."

I place the drink on the table in front of her. She sits with one leg crossed, holding her phone which has a search engine up.

"I'm new in town," she says. "What clubs or activities are there in Slidell?"

"I'm not really into the late-night scene," I start, "but I think there's a tavern that customers sometimes mention. There's also the Northern Lights Club—I think that's what it's called."

"You're sweet. Thanks," she says, raising the cup toward her dark painted lips.

"Delicious!"

"I'm glad you like it. Let me know if there's anything else I can get you."

"I will. Thank you!"

I head back behind the bar and wipe the stray milk splatters off the counter. The coffee grounds pour out of the machine, and I grab the tamp. With just the right pressure, the water flows through the coffee grounds proportionately.

The back door squeaks—must be Mr. Grant.

"How is the morning so far, son?" he asks, inspecting everything.

"Not too bad. Kind of slow," I say as a shot comes to a stop at twenty-five seconds.

"Nicely done, Mark. Say, who is that? I've never seen her here before."

"Neither have I. She didn't tell me her name, but she seems nice." Leaning in slightly, I whisper, "She was looking for places to hang out."

"Well, let me go see if I can help her. I can let her in on some of Marge's favorite spots."

He spends the next hour talking with her as the occasional laughter drifts across the room.

This is why Mr. Grant has such a loyal clientele—he takes the time to make each customer feel special. He also has a way with words and storytelling, turning even the dullest stories into captivating narratives that he tells with animated expressions.

Mrs. Grant's face, however, is harder to read, especially when she watches Mr. Grant tell stories of their life. At times, she seems to radiate joy and sentimentality—as though she wishes she could go back in time and live those moments again. Other times, her eyes show despair.

"Mark, meet our newest neighbor," Mr. Grant says, leading the woman by the hand to the front of the bar.

"Hi, yes, we've met," I say awkwardly.

"We did? Then what is my name?" she asks in a subtly flirtatious voice.

Shoot. How did I not ask for her name? I never ask for customers' names. Mr. Grant taught me to call out drink orders by the name of the drink, not the customer.

"I was going to ask, but then we started talking about the local clubs. What's your name?" I ask, feeling thrown off and uncomfortable.

"My name is Elizabeth, but my friends call me Liz," she says, extending her hand in a way that almost suggests she wants me to kiss it.

I awkwardly shake her hand.

"Very nice to meet you . . ." Do I call her Elizabeth? Or Liz? Does she consider us friends now?

"Liz," I say.

That feels safe.

"Ravi de vous rencontrer," she says with a perfect French accent.

"Well, aren't you full of surprises," interrupts Mr. Grant.

The door chimes, filling me with relief at the prospect of escaping this awkward conversation.

Liz comes running in—the other Liz. Mr. Grant and Liz—the put-together Liz—are gone.

The Liz standing before me is wearing sweatpants and a sweatshirt, her hair in a disheveled bun. Her fingernails are short and chipped, and the makeup under her eyes is slightly smeared.

"Good morning, Mark."

"How are you doing, Liz? Welcome in!" I almost forget to say the usual greeting.

"Awful, but better now, seeing you!"

I smile. "What can I get started for you?"

"Oh, I don't know. What kind of tea today?"

"It's a vanilla lavender tea to pair with the morning spring buds," I say, cringing at my words.

"Oh," she says, scrunching up her nose in slight disgust. "Lavender is soapy, don't you think?"

"I guess so, but it's soothing," I say.

"What are you drinking?" she asks, pointing to my cup.

"This is 'simple beauty' drip coffee." I say with a smirk, seeing her recall our first encounter.

A smile forms on her otherwise forlorn face.

"I'll do that with a cinnamon, uh . . . what is that?" she asks, pointing to the scones in the glass case.

"They are scones."

How does she not know what these are? Especially since she knows French. Maybe it was only an act.

"Yeah, that. Thanks."

I bring over her pastry and coffee and she slams her phone on the table.

"Everything ok?" I ask, trying to imitate Mr. Grant's accommodating nature.

"Yeah, I'll be fine. Want to join?" she asks, gesturing to the seat across from her.

I look around at the empty shop and decide that it might be nice to get off my feet for a second. Also, something about Liz is appealing.

"Mark, you seem like a nice guy. Why do all the ones I seem to get have to be arrogant, lying, abrasive, narcissistic, manipulative, scumbags?"

The list of insults makes me wonder who she's talking about.

"Want to take me out tonight?" she asks casually. "We could get dinner or something and see a movie."

Where does she get her confidence? She *is* a beautiful woman, but her lifestyle choices have deteriorated her once immaculate looks over the years. It might have been tempting the first time we met—if I didn't have Esther. Not so much now. I also refuse to be somebody's rebound.

"I would love to. I'm just in a relationship already that's been going on for some time now. It's pretty serious. You would love her."

The woman vanishes, and the door flings open as I quickly head over to the register.

"Welcome to the Lil' Cup, what can I get . . ." My words trail off as Liz walks in with her black fingernails that mask the nicotine underneath. Her eyes are swollen.

"Mark, you could have been the one."

"What?"

"You could have saved me from my life. You could have saved me. Why didn't you save me?" she says as she walks behind the bar and punches me repeatedly with her fists.

I move my arms to block the punches, but they become more intense. She's crying and saying the same words over and over again.

"You could have saved me. Why didn't you? . . . You could have saved me!"

I'm unable to move. I'm stuck.

I finally break free and grab onto her shoulders to look at her. The face that stares back isn't Liz.

"Why didn't you save me?" she repeats in a monotone voice.

Her head gushes blood from the wound that was embedded in Liz's head.

"You promised you would free me from my prison," says Esther.

I jerk awake as those haunting words echo in my head.

CHAPTER 31

Sunrise

The sky lights up as the earth spins at thousands of miles an hour, bringing the sun into view. I try to blink away the nightmare that still wants to merge with reality. It was so vivid, so real. I'm grateful to wake up, despite my current circumstances.

I sit up and take in my surroundings—a child's play palace. The slides and swings, along with the various pieces of equipment designed to keep a kid's attention for hours, make me imagine how simple life would be if I were just a carefree kid again. My parents always did their best to shield my childhood from the stresses of adult life. Though what I've endured in the past ten hours is hardly typical of adulthood. The way I long for childhood isn't something Esther could ever relate to. She yearns to be free from the father who robbed her of hers. Meanwhile, I'm stuck thinking about how nice life would be if I were six again.

I shake my head to snap out of my pointless and self-absorbent daydreams. It's time to man up and put an end to this nightmare. Both mine and Esther's.

I stand up, stretching my spine, feeling the tension in my shoulder blades release after hours of being curled up on the uncomfortable bench. I look at it, and the familiar faces of the Grimaldi brothers stare back at me, their arms outstretched in a pose meant to convey warmth. Is there a single bus stop in town where these two buffoons haven't bought up all the ad space?

The irony hits me: I've spent the night in the protective arms of the Grimaldi brothers. I laugh out loud. Next, I'm going to need a more literal form of protection from them.

Then, thoughts of Meg bring up feelings of guilt. Did

Phillip find her? Did he kill—? *No*, I can't think that way. I need to focus my thoughts on one goal at a time now. I need to get to the Grimaldis' office.

The bus has to arrive soon, and I can ride it into town. The Grimaldis' office hours are from 7:00 a.m. to 7:00 p.m. Esther had to make sure their coffee was sitting on their desk no later than 7:15 a.m. That's why she would always rush off, not because she didn't want to spend more time with me.

"Their number!" I say audibly as I pace around the bus stop, searching for it.

Esther is probably at work by now. If I could call her, they might pick me up. That would be so much faster than waiting for the bus.

I spot the number on the bottom corner of the sign. But what good is a number without a phone? Why can't things come together for once?

I quickly scan the area, looking for anyone or anything that could help. There's bound to be a morning jogger. This is exactly the type of neighborhood where people take up early morning rituals. I stand on the bus stop bench to get a better view of my surroundings.

A small cross comes into sight. It must be a church about a block away. I race over toward it, through a pleasant neighborhood block. The few hours of sleep have rejuvenated me just enough to run again.

The street leads me to a highway, and right across from it, familiar train tracks come into view—the ones I'd hoped to never see again. Churches run up and down this highway, along with some auto part stores. I will have better luck with one of those. I walk up to an old run-down building with junky cars parked outside. Crappy cars line not only the front but the side and the rear. This looks more like a junkyard than a car shop. Maybe the two are more similar than I've ever cared to notice. I wonder how many people get work done on their vehicles and then decide to abandon them, realizing that the price to fix it is worth more than the car.

THE CUSTOMERS

I walk up to the double glass doors and use the expected force to pull one open. The door doesn't budge. I pull at it again, as if somehow it would magically unlock this time. I've seen customers do this countless times at the Lil' Cup. They'd arrive early and pull at the door several times. It would always piss me off, and I would deliberately avoid looking up. I guess it's just part of human nature because now I find myself on the other side of the locked door doing the same thing.

"We're closed today!" says a man, coming from behind the shop. He's wearing grease-stained overalls with a matching denim hat.

"Sorry, sorry. I'm looking for a phone to make a call. Any chance I could use—"

"If you're looking for charity, check down the street," he says, pointing to the line of churches I had just passed.

This timeworn guy, unhelpful and rude, embodies the stereotype my dad spent decades trying to break. My dad is an honest, hardworking man in a profession that often seems anything but.

"I'll pay for it," I say with persistence.

"Yeah, how much you got?"

I guess I should have grabbed some of the change I left at the gas station store. I pull out the crumpled bills from my pocket and start counting.

"I have $11."

He approaches me slowly and haphazardly, and I can guess how he spent the previous night. My suspicions are confirmed in the most disgusting way: he belches in my face. I turn my head to avoid the stench of morning breath and alcohol, but it invades my nostrils.

He grabs the money out of my hands. Licking his blackened thumb, he counts it.

"Follow me!" he commands, clearing his throat from the mucus that has sat there all night.

I gag as he turns around, and my eyes fill with tears. I blink them away and hold my breath as I follow him around back.

More cars come into view—with rusted paint, broken windows, and crushed bumpers—parked every which way.

He leads me to a garage door and clicks it open. "Back there to the right. Touch nothing but the damn phone," he spits, making me flinch.

I step inside and find car engines, oil pans, and cluttered tools, all in disarray. The garage door starts to close behind me, and I turn around, protesting, with my arm outstretched.

"Wait! Wait! What are you doing?" I shout as an all-too-familiar darkness inundates me.

An old fluorescent motion sensor light flickers on, and I walk in the direction I was told.

Once again, I'm trapped by a lunatic. If he attempts to kill me, I probably won't protest. At this point, I deserve it for my stupidity.

A wired landline phone hangs on the wall in front of me. I race up to it and dial the number to the Justice for All law firm.

"Please answer Esth, please," I say under my breath.

"Good morning, Grimaldis' Justice for All," a female voice responds. "How may I direct your call?"

"Esther?"

"I'm sorry, I didn't get that. Who may I direct your call to?"

"Esther, it's me. It's Mark. I need your help."

"I'm sorry, sir, you may have dialed the wrong number. This is a Law Firm in Slidell, Louisiana, and my name is Marcy."

My heart sinks to my stomach. Marcy? Who is Marcy? Where is Esther?

"Yes, I know, sorry. I need some help. I'm out off the highway. Highway 3081. By the train tracks. I'm desperate and need a ride."

"I'm sorry to hear that, sir. We're located off Brownswitch Road," she replies.

"I know, I know where you're located, but I'm stuck here with no way to get there."

I probably sound crazy. But isn't this the type of people they specialize in helping?

"Give me one second!" I say, closing my eyes shut, trying to think of how to persuade them to pick me up.

"Ok, sir," says Marcy.

Then I hear a different voice: "How's my favorite couple doin' today?"

"Doing great, Lyda!" Esther said, standing up to hug her, "We just got back from New Orleans late last night."

"You did? I hope y'all went to The Gumbo Shop. Best food in the entire city," she said, closing her eyes. A warm smile spread across her face like she was being hugged, not just by Esther, but by a memory.

"We didn't get to go there this time, but it gives us a good reason to go back," I said as Esther sat back down.

"You better! And take me too. What kinda pie can I get for y'all today?"

"What did they make fresh this morning?" asked Esther.

"Lemme go check. Hang tight, you two cuties," she said, pinching our cheeks.

Esther and I rubbed the spot on our cheeks where Lyda had just aggressively pinched.

"Good ole Lyda," I said as the door chimed, making Esther turn her head.

The Grimaldi brothers entered, and the diner instantly filled with the spicy smell of their colognes. Esther slid down in her seat.

"Those are my dad's lawyers," she whispered.

I stood up slightly to get a better look.

"Sit back down," she pulled me by the strings of my hoodie.

"What's the big deal?"

"I don't want them to see me with you. They will tell my dad and—"

"Wait, your dad doesn't know about us?"

She paused for a long moment, then said, "My dad is an intolerable man. I didn't know how to tell him."

I wanted to feel mad, and maybe I should have. But I

swallowed the feeling, knowing it wouldn't do any good. And I understood why she didn't want to tell him. It wasn't because she was ashamed of me; she was just terrified of him. So I just felt sympathy for her.

"I get it. Stay low. They won't recognize me."

"Ok kiddos, it's huckleberry today," Lyda said in a loud voice, making the Grimaldi brothers look in our direction.

One of the brothers nudged the other with his elbow and pointed at me.

"Shoot!" I said under my breath.

"What was that dear?" asked Lyda.

"Oh, uh, two slices of that, please. Thanks!"

"Coming up. How 'bout a couple glasses of milk?"

"Sure, sure," I said, trying to look down at my phone.

The Grimaldis casually walked over. Esther noticed the discomfort that must have instantly appeared on my face.

"What? What is it?" she asked, still whispering.

"They're coming," I said through gritted teeth and a fake smile.

They approached, but instead of coming to us, they sat at a booth next to ours.

I pulled out my phone and started texting Esther.

"What can I get started for you two?" asked Lyda, serving the Grimaldis their menus.

"Two double-shot lattes," one of them demanded.

"Where on earth do you think you are, sugar? I have whatever's left on the pot from this mornin'," she said, not in the least bit phased.

"Fine, give us three mugs and the pot. We're also expecting someone."

"Coming right up," Lyda said.

"What time is he supposed to get here?" one of the brothers asked in his Eastern Italian accent.

"I told him 3:00 p.m. He's an old man, Freddy. The poor guy's probably just moving slowly this morning. It will be worth the wait, though," the other brother responded.

Esther put her white hood over her head to better hide herself. The brother not called Freddy lifted his arm over the top of the booth and looked back at me. Once again, I got caught staring.

"Hey kid," he said, pointing at me.

Faking surprise, I pointed at myself. "Who, me?"

"Yeah, you. Who else? How long are you and . . ." he said, trying to look at Esther, who was hiding, "your buddy there going to be?"

"We just ordered some pie. Shouldn't be longer than half an hour."

"Think you could move to the front? We're going to be conducting some confidential business with a client any minute now," he said in a tone that made it more of a demand than a request.

"Oh, uh," I glanced at Esther and she nodded. "Sure thing."

We got up, and Esther looked the other way, but in vain.

"Hey, don't I know you?" asked the one called Freddy.

"No, I don't think so," Esther responded in a deep voice, keeping her head down and walking forward.

He reached out to grab her arm. "I know you."

He paused for what felt like an eternity and finally said, "You're Brandon's girl."

"It sure is!" the other brother loudly said. "Oh god, what's your name again? It starts with a T—I know that!"

"Esther," she said, pulling the hoodie off her head in defeat.

"Esther! Oh well, close enough. Hey, how's Pops doing? He still likes that job we got him right?"

"Yeah, he still likes it."

"Freddy, remember how much trouble that guy's bum was in? Wiped the whole slate clean, if you know what I mean," the brother said, winking and then laughing obnoxiously.

"Hey kid, tell your pops 'Hi' from the G's, will ya?"

"Will do," Esther said, nodding goodbye.

I smiled and followed her. She didn't stop at any of the

other booths but went straight outside.

"Esther, wait up."

"I gotta get home."

"Why? We can still have our pie and then I will take you."

"No! I need to get home now!" she pleaded with tears in her eyes.

"Why? What's going to happen?"

"My brothers will find out because they work for those two horrible men, and they'll tell my dad."

"I'm sure they won't remember. You heard them. They didn't even remember your name." I tried to calm her, bringing her into my arms.

She pushed me away. "No, you don't understand. They will, and they will tell them they saw me with you. I'm going to get into so much trouble. I need to get home before my dad finds out from them. It will at least be a little better coming from me."

"What if I go with you and we can tell your dad together?"

She smirked and raised her eyebrows. And that was enough to tell me it was a foolish idea. I brought her back in and whispered, "I'm so sorry baby, we will be gone soon. I promise."

An older man hurriedly walked past us and through the doors.

I looked back to see where he was headed, and sure enough, he went to the Grimaldis' booth.

"My name is Mark Stratford, and I work with Brandon Foster," I say to Marcy, "Tell the G brothers that we need their help!"

CHAPTER 32

8:36 AM

"I'm sorry sir, I'm not sure what you want me to tell the Grimaldis," says Marcy.

An old clock hangs crooked on the wall. It's 8:36 a.m. if the clock is working.

"I want you to tell them that their client is in trouble, and I'm calling on his behalf."

"And what exactly is your connection to Brandon Foster?"

That's a good question. What *is* my connection to him? I always thought he would be my scumbag father-in-law. Besides Esther, we don't have any connection. We've never even exchanged a single word. But this is my strongest option.

"I work for him. Isn't that enough? Can I talk with Freddy?"

"I'm sorry, Federico Grimaldi is not in the office today, and Giovanni Grimaldi is with a client. May I take a message?"

"Tell them I will be in later today. I need their help. *Brandon and I* need their help."

"Let me put you on hold for a moment. I need to check their availability for today."

"No, don't! I just need—" My words are interrupted by music.

The garage door rolls up slowly, the way Mr. Grant moves, and then it stops only a quarter of the way as the mechanic ducks underneath. Why is he so insistent on keeping it closed? What is he hiding within these walls? It can't be significant; otherwise, he wouldn't have allowed me to enter for any amount of money.

"Time's up, kid. Unless you got more money."

I put up one finger, hoping he would give me another moment.

"One more minute, and that's it," he says, fiddling with a car behind me.

I hadn't noticed it until now—a gorgeous red '90s Corvette with pop-up headlights rising out from the hood. I used to own a small model version just like this one, but I can't remember what became of it. Is this why he's so protective of the garage? I guess I'd be the same way if I owned something this nice. I *was* very protective of my model cars, carefully storing them in glass cases to keep the dust away. This garage feels like the adult version of that.

"Ok, Mark, are you still there?"

"Yes, yes. I'm here!"

"Ok. I have some good news for you. The Grimaldi brothers agreed to meet with you today. They are sending someone to pick you up now. What was the address again?"

I can't believe this actually worked.

"I don't know the exact address, but it's right off the highway past a line of churches. I think one was a Baptist church."

"Do you know how many churches are in Slidell? I'm going to need an exact address," she says, annoyed.

"Excuse me," I say, covering the phone speaker with my palm. "What is the address of your shop?"

"Who wants to know?"

"My . . . friends. They're picking me up."

"I don't think so, kid. Get the hell out of my shop!" he demands, storming toward me with an extended lug wrench in hand.

"Marcy, tell them to pick me up out front of the church across from the tracks," I shout and drop the phone, hearing her inaudible reply as the landline swings.

I leap over an engine in the middle of the shop and feel the whoosh of the mechanic's tool slicing through the air, just inches from my shoulder.

"Get back here, you thug!" he shouts.

I crawl under the partially open garage door and sprint toward the main highway. For a moment, I glance behind and see the man standing, waving his weapon in the air as he shouts profanities.

Blocks come and go as I reach the row of churches. Opting to go farther than the Baptist church, I wait at another one down the road, optimistically hoping that someone from the Grimaldis' office will show up. I wish Esther had answered the phone. It would've been much simpler than fabricating a lie. I look behind me, relieved that the crazy mechanic is no longer in sight.

But then I see it—a red Corvette pulls out of the parking lot from what must have been a body shop. I hear the roar of its muffler as the driver accelerates down the street.

I desperately pull on the church's door handle. But it's locked. I need to come to terms with the fact that doors are not going to open for me today. They didn't open at Liz's house, and neither will they here. The car pulls up in front of me, and the mechanic yells profanities.

"Get back here, you—" he yells as I sprint into the church's parking lot.

"Oh, no you don't!" The Corvette's gears grind as he shifts it into first and follows me.

Beads of sweat form on the crest of my hairline as the sun beats on me. *I can't outrun a car.*

Just ahead, a tour bus sits on the grass. I push my legs beyond their limits as the Corvette's growl grows louder. With a leap, I dive toward the rear of the bus, and the car launches right past me.

"Damnit!" he shouts as I spring to my feet and sprint in the opposite direction toward the neighborhood houses. A car can't navigate through their backyards.

I spot a front porch and slide underneath. I stay hidden, watching the Corvette circling around the block. Cobwebs from the deck's underside cling to my skin. Thankfully, it's filthy and abandoned, so I pray no creatures will add to the swelling on the back of my neck.

The car screeches to a halt outside the house. The door swings open, and the driver steps out. Coughing and spitting, he staggers in my direction. Still hidden, I hold my breath and stay perfectly still as he stops right in front of the deck. Then slowly and silently, I inch myself further beneath the deck.

CHAPTER 33

Unknown

Storm clouds rage around me, and I'm no longer under the deck. Through my bedroom window, I watch the rain lash against the earth. The trees outside my childhood home move angrily in the wind as aggressive raindrops pelt the glass.

The weight of my depression presses heavily against my shoulders. It's a crushing weight, like the kind I put on the power bar for squats at the gym. I want to lift it off, but it won't budge. And it feels like someone keeps adding more weight on either side of the bar.

But I took on this burden willingly, so the love of my life could leave Slidell without guilt. And now, the regret is too painful to bear. It's like the ache of growing pains, though the term itself is a misnomer—there's no scientific evidence that growing hurts a child. Yet, growing in a figurative sense often hurts.

Is that why my whole body throbs? No. I'm not growing. If anything, I'm shrinking—shrinking back to my tired life. For the next five years, I will remain home, making no progress toward my goals with Esther.

These must be shrinking pains—the kind that come with aging, when bones become brittle and the spine compresses from muscle loss and tissue depreciation. That's what I'm suffering from. But self-diagnosis is always dangerous and dooming.

I gaze out the window, wondering how many other people have the next five years of their sorry, pathetic lives planned out. I'm fighting against the urge to pity myself. My mother, Esther, and the hundreds of thousands of children out in the world without a warm meal deserve my sympathy. Not my tragic little sorry self. There I go again. The self-pity happens so easily.

It's been only two days since the dreaded breakup. Is it even fair to call it a breakup? We were still in love. But we're taking a break—a five-year break. Could we still be friends? Would she even want to be friends? I wouldn't if I were her. In fact, I wouldn't have a sliver of respect for me.

A knock on my door pulls me from my thoughts.

"Honey, it's mom. Someone is here to see you."

I approach the door, wondering who it could possibly be. The fresh air outside my stale room flows into my face, and with it comes the unmistakable scent that makes my heart somersault. It must be Esther.

The only person outside my door is my mom, sitting in her wheelchair, awkwardly cramped in the hall.

"Where is she?" I ask, looking left and right down the hallway.

"How did you know?" Mom replies.

So, it is her. What is she doing here? How could she bear to see the sight of me?

I silently lean down, give Mom a kiss on her forehead, and start toward the living room.

"Hold on a second, sweetie," she says, grabbing my arm. "Wheel me into your room so we can talk really quick. I promise it will only be a minute. I told Esther you were sleeping, so you have time."

I move behind her chair, carefully avoiding her injured leg, and push her back into my room. I position her by the window. Closing the door softly, I stand by her side. The weather finally matches the mood.

"Please, take a seat, Mark. I want to look you in your eyes when I tell you this," she says, gesturing toward my worn-out gaming chair.

I sit back down in my chair that's still warm from hours of sulking. She looks into my eyes as I look down, not wanting to appear so vulnerable. But my mom can read me as easily as a children's book.

"Honey, look at me, please. I want to see your eyes."

I glance up and meet her gaze, now feeling tears welling up behind my eyes. I blink, and the tears break through, but I don't fight them.

"That's what I thought. Esther had much of the same expression when she came in moments ago. What happened, Mark?"

I let my mother's question float between us. How do I answer that? My mom will feel responsible for the breakup, and she is not. It was my decision, but one that I don't think I could relive again. If I had to relive that day outside the school a hundred times, I don't think I could break Esther's heart even once more.

But what kind of selfish, ungrateful, disrespectful son would choose anyone over his own mom?

"Esther and . . . We . . . I . . . It doesn't matter, mom. It's between me and her. Things are better this way. Trust me."

"Mark, look at you. Look at her. When you do, you will see that this is not what's best. I know you. You have always been able to see beauty in the world. You saw beauty in the starry nights when most of the time we couldn't see a single thing. You see your father and me as if we're the world's best parents. Trust me—we're not."

"What are you talking about? You and Dad *are* perfect parents. It's not just the biased opinion of a son. I'm more cynical than you might know."

"My point is, Mark, you have a one-of-a-kind girl that is sitting out there on our couch right now. And I would not be doing my job as your mother if I did not intervene at least a little and see what is going on."

"Mom, I know she's special. She's my whole world. I'm in love with her. But I can't leave you and Dad."

"Why would you have to leave me and your father?" she asks with restrained bewilderment.

I look down, wiping my eyes from the tears I can only cry

with my mother. In this moment, I'm a child again, crying to my mom just as I have since the day I was born.

"Esther's life is terrible here. She's . . ." Do I divulge all of Esther's deepest, darkest secrets? "She's . . ."

The words my mom said on the day we followed Esther home and watched the cops arrest Brandon Foster now replay in my mind.

"Always go to the proper authorities."

My mom will understand, and she could prove to be a mom to Esther if we let her.

"Mom, Esther's family is extremely abusive—physically for sure. It's terrifying to see her show up to our dates with bruises covering her arms and legs. I'm pretty sure she has them on her face too, but she hides them pretty well."

"Is it only physically, Mark? Or more?" my mom asks, placing her hand on mine.

"Only? That's pretty terrible, mom; I don't think we should downplay it."

"No, I'm not belittling it. That is terrible. You misunderstood me. I was asking if you know whether she's experienced any other forms of abuse besides the bruises?"

"Like verbal? I'm sure!" I say, not knowing where this line of questioning is leading.

"No, like . . . sexual abuse?"

"Oh god!" I say instinctively, repulsed by the idea.

But then I allow the question to sink in. I think back to all the times Esther flinched—not when I held her or kissed her, but when I made sudden movements.

"I don't think so."

"Ok honey, we can always cross that road if it ever comes up. So, you were planning on leaving Slidell with Esther to get her away from her family?" she asks.

Knowing that my mom is aware of our plan fills me with an overwhelming amount of guilt.

"Yeah. But I was going to tell you guys. And it wouldn't have been forever. She just needed to be freed from this hell that she's been living in," I say with too much intensity and defensiveness in my voice.

"It's ok honey, I understand. I think it's very sweet and noble of you to want to do that for her."

Then I see the realization dawning on her face like someone finding a new piece to a complicated puzzle. In my mom's case, though, I'm not very complicated.

"You broke up because of my condition, didn't you? You don't want to leave me, but you don't want her to have to stay. And knowing what I do about that saint of a girl out there, she would stay without a second thought."

How is my mother capable of reading human emotion and navigating the complexities of life the way she does? For her, it's not even like reading a children's book—it's more like flipping through a baby's picture book filled with oversimplified and animated images. Meanwhile, my attempts to read anything in life feel like trying to decipher a doctor's illegible scribble on a prescription pad.

All I can do is nod my head while still looking at the old, stained carpet in my room. The fibers are now soaking up the few tears that have fallen off my cheek.

"We don't need you to do that, Mark. Go, go out there right now and tell Esther you're going to take her wherever it is she wants to go. Your father and I will support you."

I hug my mother and ask, "But, what about you?"

"What *about* me? Your father is the one who has promised to take care of me for 'better or worse, for sicker or poorer.' Not you. You do that for your girl out there. If she's sick, so to speak, of being here, then get her out."

I can't believe what I'm hearing. My unsolvable problem has a simple solution, all thanks to a five-minute conversation with my mom.

"What will dad think?"

"I will take care of your dad. Don't you worry," she says. "Now what are you waiting for? Go! Run to her, sweetie!"

I give Mom one last kiss on her forehead and run to the

living room. There on the couch is a girl—my girl. I put my hand on her shoulder, and she turns to look at me. I stumble back, yelling.

"What in the hell?"

"Why didn't you save me, Mark?" asks Liz.

In my periphery, I see my mom wheeling out of my bedroom—but it's not her. It's Mrs. Grant.

"Mark, why did you run from me? I was trying to help you. I was trying to save you."

I look back at the couch, and Meg is sitting there now.

"Why did you leave me? You left me, and now you will pay!" Meg says, standing up.

She pulls a knife from behind her back and tackles me to the floor. Then she digs the knife into my heart. I gasp for air as the taste of metal fills my mouth and blood comes pouring out.

I look up at my sister, but she's no longer my sister. She is Esther. Liz's wound is still embedded in her skull and blood drips down her face.

She leans in and whispers, "Now we're both free."

She rolls off, and we lie together, side by side, on the living room floor. My hand finds hers, and I hold on tight.

"I love you, Esth."

CHAPTER 34

Unknown

I look into the eyes of an old man who has lowered himself to meet my gaze while I lie helpless beneath the deck. The hallucination has faded into a grim reality.

"Now I've got you," he says, spitting.

He tries to pull me out as I fight with every ounce of strength. His hand tightens around my filleted arm, and I scream out in pain, but the sound seems to only tighten his grip. Desperate, I sink my teeth into his arm, tearing into his disgusting flesh. But he doesn't even flinch.

His fingers wiggle their way through the tape on my wound, and I can sense my skin tear as he does. Blood rushes to my head, and I struggle, desperate to free myself from his unexpectedly strong grip.

The edges of my vision darken, and stars appear. Just when I fear I may be blacking out, I sense someone pulling the man away.

From under the deck, I can now see him lying on the grass, receiving a forceful kick to the stomach as he clutches his gut and gasps for air. Two men kick him repeatedly, and I turn my head away from the scene. Eventually, he stops grunting.

I reach for my arm with my shaky hand, grimacing from the shock.

"Come on out of there!" commands one of the men.

I crawl out slowly, my eyes falling on the two men who have frequented my nightmares throughout the years: Moab and Cain Foster. Their imposing builds tower over me, and I take in their terrifying features. The scars on Moab's face and the bent, mangled nose on Cain's. Their beards are gone, revealing prominent jaws now clenched at me.

"How do you know our father?" one of them asks pulling me by my injured arm up and to my feet.

He pulls away, seeing the blood on his hands. He bends down to wipe it on the lawn in a measly attempt to clean it.

"Answer him!" demands Cain.

"I don't know him," I sigh as I look down in defeat.

"Then why'd you say ya did?" he asks, stepping forward until we're chest to chest. His height forces me to tilt my head back, but I keep my gaze lowered, knowing eye contact could be seen as defiance.

"Look at me!" he says, grabbing my head and forcing eye contact.

"I used to date your sister! I only know your dad through her. My sister and I desperately need the Grimaldis' help," I blurt out, the words tumbling out without thought.

They exchange a look of confusion—or at least that's what it seems like. My mom would have easily identified exactly what emotion that look conveyed.

"Come with us!" they command, gesturing toward their car. I chuckle audibly at the site of the car—a black Rolls Royce—then quickly realize how stupid that was.

"What was that?" Moab asks, grabbing me once again by the arm.

"It's nothing," I wince in pain. "I like your car, is all. I used to have a model of it."

"Good for ya! Keep movin'."

"What are you going to do with him?" I ask, looking at the now passed-out mechanic, his face swollen shut from the beating. Cain and Moab got lucky no one was home to see this. Or maybe they knew nobody was home.

"Where'd he come from?" Cain asks, flinging the mechanic over his shoulder.

"A car shop a few blocks that way."

I settle into the all-leather black seat, and the scent of leather conditioner fills the air as the door slams shut behind me. The illegally tinted windows make it difficult to see through. I hear the trunk pop open and feel the weight of the body being tossed inside. These guys are not in the least bit concerned about being noticed. A shiver runs down my spine as I wonder about all the crimes they've gotten away with.

They hop in on either side of the Royce and pull out down the main highway.

"This one?" asks Moab, approaching the mechanic's shop.

"Yeah, that's the one. The front door is locked, though. Your best bet is to pull around back."

They do as I say, and to my reprieve, the garage is open. They pull all the way in and get out of the car.

They grab the body from the trunk, but I don't know where they put him. I hope it's at least in a respectable position —even if he doesn't deserve it. I feel the car frame shift as their large bodies get back in.

"Ok, Mark. You got your way. You 'bout to see the Grimaldis. Be careful what ya wish for."

CHAPTER 35

9:06 AM

Be careful what I wish for. The words reverberate in my mind, setting off internal alarm bells. I instantly try to rationalize my decision to call them for help. This has to be the best, no, the *only* option. There was nothing else I could do. I'm a criminal who needs help from other criminals.

The drive back into Slidell takes much longer than it should. Brandon and Cain have already made about half a dozen stops along the way. After the second pit stop, I stopped asking questions.

"When it's time for you to talk, you'll know. Till then, sit back and shut up," Cain said with contempt.

I have no desire to be friends with these two, ever. But in times like this, when I'm completely alone, trapped by my own thoughts and hallucinations, any human interaction would be appreciated.

But these two aren't human. They were created by scientists in a lab. The lab that produced these otherworldly mutants was a broken home; the scientists were Brandon and the G brothers. They never really had a chance.

That's not entirely true. Esther isn't like them. She could have been, but she broke free. In poker, when a hand is unevenly dealt—maybe two cards get stuck together—a player can request a re-deal. Esther had been dealt a bad hand in this world, stuck with a rotten family just by the cruel randomness of life. But she made a choice: to demand a re-deal and play life with a fair hand. Moab and Cain, on the other hand, either didn't know they had a choice or simply chose to be evil. Maybe no matter the hand, they would have chosen this life.

We're not driving on the main highway. Moab is taking every isolated road and alley on the way to the Grimaldis' Justice for All headquarters. He must have this city mapped out in his mind, inside and out. What kind of errands are they running anyway? On second thought, I don't want to know.

Instead, I decide my time will be better spent rehearsing what I'm going to tell the Grimaldis. Sitting in the back seat, I whisper the words to myself before the Foster brothers return to the car.

"I went to purchase a food truck from an ad listing. When I got there, I realized the seller was someone I knew. She invited me inside, then handcuffed me and held me at gunpoint. She said she killed her husband. My sister saw what was happening, broke in, and smashed a rock into the back of her head. We panicked because my sister had drugs in the car, so we didn't want to call the cops. We cleaned up the crime scene and then realized we should have just gotten rid of the drugs. But it was too late. We then looked for the husband's body but found nothing."

This sounds awful. I start again.

"My sister and I went to purchase a food truck out past Oil Well Road. I let my guard down when I saw that the seller was one of my regular customers at the Lil' Cup. She invited me in and tried to seduce me. When I denied her advances, she took a knife from the kitchen and forced me to handcuff myself to the staircase railing. Then got a gun. But right before she could blow my brains out, my sister broke in and hit her in the head with a rock."

Yeah, that's a little better.

The brothers get back in the car, but this time, Moab takes the passenger seat. He stretches his right hand and I spot bruising and blood on his knuckles. What am I doing here?

The sun disappears as the car drives downward into an underground parking garage. Cain drives over the obnoxious speed bumps without any care for the undercarriage. This must be the Grimaldis' car. I can't imagine driving my own car this carelessly, and my car is a piece of crap.

That's right! *My car*. I need to tell them about my car. I wish Meg were here. I have a feeling I'll leave out important details from the night.

The car comes to a stop, and the door opposite the one I entered slowly opens. I'm ordered out. Cain puts his hand on top of mine and escorts me out like a criminal from the back of a cop car. I wonder if they remember who I am. Are they enjoying this?

This isn't a traditional parking garage—it only has five spaces—each occupied by a luxury car. As I'm quickly ushered past them, I spot a Mercedes Benz, a BMW, and a Porsche. Do all of these belong to them? Or do they belong to their clients?

I'm directed to an elevator in the back corner of the garage. It seems ordinary at first, with stainless steel double doors that slide open, but stepping inside reveals a second set of closed doors on the opposite side. The panel lists floor 1 at the top and -3 at the bottom. We must have been on floor -1.

The elevator doors shut, and an agonizing amount of time passes before I sense movement. But when it finally moves, I'm filled with more terror as it doesn't move up but descends deeper into the earth.

"Where are we going?" I ask. The words ricochet around the walls and back at me with no response.

Claustrophobia sets in as the elevator moves at a snail's pace. Cain and Moab stand on either side of me, like officers escorting a prisoner to a courtroom. I might as well be in prison—only this is worse because of the unknowns. I grin at the irony, thinking back to the boy who cried in his room years ago because the next five years of his life were planned out. If only I could know what the next five minutes hold.

The doors slowly open as if to say that down here, time stands still, and everything moves at a slower pace. I don't make the first move, letting Cain and Moab direct me like they have been. An uncomfortable shove signals me to move forward. A hallway of about thirty feet in length greets us, with bright white overhead lights leading all the way down. It's about eight feet in width. I stumble out, feeling like an inmate walking down death row. Behind the closed doors we pass must be electric chairs. We go to the very last door on the right, and Cain knocks in code: once, then three times in succession, and then two more to finish.

"One moment!" a voice calls from the other side,

Cain and Moab whistle in sync, and the familiar bedtime melody—*Catch a Falling Star*—makes the hair on the back of my neck stand. The lyrics fill my mind.

I've always loved stars, and I found the brightest one of all in Esther. But I let her fade, all because of my stupidity. I allowed her light to fade from me. Catching a falling star twice in a lifetime is nearly impossible, but I'm determined to make that impossibility a reality.

I reach out and knock on the door, not worried about the rhythm. I pound on it with all my might. Suddenly, I feel trapped in this narrow hallway and realize I'm racing against time.

"What do ya think you're doin'?" Cain asks as he yanks me back from the door and forces me to the ground.

"I need to talk with them now! I've waited long enough."

Moab kneels beside me, examining everything about my face. So, I decide to do the same. I study his scars, etched deeply around his eyes and across his upper lip and cheeks. They mark the areas where the skin is thinnest and would be met with bone if punched. He doesn't fear anything. I can sense that from his demeanor. Nothing that life might bring his way will compare to the torture he's already lived through.

"I know ya," he says as a smirk spreads across his face.

"We've got ourselves here that spineless kid who came to pick up our lil sis from the house that one day."

My Adam's apple rises and falls as I take a long, painful swallow. My mouth is dry from dehydration.

"If I remember correctly, the last time you tried somethin', it left you gasping for air. So, if I was you, I'd sit there patiently, mind my manners, and pray to God, thanking him for every moment ya still breathe air freely. Because between you and me,

I wanted to leave ya the same way we left that lowlife back in the shop. I'm not even sure if he'll wake up again. I don't give a—"

The door opens before he can finish, and a lady steps out of the office. She's dressed in a grey massage therapist uniform and holds a collapsible table under her arm. As she makes eye contact with me, there's no sign of shock on her face at seeing me on the floor being threatened by Moab. If she's worked for the Grimaldis for any length of time, she's probably seen far worse.

"Boys," she says, scooting past Cain. He ogles her as she walks down the hallway.

I look past them into the room, where a large, hairy man stands with his back to me. He grabs his shirt, buttons it up, and turns around to step out. The three top buttons are left undone —intentionally, of course.

"So, who is it? Who was demanding to see me today?" Giovanni asks as he comes out of the room.

"He told us his name is Mark," Cain replies, his eyes still following the woman down the hall.

"Mark? Mark what? Come on, if I'm going to work with you, I need your name."

"Stratford," I say as Moab stands, pulling me up by my arm.

"Stand when you're in front of the Grimaldis," he says, millimeters from my ear.

I can sense his anger and the tightness in his jaw as he mutters the words.

"Come on now, Moab, that's not how we treat our clients. Did they offer you any water yet?" he asks, slapping Cain on his stomach to snap him back to reality.

"Get our friend Mr. Stratford some water. How about a Coke? Do you like Coke? If you don't, I can have them get you anything you like. Pepsi, orange soda, Modelo—actually, I could use a Modelo. Yeah, get us a couple of cold ones. On second thought, make it a Peroni. Ever had an Italian beer before? They're so refreshing."

He rambles on as he motions for me to follow him into his

office.

Moab and Cain glare at me as they walk back out the way we came.

"Take a seat, Mr. Stratford, and call me Gio."

Gio gestures to one of the two maroon leather chairs in front of his larger-than-life desk.

Behind him, a mural of a villa and vineyards adorns the wall—probably a scene from his homeland. The surrounding walls are painted a dark red, and crown molding lines the ceiling and baseboards. Warm dim lights illuminate the room, and a brighter light shines from below onto the mural. A cinnamon-scented candle flickers on a small table in the corner.

"So tell me, boy, how do you know Brandon Foster? And before you come up with the story, I want you to be aware of something. I already know that you don't work with that lowlife," Gio says in a casually intimidating voice. "All I want to know is why you used him to try to get a meeting with my brother and me?"

Where *is* Freddy, his brother? I thought Marcy had said they both agreed to meet with me. Was meeting with me Gio's decision alone?

"He was the only person I knew that you had worked with."

He bursts into laughter and leans back in his chair.

"Kid, we work with the whole damn city. Brandon's the only guy you could think of? I'm shocked you didn't mention a higher-end client that you're more closely affiliated with."

Who is he talking about? I don't socialize with anyone who would choose to hire these criminals—unless he's referring to Esther. But she's just an underpaid employee, not a client.

"You really don't know who I'm talking about, do you? Well, if he's gone to such great lengths to keep it secret, I suppose I don't want to say anything to jeopardize that."

Once again, I have no reply. I have no clue what he's talking about.

"Do you realize why you even made it this far, Mark? Do

you know why I didn't have Marcy hang up on you, or why I didn't let Cain and Moab hurt you? I played it like I didn't know you to keep those two meatheads in the dark. When Marcy told me you'd called, I was intrigued. I like the way you came knocking on my door, like you had any sort of power or authority. Some might call it delusion. But I see potential—if it's harnessed properly."

Why would he be intrigued by *my* call? My family has no dealings with the Grimaldis. The only interaction I've had with him was that one time at the diner.

"I appreciate that," I say, trying to balance humility and confidence.

"So, you've gotten yourself into a little trouble? Or maybe someone you know is in trouble. You can rest assured there's no situation in this godforsaken life I can't get you out of. I'm only going to need one thing from you, other than payment."

Payment. How on earth am I going to afford this? Doesn't matter; I can worry about that later. I'd rather pay off this debt for the rest of my life than spend it rotting away in prison.

"Do you know what that is Mr. Stratford?"

"My undying loyalty?" I ask.

"Your undying what? No, of course not. I'm just your lawyer, kid. I was going to say, 'I need the whole truth and nothing but the truth.'"

As the old line slips from his lips, he bursts into laughter.

"So, go on. I want to hear the whole story. Start from the beginning and don't leave anything out."

CHAPTER 36

12:15 PM

I spend about twenty minutes trying to recall and explain everything that happened last night and this morning. The effort feels tiresome, like trying to remember a ridiculous dream after waking up.

I begin by explaining my business plan, which led me to browse food truck listings. I tell Gio that I'd been messaging a profile with the name Mike Hill. Immediately, Gio types the name into his computer.

"Mike Hill, forty-eight years old, born in Washington State, married to Samantha Mallory, now deceased. He has a bachelor's degree in accounting from Washington State University," he says, adjusting a small pair of reading glasses on his nose as he scrolls through what seems like an endless page of information.

So, Mike was married before. I wonder what happened to Samantha, but that's a rabbit hole I don't care to go down.

"So, this is the guy that's supposedly dead?" he asks.

"Yeah, that's what she told me, at least."

"And you didn't see any sign of a body?"

"No, I looked everywhere. That was my ticket out of this whole mess."

"Yeah, it sure would have helped," he says, still gazing into the computer monitor.

I then walk him through my steps in cleaning up the crime scene, trying to remember every detail about what we did and in the right order.

"You're a world-class criminal, aren't you, Mr. Stratford?" he says with condescending laughter.

I explain my connection to Liz.

"You said she was a regular. How often would you say she came into the Lil' Cup?" Gio asks.

"At least four times a week. I work Mondays, Tuesdays, Thursdays, and Saturdays, and I saw her on almost all those days. I think Mike Hill worked across the street in one of the office buildings."

"Why do you make that assumption?"

For a moment, I hesitate, not wanting to explain the observation games I play to keep my mind preoccupied during the long workdays. But he needs the whole truth.

"I pay attention to all the usual cars that park across the street. There's always the row with the same car brand that park on the block. Across from those cars, parked all by itself, is an orange square car. It's always there when I arrive at work in the morning and when I leave. That car is currently parked outside Liz's house."

"Kid, I don't mean to discredit your little detective work, but to assume they're the same car is a bit of a leap. I can understand if the car was a rarer brand, but that's a cookie-cutter car."

"I know, but the car was gone last night when I left the shop. First time. I think it's connected. Is there any way you can search what kind of car he drives and where he works?"

"Who do you think I am, a police officer or a private investigator? Let's ditch that little theory of yours and focus on Liz. I assume that's short for something?" he asks.

"Yes, Elizabeth Hill."

I can see the monitor as he types in the name and scrolls through the various options that come up.

"Ok. Elizabeth Hill. . . I'm going to go out on a limb here and say the woman trying to seduce you in lingerie wasn't eighty-five years old," he says, cackling to himself. "*This* might be a match. Elizabeth Hill, born in Spokane, Washington, age thirty-seven, has a high school diploma from the local school. Married to—yup, it's a match—Mike Hill. Nothing too exciting about her. Let me do a little more cross-referencing here," he says, leaning into the monitor and furrowing his eyebrows in deep concentration.

"You're in luck, kid. Her parents are dead, and there seem to be no relatives. Nobody should be looking for her anytime soon."

I feel an ache of sympathy for the woman, but it doesn't last long as Gio continues.

"Can you think of any more details about last night?"

I look up at the dark maroon ceiling as if the change of visual will unlock another part of my memory.

"I told you about the messages, Liz's body, my car, not finding Mike's corpse, and that we tried not to leave behind any evidence. We cleaned everything, even objects I'm certain I didn't touch."

"I'm not too concerned with the cleaning. My guys are going to go in and take care of all of that, anyway. Think. This is it. The home stretch, kid. If you want me to help you get out of this situation, I need full disclosure."

I think quietly for a moment, then finally say, "I connected to the Wi-Fi."

"Wi-Fi," he repeats as he scribbles on a notepad.

"This is important to know. My guy will need to wipe your phone and all their devices to remove any trace of connection. This is the kind of stuff that makes me the best at my job. Hold on a minute. You said, '*We* tried not to leave behind any evidence.' Who's we?"

My heart sinks. I didn't want to implicate my sister in any of this.

"My sister," I say. The mention of her stabs pain through my body.

"Your sister. She was with you. Where is she now?"

"I don't know, I haven't seen her since this morning."

"Come again?" he asks, lowering his glasses and looking into my eyes.

"It's hard to explain."

"I had two rules, Mark. Can you repeat them to me?"

"I know what they are. Meg and I crossed the train tracks over the river."

"*Which* river? Details, Mark!"

"Yes, sorry, sorry. Old Pearl River. We crossed it and went to a gas station. I made a phone call to my boss, Mrs. Grant."

I go on for the next couple of minutes, describing Phillip, my encounter with him yesterday morning, and what happened to Mr. Grant. I tell him about calling Mrs. Grant and that she already knew Phillip.

"She told me Mr. Grant never came home. And then I think she sent Phillip to come pick up my sister and me. I don't trust him, so I ran out of the store when he showed up, and that's when I lost my sister."

"Mr. Grant is missing?" he asks as if that's all he heard.

"So, you *don't* know everything," I say, hoping he'll appreciate my confidence.

I'm right. He looks at me with wide eyes and bursts into laughter. With a firm grip on my shoulder, he says, "I like this kid!" as if addressing a room full of people.

His excitement dissipates instantly as his business face returns.

"Any idea where your boss is?"

Why does he care to know? What does it matter to him what happened to a random old man in Slidell? As I ask the question in my head, the pieces come together the way they did outside Liz's door, just moments too late.

"Mr. Grant is a client of yours, isn't he?"

The memory resurfaces—the old man who brushed past Esther and me that day at the diner when the Grimaldis were meeting someone. Was that him?

"Not too bad, kid. I'm shocked you didn't know. Mr. Grant talks about you all the time. That's why I agreed to meet with you. I've been looking for him all night."

He leans over and clicks a button on his answering machine.

"You have one saved message," the automated voice says, followed by Mr. Grant's panicked voice: "Giovani, I need your help. Someone's after me. They know. I have to get out of town. Call me back."

"You haven't heard from him?" asks Gio.

"No, not since he left early yesterday morning."

"What time was it exactly?"

This is the most interest he's shown since I walked in here. He's not concerned about me. He's only worried about Mr. Grant.

"It was shortly after we opened. Most likely 7:10 a.m., but no later than that."

"And he didn't tell you where he was going? You can't remember anything about his conversation with this man, Phillip?"

"Like I said, he came in asking about the coffee, and then he wanted to know more about you and your brother."

"What did Edwin say?"

"Nothing, he said that if they wanted information to ask you directly."

"Good man. Nothing worse than somebody snooping around where they don't belong."

"Has he tried to reach out to you?" he asks.

"I wouldn't know. My phone is dead, has been since late last night."

"Come on, kid. Work with me here. Use your head," he says, pointing to his own.

I hand him my phone and he plugs it into one of his many chargers. He taps his finger impatiently on the desk, waiting for the screen to illuminate. Another thought about last night comes to my mind as we wait.

"You know how you can share Wi-Fi networks with someone who requests to join?"

"What was that?" he asks, still hovering over the phone.

"I'll show you."

I take my phone as it lights up and go to my settings to connect to his Wi-Fi.

"Is this your network?"

"Yeah, that's it. The password—"

"No, don't tell me. I'm just going to click on it. Now open your phone. Do you see any requests to share the password?"

"I do. Pretty neat."

"When I was trapped inside the home, I waited, hoping that my sister would try to connect to the Wi-Fi. I got a notification like the one you just got and shared the password with who I thought was my sister. Later, we realized she never requested to join. So, someone else must have been at the house."

"That's an interesting theory. We'll look into that later. I need to find my client first. Did he contact you?"

I scroll through my phone, waiting for the messages to load. My emails come through, mostly advertisements. I can feel Gio's tension rising as he leans further across the desk. Finally, the missed calls appear: one from my father, one from Mrs. Grant, and dozens from Meg.

Then I spot a lone text message from Dad—the one I must have heard come through last night when I was cuffed to the railing. It reads: *Mom and I are going to bed. Missed you at dinner. Meg said you wouldn't be home until late. I'll call you in the morning.* His call came about three hours ago.

"Mr. Grant's wife called me," I say, holding up the phone to show him.

"Did she leave a message?" Gio asks, snatching the phone from my hand.

"No, she probably called my phone after we disconnected from the payphone."

Gio leans back in his chair like he's contemplating everything. We sit in silence for a long while. Is he even going to help me now that I have nothing else to share with him? I regret revealing everything I know.

He picks up his phone and taps one of the speed dial buttons. Holding the phone to his ear, he gives me a playful wink.

"Freddy, call me back. I have a little more information

about our client."

"Ok kid, you've been very helpful. I trust you'll keep everything we discussed confidential. We wouldn't want this information to end up in the wrong hands. If you can keep that promise, I'll make sure you and your sister get off the hook for Liz's death."

"Yes, I promise. Thank you so much. I can't tell you what a relief this is. What are you going to do, if you don't mind me asking?"

"A magician never reveals his secrets," he says, once again picking up the phone and pressing a button.

"We're done."

The moment the words leave his lips, the door behind me opens. Cain and Moab walk in with a six-pack of ice-cold beer and set it down on the desk between us.

"Salute!" Gio shouts, raising his bottle. "To truth and justice."

Then he takes a long sip.

CHAPTER 37

1:05 PM

I force my beer down, wishing it were water instead. It is tasty, though—refreshing, with a crisp, smooth taste. Still, the combination of dehydration and an empty stomach made even a little bit of alcohol hit me harder than it should.

I stumble out of the room as Moab says, "The twig got drunk off a sixteen-ounce light beer."

"Leave the kid alone," says Gio. Then he looks my way. "Where are my manners? Come back in here and let me get that arm of yours taken care of."

I protest at first, fearing the pain of pulling the duct tape off.

Next thing I know, I'm sitting back in my chair, and Gio is helping me free my arm from the sleeve.

Seeing my shirt covered in dry blood, Gio says, "Cain, go get this kid a fresh shirt. What color do you like? How about a nice baby blue? Yeah, go get him a light blue dress shirt and some new pants. Camel chinos."

Esther would love that I'm getting some new clothes. But why is Gio going to such great lengths for me?

"Did you even think these clothes might contain Liz's DNA?" he asks after Cain and Moab walk out. "If you're going to work for me, I need you to get your head in the game."

As his words come out, pins and needles poke through my entire body. Work for him? I would never work for someone like him. And yet, there is something about the guy that makes me really like him. He's been extremely helpful and he exudes competence, even if it's competence in breaking the law.

"How would you dispose of these clothes? Imagine I'm

not here to tell you what to do."

What *would* I do?

"I was probably going to go home and throw them in the garbage."

He rips the duct tape off without the slightest bit of restraint, probably displeased with my response. My skin tears more, too.

"What would happen then if the cops linked you to the crime and wanted to search your house?"

"They wouldn't know to look at me," I say through gritted teeth, "And like you said, they won't go looking for her anytime soon. My clothes would be long gone in the dump."

"That's the problem with your generation," he starts while pouring hydrogen peroxide on the cut.

"Ah! Ah! Ah!" I scream, tightly gripping the chair with my other arm.

"Oh, I should have warned you. This is gonna sting," he says, laughing as he pours more of the liquid onto my wound.

As it foams up, I picture tiny chemical warriors battling any infectious enemies that might threaten my body. The visual helps distract a little from the pain.

"That's the problem with you kids. You don't think worst-case scenario. What if the cops link you to the crime within the first forty-eight hours? Plan for the worst. Have contingency arrangements."

"Ok, well tell me. What would you do with my clothes?"

"I would disintegrate them in a barrel of acid."

Chills run through my bones as I envision him doing this, and not just with clothes.

"Play the 'what if' game? What if this, what if that? Pessimism over optimism. If you learn that early enough in life, you just might make it."

He threads the needle and looks at me. "Hold still. This is gonna hurt like a mother…"

The profanity is an understatement, and I can't help but let a few of my own euphemisms slip as he stitches me up.

"All set, kid. Now go on and rest up. I will call you when your car is ready for pickup. In the meantime, stay low and find your sister. And for the love of God, don't share any of these stories with mommy or daddy, or papa and nana or whatever the hell you call your family. And if you hear anything from Mr. Grant, you call your old pal Gio. You understand?"

"Yes."

"Not good enough. Get down on your knees and repeat after me."

The command feels cultish. I hesitate for a moment, and I'm sure my face shows my discomfort. But I lower myself down on both knees.

He stands, setting the sewing kit on his desk.

"I, Mark Stratford," he starts.

"I, Mark Stratford," I repeat

"Swear my undying loyalty to the all-powerful Grimaldi brothers."

I look up at him, and the moment our eyes meet, he bursts into uncontrollable laughter.

I rise to my feet and examine the flawless stitching that now replaces the open wound on my arm.

"I had you going, didn't I? You know, I would have never thought of that if you hadn't come in here with your tail between your legs, thinking that's how we conduct business. You should've seen your face."

"Ok, ok, I'm an idiot. You got me. Am I free to go?"

"Yeah, go on, but take off your clothes first and leave them here."

I look at him with a face that says I won't fall for any more of his humiliating pranks.

"What's with the face, kid? Go on, take them off. Unless you have a barrel of acid lying around."

Oh no, he's serious. I stand in front of him, imagining how vulnerable I will feel in nothing but my boxers.

"Don't be shy, kid. Nothing I haven't seen before."

I do as he says, taking off everything besides my boxers

and bunching my disgusting clothes onto the chair.

"Go on now, up the elevator to where you came in. Cain has your clothes in the car. You can change there."

"You can't be serious?"

"As serious as a heart attack. Now get the hell out of my office!" he says, pushing me into the hallway.

What is with this man? One second, he's the most accommodating host, and the next, he's forcing my nearly naked self out of his office. I feel extremely uncomfortable as I walk back down the hallway. The elevator dings up ahead.

"Shoot, shoot, shoot, shoot," I say, scrambling to get into one of the doors I just passed.

I don't care if there's an electric chair on the other side. If someone comes out of the elevator and sees me like this, I will die of embarrassment anyway.

I was dumb to even try—it's locked, of course.

The elevator doors slide open, and a cute girl about my age steps out. She's looking at a file in her hand as she walks purposefully toward me. I squint my eyes shut and stand frozen, hoping she'll simply walk by. Her heels click in succession as she approaches.

The clicking heels pass me, and I open one eye to confirm. She has passed. Was she so engrossed in her papers that she didn't notice? I glance behind, and to my mortification, I see the girl standing at the end of the hall, near Gio's door, looking at me. Instinctively, I cover my more vulnerable region with my hands.

"Nice to see you again, Mark," she says, smirking.

Aside from that, she seems completely unfazed. She's wearing a tweed pencil skirt and a matching blazer with a burgundy blouse underneath. Her hair is pulled up into a ponytail, the way Esther typically wears hers.

"I . . . uh, do I know you?"

"Yeah, it's Marcy. Don't you remember me? We spoke over the phone this morning. I'm glad you could get some help. If I'd known it was you, I would've been more helpful."

All I can do is stand there frozen. Warmth rushes to my

face, and I can't help but imagine she's noticing my cheeks are turning a rosy red.

"Don't worry. You're not the first guy down on his luck that's come out of Mr. Grimaldi's office in his boxers," she says, smiling at me like we're long-lost friends. "I hope your day turns around."

She opens the door and steps into Gio's office.

I'm left mesmerized by her confidence. Shaking my head, I whistle the catchy tune Cain and Moab had been whistling about an hour ago.

As the elevator doors open to the floor where we parked, Cain greets me by shoving my new clothes into my chest. The small power I hold over him is more satisfying than I'd like to admit. These two goons are working for me now.

I call my dad and leave a voicemail: "Hey Dad, sorry for not getting back to you sooner. You're probably at work now. I'll see you tonight for dinner."

The clothes fit like a glove, filling me with a newfound confidence about everything working out. Nothing like a fresh set of threads to get you out of a funk.

I sit in the backseat of the car, waiting for Cain and Moab to drive me wherever I direct. But in this moment, the all-too-familiar sense of dread starts creeping into my thoughts. What is it now?

Is it the guilt for not feeling more remorse over hiding Liz's murder? But *I* didn't kill her, and Meg killed her in self-defense. Would she have done it if she weren't under the influence of drugs? Probably not. Then again, if she hadn't been, we might both be dead. Not "might." *We'd both be dead.*

No, it's not guilt gnawing at me. It's the feeling of leaving something behind, the same feeling I had leaving Mike and Liz's house. My gut is trying to communicate with me, awkwardly and unclear, the way a foreigner asks a local where the bathroom is. It's the feeling you get when you've left your wallet or phone behind.

But what is it?

CHAPTER 38

1:37 PM

"Where do ya wanna go?" demands Cain. Moab is no longer with him.

I'm making my fifth call to Meg, and once again, I hear: "I'm sorry. The person you are trying to reach has a voice mail box that has not been set up yet."

I need to find her. The thought of Meg lying in a ditch somewhere is slowly rising into my consciousness, as unwanted as the orange box car.

"Would you mind driving me around to look for my sister?"

He looks at me from the driver's seat with a look that says he wants to murder me.

"Who do ya think you're talking to?"

The question is rhetorical, of course. I'm not sure what is coming over me, but the fear I once felt for this man has vanished—maybe forever, like Virginia Rose McKinley.

"Do you know who *you're* talking to?" I respond, leaning over the center console, just inches away from his face. "I'm a client now. Gio said to take me wherever the hell I need to go. What I need is to find my sister."

My words tumble out, probably fueled by beer, sleep deprivation, and the pain coursing through my arm.

"Esther told me 'bout you. She said you were the most honorable, honest man she'd ever met. If only she'd see ya now," he says, turning to face forward and shifting the car into reverse.

I lean back, defeated once again by one of Esther's brothers.

We start by driving back to the gas station where I had

left Meg. I get out to search around the building and main road, hoping to find any signs pointing to where she had gone.

"She's not here," barks Cain. "Get back in the car. I'm taking you home."

"I'm going to check inside really quick."

I run up and pull open the door. The lady at the register, a white middle-aged woman, glances up, then looks back down at her phone, disinterested in greeting me.

"Hey, I was in here early this morning, and a young guy helped me. He doesn't happen to be here still?"

She continues looking at her phone as I speak, then slowly looks up.

"You talking about Diego? He left hours ago."

Of course, he did.

"I know this sounds strange, but he might have information about a missing person. I'm looking for my sister, and I think he might have seen her. Do you happen to have his number?"

"What's in it for me?" she asks.

"I don't have any money. I promise to come back and give you some if you help me."

"Forget it. I'll give you the number. You don't seem like you got much anyway."

She scribbles the digits on a piece of paper and slides it to me.

"Thank you so much. You have no idea how much I appreciate this," I say, running out of the store.

I dial the number. "Hi, you have reached Diego."

He's probably sleeping after his night shift. I call and call and call until finally, I hear, "Hello?"

"Hi, I'm so sorry for calling so much. Is this Diego?"

"Yeah, who is this?"

"My name is Mark. I spoke with you early this morning. My sister and I were using the payphone."

"Oh. How did you get my number?"

"I got it from a co-worker. I'm calling to see if you have

any information about what happened to my sister. I haven't seen her."

"Yeah, I know what happened to her. After you sprinted off, the older guy went out looking for you. Your sister came out of the bathroom shortly after that asking for you. I told her you left."

She must have gone into the bathroom right after me when I was distracted with looking at Phillip. My sister probably thinks I left her.

"Do you know where she went?"

"Yeah. She left with your friend, the older guy. They spoke outside and then hopped in his car."

What could possibly have been her rationale for leaving with Phillip—a stranger? Stupid, stupid, stupid girl.

"Did they say where they were going?" I ask, pacing back and forth.

Hard to believe that just ten hours ago, Meg and I were frantically trying to remember phone numbers right here by this payphone. It feels like a lifetime ago.

"I'm sorry. She never came back in. I wish I could be of more help, amigo," he says, his genuinely helpful nature easing my sense of guilt just a little.

"Thanks, bro. I really appreciate it. Sorry for waking you up."

I walk back up to the Royce and hop in the front seat, forgetting who I was with for a moment. The preoccupation with Meg's whereabouts could be blinding me to my own.

"What'd ya think you doing?" asks Cain.

"What? Oh, sorry. I'm used to sitting up front."

"Not with me. No client sits in front."

I ignore his attempt to intimidate me and give him directions.

"Go to August Road," I say, buckling up.

It's time to see what Mrs. Grant knows.

CHAPTER 39

2:30 PM

Cain barrels down the highway at an alarming speed. He looks angry. I hope Mrs. Grant is home. I don't think I'll be able to convince Cain to take me anywhere else.

The lush, vibrant trees that line either side of the highway blur into a streak of green, as hazy as the memories of last night. In what order did things happen? Did we search the house before going out to the shed? When did I go to the van? I never told Gio that I think the van was spray-painted. I also forgot to mention the crushed sprinkler heads that created the mud that trapped our car. What about the tire marks that ran over them? Could Liz have caused that? Should I have mentioned the lack of family photos in the house?

Even my memories from years spent with Esther have started to blur. Besides the big moments that will always be imprinted on my mind, the little things are fading. The dates we shared, the movies we watched, our mini golf games, the jokes we couldn't stop laughing at. I can't even remember one of those things that made us laugh endlessly. Who won the last time we played golf? What was the last movie we watched? When did I last see her smile? What was she wearing when she came into the coffee shop this past Friday?

A surge of panic rises as I struggle to piece together the memory. She was wearing slacks with a blazer, oversized but purposefully so. She had her hair up in the usual ponytail, and she wore soft pink lipstick. God, I miss her.

"Do you know where your sister is?" I ask, still staring out the window at the endless blur of trees.

Silence stretches between us.

"How'd I know?" Cain finally says.

There's no trace of love for his own little sister.

"I figured you would have some idea," I say. "She wasn't in the office today, so I thought maybe she took the day off."

He looks at me with disgust, but in his expression, I notice a hint of something else. What is it? Is he truly evil, or simply a product of his horrible environment?

We exit and take the same roads that Meg and I followed to the Grant's house last night. I glance down at my phone again—still nothing from Meg.

"Which house?"

"It's the seventh house on the right. You can pull into the driveway and loop around."

Even the simplest instructions make Cain radiate anger. He's probably been told what to do his whole life, trapped—like Esther—by the same abusive father and criminal employers.

"Listen, man, I'm sorry for making you drive me around," I say. "I really appreciate it."

He doesn't respond.

"I think we got off on the wrong foot when I used to date your sister," I continue. "I would like to be friends if at all possible. Your sister is very special to me."

"Do ya want me to kill ya?" he asks casually, the same way I would ask Esther if she wanted to get ice cream.

His contempt for me is palpable. I'm wasting my effort trying to be polite with him.

"I can explain things pretty easy to boss man," Cain says. "I'll gladly crash this car in a way that makes it seem you died from the impact. Do ya wanna push ya luck? You've got no right to talk about my family."

These are the most words I've ever heard him say in succession. They should leave me terrified, but I sense that his threat holds no weight.

"Ok, I'll shut up."

The next few minutes fill me with the most potent tension, which is saying a lot, given the stress I endured with Liz less than a day ago.

As the car comes to a stop, I extend my hand for a shake. "Ok, I guess we'll see each other around."

He ignores the gesture, his gaze fixed straight ahead. I keep my hand there for a few seconds longer, hoping the awkwardness will move him to shake it and be done with me. But he doesn't budge.

I get out of the car, the tight knots of tension pulling at my shoulders. This is where all my stress and anxiety seem to settle—better here than my gut.

In front of me stands Mr. and Mrs. Grant's run-down house. A single car is parked outside, but it's not the old Volvo Mr. Grant drives. He's not back home yet.

"Shoot!" I mutter, turning around toward the car.

As I do, the wheels kick up the dust and rocks from the driveway as Cain speeds off the property. I wave my hands in a futile attempt to stop him.

Mrs. Grant is likely at the Lil' Cup to open today. It will probably take about an hour to walk there. Why did I tell Cain to drop me off at their house? What a stupid choice. I should have gone to the Lil' Cup or back home.

I stroll dejectedly to the rotting steps and slump down in defeat. Exhaustion settles in, my energy fading like a phone running on its last five percent of battery. I shut my eyes, and once again, the image of Esther in that beautiful red dress fills my mind—the one I saw before the fictional train came crashing into me.

"Run to her, sweetie!" my mom says as I walk out of my room toward the girl on the couch.

As I stretch out my hand to touch her shoulder where the red strap clings, I feel her soft, gentle skin meet my fingertips. Goosebumps run up and down my arms, and butterflies flap their wings in my stomach. I close my eyes to soak in the moment.

When I open them, I'm outside the Grant's house again. I force my eyes shut to bring Esther back. Is this a memory?

Esther turns to look at me, her eyes are wet with tears, but they don't fall. She's strong, determined. Despite the rain, her hair is straight and dry. How long has she been here? Must have been before the rain started. Her glossy lips make me want to kiss her.

"Hey," is all she says in her gentle, beautiful voice.

I move around the couch to sit beside her.

"Hey."

She reaches for my hand, and our fingers intertwine. We sit in silence, besides the occasional chirping from the dying smoke detector. The dress she wears is the same one I saw her in on the train tracks.

The front door creaks open, and we both turn to look. But it remains closed.

"Mr. Stratford," I hear a voice call behind me.

I turn around, and Esther fades.

"There are some matters we need to discuss," says Phillip.

CHAPTER 40

2:59 PM

"What did you do with my sister?" I demand, springing from the stairs where I'd been dreaming.

The sudden movement sends dark spots flashing before my eyes, but I stride with determination directly toward him.

"Calm down, please," Phillip says. "I'm a friend. We're on the same side."

I don't buy it. This guy has known far too much since I met him yesterday morning. His knowledge makes him arrogant, like a chess grandmaster who's already planned every move I might make. Nothing I do will surprise him—he always has a plan for my next step. If I had gone to the Lil' Cup, he'd have been there. If I'd gone home, he'd have shown up. He knew that I'd come here, and low and behold, here he is, waiting for me.

As my thoughts spiral into paranoia, I ask, "How'd you know I'd ask to be dropped off at this house?"

What is it about this house that makes me feel so exposed? I felt a similar vulnerability last night when I imagined the Onionhead watching me. Was it him? Or was it Phillip? Was it his gaze from the tree line that left me feeling so susceptible outside Liz's house as I walked to the shed.

"You give me a little too much credit, Mr. Stratford," he says calmly. "I didn't know you would come here. I heard a car drive off abruptly and came down to check what all the commotion was about."

"What in the hell are you doing here?" I ask, angrily. "This isn't your house! And what did you do to poor old Mr. Grant? Are you taking advantage of these people?"

"I'm sorry if I gave the impression that I'm some kind of

menace to society," he says. "We obviously got off on the wrong foot. If you would come inside, I can explain everything to you."

Remorse hits me like a ton of bricks. Why am I treating Phillip so poorly? I was far more polite to Cain and Gio, and they're actual criminals. This man hasn't done a single thing wrong. He asked Mr. Grant questions, complimented me on my coffee, and was ready to pick us up when we needed help. My suspicion of him stems solely from the fact that he knows too much. And that's no excuse to treat him badly.

Suddenly, I fall back against the worn-down wooden railing, my head spinning. I touch the back of my neck, wondering if the poisonous bite might be the cause of my unsteadiness. He reaches out to catch me, but I can see his hesitation, not wanting to overstep.

"Are you ok?" he asks with sincerity. "Is there something wrong with the back of your neck? That's a nasty cut on your arm. Do you mind my asking what caused it?"

It's comforting to consider that he might genuinely be oblivious to what caused my wounds. I hope that's the truth.

"I was grabbing something from our shed, and I got bit."

"Oh boy? Do you know what got you? I spotted several spiders that I don't recognize in the short time I've been here."

"Where did you come from?" I ask, ignoring his question.

"I move around quite a bit. I'm currently living in New York, but I'm originally from Rhode Island."

Maybe I have this man all wrong. His eyes look kind and his tallness doesn't make him intimidating—he carries his stature with ease.

"Listen, I'm sorry for losing it. You seem like a decent guy. I just don't know what you wanted with Mr. Grant yesterday, and now he's missing. And what was with you telling that gas station worker I asked you to pick me up? How did you even know where we were? Oh, and what did you do with my sister?" I demand the last part, my calmness breaking as the words leave my mouth.

The sudden realization makes me upset for almost

forgetting about Meg again. My mind is overwhelmed, and it's becoming harder and harder to keep things straight. I had wanted the dominoes to start falling, and now that they have, I can't keep up.

"These are all valid questions, and I'm more than willing to answer them. Would you be comfortable coming inside?" he says, gesturing to the open door.

I want to trust him. I want so badly to hear him out. My gut says I should, but my gut's been wrong before. What if he's trying to lure me into some sort of trap? What if Meg and Mr. and Mrs. Grant are all dead? No. That's absurd.

"Why can't we talk out here?"

"We can. I have some water boiling in the kettle inside. If you would give me a moment, I can go inside and get some tea for us. We can sit right over there and talk."

He glances at the table and chairs facing the hideous front yard, which must have once been appealing enough for them to buy the set.

The angry hiss of water boiling in a kettle alerts us both.

"No, we can go inside. Lead the way," I say.

I step inside a house I've never entered before, feeling strange that it isn't Mr. or Mrs. Grant who invited me, but a man I hardly know.

A dark oak banister is the first thing that greets me as I enter, leading to a hallway that stretches into the house. To my right is a dining room, and to my left, a formal sitting room. Old paintings depicting nature scenes line the walls, hanging atop floral wallpaper. The house is dim with heavy blinds and curtains covering the windows. The ancient wooden scratched-up floor creaks beneath my feet, and much like the porch, could desperately use some oil rejuvenation. I hear Phillip rummaging through cabinets from somewhere in the back of the house, probably the kitchen.

"Mr. Stratford, there's a perfect spot to sit right back here. Mrs. Grant doesn't like shoes on the carpeted areas."

I notice the wooden floor continues to the back, but

THE CUSTOMERS

golden carpeting covers the dining and living rooms, vacuumed into pristine lines. I picture Mrs. Grant tirelessly and perfectly maintaining this part of the house, and something about that makes her endearing to me. How could I not trust her?

I walk down the dark hallway that leads to a far brighter kitchen, examining the pictures on the walls. One picture shows the Grants on their wedding day. Mrs. Grant looks beautiful, with a classic curly cut and white veil. But her face is so emotionless as she poses next to her groom. Mr. Grant looks at least ten years older. Maybe it's just a bad angle.

I examine more photos from their world travels and adventures, picturing Esther's face in place of Mrs. Grant's, and my own in place of Mr. Grant's. There are no photos from their childhoods, no other family members, and no children.

"Mark, would you like chamomile, green, or honey lavender? I think she has lemon ginger as well," Phillip says, looking through a cabinet full of tea boxes.

"Green is fine."

I could use the caffeine.

I sit at the coffee table and fiddle with the white knitted placemat in front of me. Phillip carefully sets the steaming tea on top of it.

"Thank you for your patience, Mark. So, what would you like me to answer for you?" he asks, clasping his cup.

"First off, what did you do with my sister?" I ask, but with less intensity than before.

"She's safe at home. I took her to her car upon her request. I would've taken you too—if you had let me," he says blowing on the tea.

"How can I be sure you're telling the truth?"

"I guess you're going to have to trust me. I understand why you don't. You hardly know me."

I don't trust him. This is going nowhere.

"How do you know Mrs. Grant?" I ask, hoping to get more information.

"Mrs. Grant hired me," he says, without elaborating.

205

"Hired you? Hired you for what? What exactly is your job?"

"What I'm about to disclose is extremely sensitive information. Of course, I can't get into specifics, at least not without Mrs. Grant's consent. But I will tell you what I can."

He pauses, contemplating where to start.

"I run my own private investigation business. Mrs. Grant wanted to hire someone who wasn't local to do some digging on her husband."

"What kind of digging?" I interrupt, finally feeling like I'm getting somewhere.

"How close would you say you are with Mr. and Mrs. Grant?" he asks, and I feel annoyed for having to answer questions again.

Swallow your pride, I tell myself. *It does need to be a give-and-take. Answer his question, but only the one.*

"I'm a lot closer to her than to him. I do know he loves coffee and is friends with almost everyone in town."

That Mr. Grant is a client of the Grimaldis almost slips out, but I catch myself.

"And what do you know about her?" Phillip asks.

"I know her maiden name was McKinley. I know she had a younger sister who went missing at twelve. Her name was Virginia. Marge adores her husband. Almost every story she tells is about him or their experiences. She doesn't like coffee as much as she likes tea," I rattle off another dozen details about Mrs. Grant, as if I'm being graded on this question.

"So, she has told you about her past, then? Well, at least a little bit of it?"

"Yeah, why?"

"Part of the reason I'm here is closely related to Virginia."

The eagerness I feel at these words erupts like a volcano. The long-lost Virginia Rose McKinley? Is he going to help find her?

"Are you serious? Is that why Mrs. Grant hired you? Is she finally going to try to find her after all these years?"

"I don't think she has ever stopped searching."

"I've looked it up before. I couldn't find any information. Did you?" I ask.

A satisfied smile grows across his face, like the one he had when he took a sip of espresso yesterday morning.

"I bet you tried searching for it online, huh? I did too when Mrs. Grant first hired me, with much of the same luck. So, I had to go back to where Mrs. Grant told me she grew up."

"Where was that?" I ask in utter disbelief.

I always thought she was born and raised here, like me. At least, she never mentioned anything different.

"Oregon," he says, contemplating for a moment. "Medford, to be exact."

"Medford, that's nowhere close to here!" I say, unable to hide my surprise.

"Almost perfect irony, right?" he says.

I'm all for irony, but I don't really get it. I think about asking, but fear losing the momentum we've built in this discussion. With a smile, I take a sip of my tea.

Phillip continues: "I went there and used a connection with a detective to find some information on the case."

He pulls out a binder from a leather bag that I hadn't noticed until now. My observation skills have really taken a back seat lately. He places the binder in front of me, and the anticipation is enough to hurt my bones.

"Virginia Rose McKinley," he says, pausing to enjoy my undoubtedly dumbfounded expression. "You really invested a lot of time thinking about her. Is it because of the missing person cold case in Slidell?"

Missing person in Slidell? I'm taken aback for a moment, then realize he must be talking about the girl from the Onionhead story.

"Yeah, but I thought the police solved that?" I say.

"I wasn't aware they did. I couldn't think of the name of the girl. It's tragic what happened to her, and right by the train tracks, too. You would think somebody would have seen something."

"The whole story is tragic. But it was a long time ago," I say, nodding for him to continue with the file.

He looks confused for a flash and then continues.

"Born to Robert and Dianne McKinley on May 16th, 1955. Reported missing on January 2nd, 1967."

That all fits what Mrs. Grant told me. This might be the most satisfying moment in my life, as the pieces to an old, scattered puzzle finally align. I had almost given up hope of ever finding a resolution.

"Wow, so Mrs. Grant remembered correctly. Is there anything else in the file?"

"Not too much. She went missing after school and never came home. When the parents reported it later that night, the police immediately checked the last place she was seen—the playground. The only lead they had was the substitute teacher who never returned to work after she went missing. He had been hired just for that semester, and it turns out he had been using a fake name."

"What was the name?"

"Frank Garland."

"So, did they try to track him down?"

"Of course, but they had nothing to go off of. He was using that alias, and he had nothing that tied him down to any specific place. He would park his RV in various hookups all over Medford. The paper trail went cold."

"Why would the school ever hire a creep like that?"

"That's what I thought. But you have to consider the time period. People didn't take as strong of safety measures then as they do now. In an interview on file, the principal said that they were desperately short-staffed, and he hired this Frank Garland himself. He claimed to have done a background and financial check, but I don't buy it. They terminated the principal's employment after that."

"What about Marge and her parents?"

Phillip clears his throat at the question.

"I can tell you about the parents. They died sadly only two years later in a hit-and-run accident."

"Oh my God!" I exclaim, resting my head on my fist as I contemplate the catastrophe.

Mrs. Grant never told me she was an orphan. That must be why she would always change the subject whenever I would try to find out more information.

"And that's where the story ended. Until now, that is."

"So, what happened to Mrs. Grant after her parents died? Did she go into the foster care system? Did she have any other family to take her in?"

He clears his throat once again and takes a sip of his tea.

"As far as I know, Mrs. Grant has no other family."

"Except for Virginia Rose McKinley."

He smiles at what must be my optimism. It is an extraordinarily long shot for her to still be alive, but I need hope —at least for Mrs. Grant's sake. And yet, not only for her, but also for me. Somehow, it encompasses a hope for my mom to survive her terminal disease and for Esther and me to finally live the life we've spent so much time dreaming of. Finding Virginia would turn the impossible into something possible, or even, dare I say, probable.

"So, what made Mrs. Grant reach out to you for answers after all these years?"

"It's only right for me to let her answer these personal questions. But I can tell you this." He pauses, once again weighing his words. "We found Virginia Rose McKinley."

CHAPTER 41

3:20 PM

Those words, uttered so casually, delivered the resolution I'd longed for since I first heard Virginia's story—yet in such an anticlimactic way. It was like watching a suspenseful movie that keeps you on the edge of your seat, only to fall flat at the most pivotal point. When it's over, you're left regretting the couple of hours you spent watching it.

I shouldn't compare this real circumstance involving two living, breathing sisters, to some movie. My investment in their story wasn't simply for entertainment.

Meg is right—I do romanticize life. But life isn't a movie. I can't expect it to play out like a romance flick, a fictional horror, or a suspenseful mystery with a climactic ending. Maybe it's the adventurous kid in me that longs for a life I don't live. Or maybe it's how I cope with life's difficulties, spinning these wild scenarios to escape the realities of the last five years.

Unlike Esther, I haven't asked for a redeal and unlike Cain and Moab, I haven't accepted my hand. Instead, I've been imagining a different set of cards, swapping low ones for Aces and Royals. You can't win if you don't face reality.

"What are you thinking about Mr. Stratford?" Phillip asks.

I take another sip of tea before responding. I can't explain what's going on in my mind because I haven't made sense of it myself.

"I'm wondering where she is," is all I can think to say.

"I bet you are. I'm shocked it took you so long to ask."

"So, where is she?"

"Like I told you, I have to uphold client privilege. The answers you seek can only come from Margarine Grant."

"Where is *Mrs. Grant*?"

"Upstairs."

"This whole time?" I say, rising to my feet, ready to find her.

"She's been resting for a while. Mrs. Grant is processing right now, Mark."

"Processing? Is she alive—Virginia?"

I feel stupid for not asking earlier. Maybe he meant they found her tombstone or records of her death. Knowing what I do about Phillip, he's not always direct.

"Yes. She's very much alive."

I'm filled with joy at this statement.

"What do you know about psychology, Mark?"

"Enough," I say feeling a bit irritated at the sudden change in topic.

"I should be more specific. What do you know about repressed memory?"

Repressed memory? I thought it was called suppressed memory. Are they the same thing?

"Not much," I say. "I think they're memories that center around traumatic events that can be suppressed until they are no longer even remembered."

"Impressive response," he says raising an eyebrow.

I feel a bit of pride as I replay my words, which must have been spot on. Esther would have been proud if she heard me, just like I was always proud of her when she answered random questions in school.

"I'm a PI, that is true," Phillip says. "But my main specialty is psychology. I'm fascinated by the brain and what makes us," he gestures between us, "tick. I was first hired by Mrs. Grant as her therapist. Obviously, I can't discuss specifics, but as you can guess, we've been talking about repressed, or suppressed, memory."

Of course, this guy's a psychologist. That's why he's been able to read me so effortlessly, much like my mom does. He's always one step ahead, even back in the coffee shop during our first conversation.

I can understand why Mrs. Grant needed a therapist, especially since she lost both her sister and her parents.

"I might need you soon enough," I say under my breath.

"What makes you say that?" he asks leaning in.

In an instant, I feel closer to this man than anyone else. Am I really going to unburden myself to a stranger?

"My mom has ALS and is probably going to die within the year." The words tumble out, followed by my weeping.

He moves closer, sitting in the chair beside me, and gently puts his arm on my back. He's a kind man. Any fear I ever had toward him has completely vanished.

"I'm very saddened to hear that. How long has she had the diagnosis, if you don't mind my asking?"

"Five years, about," I say, wiping my eyes.

He says nothing, but his silence, filled with respect and genuine empathy, speaks volumes and imparts a sense of healing.

My phone ring breaks the silence. The caller ID shows Meg's name, and the tightness in my stomach, which I hadn't even realized was there, releases.

"Hello, Meg? Are you ok?"

"Oh my God, Mark, where are you? Where did you go?"

"I'm so sorry. I am . . ." I pause as tears come flooding out.

I take about a minute to compose myself as my sister tries to console me.

"I ran off because I thought," I start, now feeling awkward admitting that I believed Phillip was trying to kill us. "I thought we were in trouble."

"Well, you weren't wrong. We're in trouble, remember dummy," she says, trying to make me laugh. "Where are you?"

"I'm at Mrs. Grant's house."

"How did you get there?"

I glance at Phillip when she asks, recalling Gio's warning not to let anyone know about our conversation.

"Excuse me Phillip, I'm going to step outside and talk to

my sister."

"Sure thing," he says gesturing for me to go.

Outside on the porch, I quietly tell Meg everything that's happened since we last saw each other. I leave out some of the more embarrassing details, of course.

"You did all of that by yourself? Sounds like a nightmare!"

"It felt like one. But I think it will all get taken care of. I had them drop me off at Mrs. Grant's house thinking Phillip brought you here."

"Why'd you think that?"

"It sounds so stupid now, knowing what I do, but I thought he kidnapped you. Don't ask me why. I *am* extremely sleep-deprived. I'm just glad you're safe."

"I'm going to come pick you up!"

"What about mom?" I ask.

"Crap, I didn't think about that. Dad doesn't get home from work until 5:30."

"That's actually perfect. I'm still looking for some answers from Mrs. Grant."

"What kinds of answers?" Meg asks, and I can picture her in anticipation, phone pressed to her ear.

She's always one for a good mystery.

"I'll tell you about it when you get here."

A long silence ensues, filled with an unspoken understanding and mutual respect that hadn't existed before last night.

"I, I . . . appreciate you sis!" I finally say.

"Gross. Go hang out with your new girlfriend, Mrs. Grant. I'll see you soon."

The phone call ends as I literally squirm at the idea.

"Sorry to interrupt, Mr. Stratford," Phillip says, "but I thought you'd like to know Mrs. Grant is downstairs in the living room. She's excited to speak with you."

CHAPTER 42

3:30 PM

"Ok, I'll be there in a second," I say to Phillip, looking up from my phone, where the lock screen displays a photo of Esther and me. "Think I could get another tea? The lavender one this time."

The photo on my screen is one of my favorites. Esther had hopped onto my back so that I could spin her around in circles. She would've let me do this for hours if I'd been able to keep my balance. I could only go for a couple of minutes before I'd tumble onto the grass, then look up at the moving stars, as if they might tumble down, too.

I had taken the photo without her noticing, perfectly capturing the pure joy on her face, an expression I'd never seen in a photo before—and haven't seen since. Candid photos like that are priceless, much more endearing than posed ones, like Mrs. Grant's wedding photo.

I lock the phone and climb the stairs, eager to finally learn more about Mrs. Grant. I just hope the stories aren't just about her and Mr. Grant—I want to hear about Virginia. And I want to know why Mrs. Grant hired Phillip to investigate her own husband.

How could the person who has vowed to love you develop such distrust? The thought of Esther ever hiring someone to investigate me would do irreparable damage. Sure, Mr. Grant might be a grumpy old man with some minor insults up his sleeve. But surely his good qualities outweigh the bad.

As I step inside, I immediately make eye contact with Mrs. Grant. Her warm silver eyes sparkle. She wears cozy slippers and a dark green blanket that she knitted herself, just like the placemats in the kitchen. I wonder if she also painted the artwork displayed in her home.

"Oh, my dearest little Mark. Come on over here!" she says, her arms outstretched, ready for an embrace.

I take two steps forward before realizing I've stepped onto the carpet with my shoes. Mrs. Grant slightly opens her mouth in apprehension as I look at her, mortified. She waves me to come forward anyway.

"It's only carpet," she says. "It's long past the time for me to remodel this home."

I bend down to hug her, and she motions for me to sit on the small stool beside her chair. My excitement isn't typical because seeing Mrs. Grant usually means I'm stuck at work.

"Mark, I'm very sorry for confusing you. I should have told you about Phillip before he ever came in. It was very spur of the moment, and we both felt that immediate action was necessary."

"Oh, sweetie," she says, just like my mom used to.

She takes my hand between hers. They are extremely delicate and warm to the touch.

"There is so much to explain, and I don't want to burden you. I only want you to know and accept my sincerest apologies for dragging you into this mess. It was not right of me."

I feel like a little kid who's been left out of the adult conversations.

"Mrs. Grant, I understand. I need to know, though. I need to hear the story about your missing sister."

"I should have never told you about it in the first place, which I especially realized after understanding what you've been going through these last five years. You poor thing."

"No, I needed something to take my mind off my mother."

She furrows her eyebrows. "When was the first time I mentioned my sister to you?"

"Not that long ago—last year, I think."

"Yeah, that's what I thought," she says, pondering.

"I don't mean to intrude, but here are your teas," says Phillip.

As I look at him now, standing beside a woman of Mrs. Grant's age, he seems younger than I initially thought—late forties at most. His deep forehead wrinkles probably resulted from years of making empathetic facial expressions at his clients.

"Hey, how'd you know about my shots pulling at twenty-seven seconds yesterday?" I finally remember to ask my burning question.

What else am I forgetting? This feeling of forgetfulness stirs up a sense of emptiness inside me.

A smirk appears on Phillip's face, and Mrs. Grant bashfully lowers her gaze to her tea.

"You were right about him. I can see now why you hold him in such high regard," Phillip says.

The praise won't distract me from my original question.

"So? How did he know?" I direct the question now to Mrs. Grant.

"You can tell him, Phillip," she says, blowing on her steaming liquid.

"Ok. Mark, do you know where that painting hangs, right behind the cash register? The one with—"

"The one with the deli overlooking the Mediterranean Sea," I interrupt, thinking he's dodging the question again. "Yeah, what about it?"

"There's a little camera right on top of it—small enough to blend in with the wall, at least."

"For how long?" I ask, feeling violated at the thought of being watched.

"It's not the only one, Mark," Mrs. Grant adds. "I had them installed in other parts of the shop too. For security."

She must sense my unease at the hidden cameras, though my discomfort is more from not knowing about them.

"Eddy always thought that we didn't need new technology. You know that, I'm sure. So, I had them installed confidentially earlier this year."

Something tells me there's more to this than just security.

"You're telling me that Phillip watches footage from these cameras?" I ask.

"I watched it that morning before I came in," Phillip admits. "I didn't want to miss Mr. Grant, so I needed to find out what time he'd arrive. I saw you stressing over the coffee shots pulling a little long, and I let it slip. To be honest, I thought you wouldn't notice. My apologies, Marge, for my lack of discretion."

Ok, one question down. I mentally check it off. *Next.*

"Why, Mrs. Grant? Why are you having Phillip investigate your own husband?"

"Mr. Stratford, like I told you earlier, this is sensitive information. It will be difficult for Mrs. Grant to share right now. These things can take years to fully understand."

Years? I don't have years. I want to know *now*. I feel like the child inside me is begging to come out and throw a tantrum. I see it all the time—this childish instinct that takes over full-grown adults when they don't get their way. They scream, curse, mock, throw their arms up in the air, like overgrown toddlers who never moved passed their early stages of development.

But I'm not about to do that.

"I understand. I'm sorry. You don't owe me anything."

The realization that I might never know the full story sends an ache through me. Without the distraction of Mrs. Grant's secrets, the anxiety over last night's fiasco resurfaces, forming a knot in my gut.

"Look at me, Mark," Mrs. Grant says, staring into my eyes and straight through to my heart.

"Once you know, you must promise to allow me to take care of things from this point forward. Do you understand?"

"I promise, Mrs. Grant. I swear on all the people I love most."

"Oh, no need for that. I trust you," she says, giggling.

"Well, Phillip, what do you think? He's bound to find out any day now anyway."

"The decision is completely up to you. It's your life."
"Ok, Mark. I'll start from the beginning."

CHAPTER 43

3:45 PM

"Eddy and I met at school," starts Mrs. Grant. "He was my crush when I was a little girl, and I eventually fell in love with him."

I instantly think of Esther and me falling in love at school. I can relate more than Mrs. Grant knows.

"I had a difficult time with my parents, Mark. They wanted another child so desperately. My mother was unable to for years. I began feeling isolated from them as they were dealing with their grief. I felt like I was not enough. Every time I was with Eddy, he would immediately take away these feelings of loneliness. He made me feel seen. He asked me questions, he complemented me, he made me see myself as beautiful."

It dawns on me for the first time—the significant age gap between Margarine and Virginia.

"We eventually got married when I was eighteen. He gave me the life I had always dreamed of. We traveled around the country, going through almost every state. We were always moving and learning and hiking and exploring and eating local foods at the places we would visit."

The life Mrs. Grant describes sounds like the one Esther and I have always envisioned. Who would have thought that the two people I work for had already lived my perfect life?

I know my life isn't a movie, but if it were, it would be *Serendipity*. The major theme centers on the idea of fate and that the love of your life will be revealed through undeniable signs. In the story, it takes years for the two lead characters to reunite after their first romantic encounter. Despite all the odds against them, fate ultimately brings them back together. That's exactly what I want for Esther and me.

"Phillip, would you bring me that photo album over there?" Mrs. Grant asks, gesturing to the bookshelf in the corner of the room.

"Here are some of our wedding photos," she says, opening the album.

She looks beautiful in her white lace dress. Mr. Grant is just as dashing. The two of them are outdoors, surrounded by the woods, with a lake in the distance.

"Where are all the guests?" I ask.

"Eddy and I moved around so much we didn't build many friendships. I think Phillip mentioned what happened with my parents," she says, looking at Phillip.

Phillip nods, but his gesture carries more than just an acknowledgment—it carries empathy.

"Yes, yes. I'm sorry." I say, feeling stupid for already forgetting the detail I just learned.

"Don't be. That was a long time ago. And you, of all people, can relate. You have extra leeway, you see," she says, smiling.

"Ok, that was our wedding day. So, did you notice anything?" she asks.

"You looked beautiful. And it seems like you two were just perfect together."

She smiles, but a flicker of sadness appears in her eyes.

"So here we are in the California redwoods," she continues, turning the page.

That must've been where they got married. For the next half an hour, she takes me through her tour across the country. They had visited every national park, every major landmark, and most of the country's big cities.

With each story, my envy quietly grows. I've dreamed of doing these very things with Esther.

"So, what do you think, Mark?"

"I think I'm a little jealous of the life that you've lived."

"A lot of people have told me that through the years. And I believed them."

I hear a restrained anguish in her voice. How can this woman who had everything feel sad while reminiscing about her perfect life?

"Eddy and I moved to Slidell in 1999, and he took all the coffee experience he'd gained over the years and poured it into the Lil' Cup. The business took off. Between that and his inheritance that was left by a distant relative, we were very well off."

This must be one huge plan to make me feel worse about my own life. I have no money. I'm not with the love of my life, traveling the world. And now, I'm trying to avoid a prison sentence.

"Phillip, would you hand me that other photo album?" she asks, gesturing to the shelf again.

She opens it up and starts telling me stories of their world travels. They visited ten different countries and saw more in their fifty years of marriage than I would probably see if I lived three lifetimes.

Phillip moves closer to Mrs. Grant and rests his hand on her shoulder.

"You can take a break now. This is a good stopping point," he suggests.

Everything inside me wants to protest the silly suggestion. *A break from what? Sharing stories about her perfect life?*

"Mark, I can tell what you're thinking," she continues. "It's the same thing I've thought myself. What do I have to complain about? I've lived a really happy life."

I take an uncomfortable sip of my tea, realizing my facial expressions give me away.

"Through all these years and pictures and travels and successes, I've always been despondent. Guilt forced me to keep this feeling bottled up inside. I have no right to be unhappy. I have the perfect world from the perspective of anyone else. That's why I started by showing you my life through the eyes of everyone around me."

The loneliness of having it all while feeling empty must be miserable. Despite my initial lack of sympathy, a wave of sadness washes over me.

"Eddy, as you've seen from time to time, can be a harsh man. The compliments followed by the yelling and abuse felt like a whirlpool I couldn't escape. I wanted to break free, but he always sucked me back in. I grew so accustomed to it that it became like living with a terrible odor. At first, you're repulsed. But eventually, your senses grow numb. The thing is, Mark, it doesn't disappear. You just become accepting."

My heart feels heavy. Knowing what she was living through in all these photos makes me feel devastated. I've only briefly experienced Mr. Grant's behavior, and I know the impact it had on me.

"You helped me, my dearest boy. You helped me smell the disgusting odor again," she says, chuckling.

"When I saw from an outside perspective how he would treat you, it made me want to confront him. I did, and he flipped everything on me. He made me believe I was the one at fault, that I deserved it, or that I was treating *him* poorly."

Her words remind me of Liz, when she talked about catching Mike having an affair, only for him to spin things around and make it her fault.

"Eddy has always had his secrets," she continues, "and I was fine with that. But one day, about six years ago, I caught him having..." She stops.

"Having what?" I ask.

"He had a young lady over at our house. They were here while I was at the shop. I came home and didn't catch them doing anything. But I knew. I knew he had charmed her the way he had so many other women during our marriage. He had many affairs, but I thought those days were behind him. The move to Slidell was my idea of a fresh start."

The similarities between Liz and Mrs. Grant are uncanny, but probably not much of a coincidence. There's often a pattern among adulterous men and the women they betray.

"Why did you stay with him?" I ask.

"Where would I go? I had no family and no savings—everything was in Eddy's name. All our earnings from the Lil' Cup were in his social security."

"But if you got divorced, you would get some of his money, right?" I say, hoping that I just solved all her problems.

"I thought that as well. But he hired the Grimaldis. They're the most powerful lawyers in town. I don't have the money to compete with that."

The timeline adds up. Of course it does. Why did I not think of it until now. Six years ago. It must have been Mr. Grant who pushed passed me into the diner. That's why he hired them, to make sure his poor wife wouldn't leave him. If she did, Mrs. Grant would be left without a dime to her name.

The light outside is fading as the sun falls slowly to the horizon in the west.

"So, I tried to make the best of it. He promised he was showing a customer some of my art, and that's why he brought her to the house. I pretended to believe him, and life got a little better for a time."

Finally, I have some of the answers I've sought for a long time, but I'm feeling less satisfied and more devastated.

"Shortly after, I met you in the pharmacy. I sensed an instant connection. You were like a son that I could never have. You see, I inherited some of my mother's fertility issues."

My jealousy has now transformed into deep sympathy.

"We're even now," I say under my breath.

"What was that dear?" Mrs. Grant asks.

"When I first called you years ago, Mr. Grant answered," I say. "I could tell he didn't want to hire me. And after he did, he rubbed it in your face, saying that you two were even. Was that what he meant?"

"It was so long ago. It's possible, but to tell you the truth, I don't remember," she says.

But I remember, and I know that's what he meant.

This narcissistic man actually thought that hiring

someone to help his wife would somehow make up for his affairs. I don't just dislike this man—I'm starting to hate him. My level of disgust for him rivals my feelings toward Brandon Foster.

"How well do you know your customers, Mark?" asks Phillip.

"I know the regulars. Why?"

"Do you know an Elizabeth Hill?"

My heart sinks at the unexpected question.

"Maybe," is all I can say. I take another sip of my drink, hoping to hide any facial expressions.

"Have you seen any of my husband's interactions with her?" Mrs. Grant asks.

The memory of that first day she came into the shop replays like an old video reel. Mr. Grant chatted with her for a long time, basking in her attention. I thought it was friendly banter, maybe even fatherly. Nothing flirtatious. But was it?

"Yeah, they were pretty close," is all I say.

"I got the security cameras to catch him in the act. I had hoped I would gather enough proof, that with an affordable lawyer, I could make a strong enough case against him. At the very least, I thought I could threaten to ruin his reputation around town along with his customer following. I thought it might be enough leverage to force him to give me some financial help after the divorce."

This woman isn't a greedy gold digger. She didn't want his fortune, just enough to live on. From what I can tell, he had more than enough to give.

"I caught him on tape," is all she says.

What does that even mean? Did she catch him having an affair with Liz at the Lil' Cup?

"Caught him?" I say, raising my eyebrows, "Doing what?"

I'm scared to find out, hoping it's not what I think it is.

"I caught him sexually harassing her. He did something highly inappropriate one night while he was closing the shop. She was a poor, vulnerable woman, and he took advantage of that. She denied his advances and slapped him across the face."

"How long ago?"

"This was pretty recent," Phillip interjects. "Two weeks ago, maybe less."

His voice is no longer that of a therapist, but of a private investigator.

This video evidence would be more than enough to hold over his head and use as a bargaining chip.

"That is awful," I say, thinking about Liz and her unfortunate lot in life.

The remorse over her death blows a punch to my gut. I suddenly lack air in my lungs. Liz had an unfaithful husband and a man double her age sexually harassed her. All she wanted, like Mrs. Grant, was to be freed from her life.

"You could have saved me. Why didn't you?" her words from my dream replay in my mind.

If only I'd known what she'd been through, I might have been more empathetic—and maybe I could have saved her. The woman I encountered last night wasn't the real Liz. She must have snapped. But to pull a gun and try to kill someone—that was more than just snapping. A perplexing mix of emotions pulls me in every direction.

"At this moment, we possess all the evidence we require," Phillip says. "So, I went into the shop and strong-armed him a little. I was trying to intimidate him into a confession. It almost worked. Before I could get a tangible admission of guilt, he stormed off."

"So that's why he left," I say as another perfect piece fits into place.

"Yes. Unfortunately, I spooked him."

"What's the next step?" I ask.

"First, we have to locate him. He hasn't contacted you, has he?" asks Phillip, much the same way Gio had asked.

"No, I don't think he would contact me."

"He'll only reach out to the Grimaldis," adds Mrs. Grant.

"Wait," I look at Mrs. Grant, "So how did you connect with

Phillip?"

"A therapist program paired us. He was helping me with some of my issues that I mentioned to you. The two of you are the only people in the world who know the things I told you about Eddy."

Mrs. Grant's life stories and the realization that the man I've worked for the past five years is a monster have nearly made me forget the biggest question of all: Where is Virginia?

CHAPTER 44

5:30 PM

Mrs. Grant leans toward an ancient lamp and pulls its chain, illuminating the room as the sun dips lower behind the trees on this late October evening. I glance at the chiming clock—it's 5:30 p.m. Already?

Time is bizarre. It behaves differently on other planets. On Mercury, a single day is the equivalent of fifty-nine Earth days, while Jupiter has the shortest days, in just under ten hours. But years are a different story. A year is only eighty-eight days on Mercury. If Mrs. Grant lived on Mercury, she would've been married to Mr. Grant for 207—over three lifetimes of absolute misery. On Jupiter, where a year is 4,307 days, she would have been married to him for just over four years. Of course, it's all the same, but playing with time helps me to cope with my own life, wasted away like hers.

"Remember, Mark, our conversation earlier about repressed and suppressed memory?" asks Phillip.

"Yeah, but I still don't understand the difference," I say, not really caring at this point.

All I want to know is where that poor little girl, Virginia, is. Then I'm hit with the strange realization that she's no longer the little girl I've always pictured. She would be a woman now. What does she look like?

"Repressed memory takes place on an unconscious level," Phillip explains. "When you go through a traumatic event, the brain does what it can to protect you. It takes those dangerous memories and locks them away, like in a box. Does that make sense?"

"Yeah, perfect sense."

"Good. Mrs. Grant and I discussed this during our sessions. Suppressed memory is when you intentionally choose to take these unwanted memories and lock them in the box. This is a conscious choice."

"What does this have to do with Mrs. Grant?" I ask.

He looks at her as she rocks back and forth in her chair.

It must be related to her and Virginia growing up. Did she see who kidnapped Virginia, and did she block out the memory? If she did, I couldn't blame her. Even in my dream, I could hardly bear watching it happen. It wouldn't have been a choice to block it out—it would have been her subconscious shielding her.

My phone buzzes on my leg. I choose to ignore it, determined to finally find out about Virginia. It vibrates again. A third time. Then a fourth.

"I insist we take a break. Doctor's orders," Phillip says, finally breaking the silence.

Mrs. Grant's rocking has intensified. She's no longer mentally present with us.

"Mrs. Grant?" I call out.

"I was afraid this might happen. She's trapped in one of her memories."

"What do we do?"

Is this what I look like when I'm caught in my hallucinations? Her eyes stare straight ahead, filled with tears.

"Mrs. Grant, we're here. You're safe at home," I plead.

Phillip moves closer and tells her to breathe, guiding her through the exercise.

"Mark, go get her some water from the fridge," Phillip says.

I hurry to the kitchen and grab a bottle of water for Mrs. Grant and one for myself. As I reach for the second bottle, my eyes land on Phillip's binder on the table. The temptation to skim through it is palpable—this might be my only way to find out about Virginia.

"Mark, we need the water!" Phillip's voice pulls me back.

I shake my head and race back to them.

Phillip gently helps Mrs. Grant drink the water, but it does little to bring her back to reality.

"What memories is she reliving?" I ask.

"I wish I could tell. This is all so fresh for her. It might take years, if ever, for her to talk about them."

My chest is heavy with distress for not knowing. I don't have a right to the answers, but then again, Mrs. Grant said I'm like a son to her. Doesn't that entitle me to the information? The familiar tug-of-war between morality and curiosity wages in my mind.

I pull out my phone and see Meg's name—she's the one who's been calling.

"I need to call my sister," I mutter.

"Ok, I'm going to try to get Marge upstairs so she can get some sleep," Phillip says, trying to calm her.

I replay Meg's voicemail: "I'm on my way. Dad got home early. You better still be there!"

I send her a quick text to let her know I'm still here. Now, I only have one thing on my mind: that freaking binder.

I walk back to the house and see Phillip slowly guiding Mrs. Grant up the stairs. Now is my chance. I wait for them to make it all the way up and slowly open the squeaky screen door. I keep the handle twisted open until it comes to a silent close behind me, then release it.

The sounds of movement upstairs tell me I have time to do the unthinkable. Am I really going to invade Mrs. Grant's privacy just to satisfy my curiosity? No, that's not the only reason. I'm doing it to educate myself on how to help her. But even I know that's a sorry excuse.

My curiosity pulls my feet toward the kitchen while my conscience screams at me to stop. Heartburn makes its way up my chest and into the bottom of my throat, filling my mouth with the taste of bile as my intestines twist with apprehension.

One look. I'll stop at one look. I just need to know where Virginia is. I won't read all the psychology stuff or anything else that Mrs. Grant hasn't shared with me. She was about to tell me, anyway, if she hadn't had the panic attack. I'm sure of it. This winning thought pushes me to open the binder.

The first thing I find at the top is an old newspaper clipping from 1967. In big, bold letters the headline reads: *Child Vanishes from School.*

CHAPTER 45

5:45 PM

The article, dated January 2, 1967, reads:

The community of Medford remains on high alert following the mysterious disappearance of 12-year-old Virginia Rose McKinley. Last seen at her middle school at 3 p.m. on January 2, Virginia vanished shortly after classes ended for the day.

Her parents, Elliot and Marybeth McKinley, are desperate for answers and urging anyone with information about their daughter's whereabouts to come forward.

"Virginia is a sweet girl who wouldn't wander off on her own. We're beside ourselves with worry," said Elliot McKinley. "We plead with everyone to please help us search for her."

"Mr. Stratford, where are you?" Phillip's voice interrupts.

Sweat begins to bead on my skin, but I don't move. I *need* to finish.

Virginia is described as having brown hair and beautiful light-colored eyes and was last seen wearing a light blue coat and a pink backpack.

Local law enforcement has launched an investigation and is coordinating search efforts in the surrounding area, the article continues.

Footsteps approach the kitchen, and I quickly snatch the binder, slipping out the back sliding door. What am I doing? This is ridiculous. For the second time, I'm running from Phillip. I dart to the side of the house, and I can hear him behind me, opening the glass door to follow.

"Mr. Stratford, please—son, you don't have the right to read that!" he calls out.

It's a public newspaper. I have every right.

The screech of tires pulling up into the driveway alerts me that Meg has arrived. I race around the side of the house toward the front. Her bewildered expression as I sprint toward her with the open binder makes me realize how crazy I must look. I reach out to pull on the door handle and realize it's locked as papers fly out of the binder. Then I hear Mrs. Grant's front door open.

"Mr. Stratford, that does not belong to you!"

I ignore him, and Meg finally unlocks the car.

"What in the hell are you doing?" she asks.

Phillip waves his hands in protest.

"Megan!" Phillip pleads. "Please don't drive off."

"Don't listen to him, Meg," I say. "Drive! Punch it!"

"What did you do?"

"I will tell you! Just drive!"

She curses and slams on the gas.

"What is going on, Mark?"

"It's Mrs. Grant. She hired Phillip as a therapist and as a private investigator!"

"Ok, so why were you running from him?"

I spend the drive back home frantically bringing my sister up to speed on the revelations about Mrs. Grant and her disgusting husband.

"That poor woman," she says. "What is in that binder?"

"They know what happened to her sister, Virginia," I say. "Phillip said they found her. But right when Mrs. Grant was about to tell me, she went into some sort of strange mental state."

"What triggered it?" Meg asks.

"It's related to what Phillip was describing about repressed and suppressed memories. I guess her brain experienced so much trauma after Virginia went missing, that it tried to protect her by blocking out what happened."

"Oh my God. So, she witnessed what happened to her little sister?"

"That's what I think. But Phillip kept insisting she take a break and that it might take years before she'd be able to tell me."

"So, what happened to her is in that binder?"

"It's all the information about Phillip's investigation and some of his notes during her therapy sessions."

"Mark, you can't read that!"

"I know. I'm not going to look at that part. I just want to read the newspapers he found from when Virginia first went missing."

"Yeah, I mean, I guess that's public information," Meg says.

"My thoughts exactly."

"Well, what are you waiting for? Read it to me."

I start from the beginning and finally reach the part where I left off.

Friends and neighbors have started organizing search parties, distributing flyers, and canvassing the neighborhoods in hopes of finding any clues about the missing girl.

"We're all praying for her safe return," said a family friend. "This is a tight-knit community, and we'll do everything we can to bring her home."

Anyone with information is urged to contact the Medford Police Department. The McKinley family expresses their deepest gratitude for the community's support during this difficult time.

"So, they never found her?" Meg asks as I finish the article.

"That's the crazy part. Phillip said they just did. And right when Mrs. Grant was about to tell me where Virginia is, she lost touch with reality. Phillip took her upstairs, and that's when I looked. I couldn't finish in time before he came back downstairs."

I dig through the rest of the papers, mostly documentation of Phillip's measures. Then I find another newspaper article, dated May 7, 1969.

Tragedy Strikes Again: Hit-and-Run Claims Lives of Grieving Parents

The Medford community is reeling after Elliot and Marybeth McKinley, parents of missing 12-year-old Virginia Rose McKinley, were killed in a hit-and-run car accident Tuesday night.

Authorities say the couple's vehicle was struck by a speeding car as they were traveling home. The driver reportedly fled the scene moments after the collision. Police are investigating and have urged witnesses to come forward with any information.

The McKinleys were widely known for their tireless search for their daughter, Virginia, who disappeared on Jan. 2, 1967. Their deaths have left the community heartbroken.

Unanswered questions surrounding Virginia's disappearance compound the grief for many in Medford. Residents have held out hope for closure in her case, which remains unsolved.

"Oh my God! That poor lady. So, she lost her sister and her parents all in that short time. No wonder she blocked it out," says Meg.

"It doesn't make sense. There's nothing here about Virginia's whereabouts."

Abandoning any moral objections, I rifle through every piece of paper, scanning them one by one.

Still, nothing about Virginia's whereabouts, and no mention of Frank Garland. That information must have been on the papers that fell out.

"Mark, you have to stop fixating on these cases," Meg says. "It's not healthy. You need to start getting over it."

"I will once I know what happened to Virginia. Do you think they found her tombstone or something? Is that what Phillip meant? Did he tell you anything when he took you back to your car this morning?"

"No. We talked about you. The only thing he mentioned was that he's a therapist."

"Wait, so you already knew that?"

"Yeah, so?"

"So, why didn't you tell me?"

"How could I? I called you at least a dozen times last night, but your phone was dead; it would go straight to voicemail."

A sudden shift in air pressure inside the car triggers something in my brain, and I finally remember what has been nagging me.

"Shoot! Meg, the drugs at the Lil' Cup. We need to grab

them. I forgot to tell Gio about that."

That's why I kept feeling like I was forgetting something. *No*, there's more. There has to be. I just need a second to think.

"How could you forget that?" Meg asks.

"It was hard keeping everything straight in my head. I feel like there's even more that I'm forgetting."

"What are we going to do with them?" Meg asks, ignoring the last thing I said.

She's never been as paranoid as me.

"What do you think?" I respond. "I'm going to flush them down the toilet!"

She looks at me with wide eyes. "That's at least $500 worth!"

"So! What do you want to do?"

"We could sell it?" she mutters under her breath, knowing it's an absurd suggestion.

"You're joking. We're already working tirelessly to get off the hook for Liz's murder. Do you really think drawing more attention to ourselves is a good idea?"

She doesn't respond but presses down on the gas to get us to the shop faster. The thought dawns on me as to why she threw the garbage away earlier.

"Did you throw away some of your product in the trash can at the Lil' Cup?"

"I had dropped some, so yeah. I scooped it up and tossed it in there."

She wasn't helping me out when she took out the trash; she was covering up her addiction. And what's with her carelessness—especially with something so expensive and illegal?

"It was that left!" I shout as she speeds past the street leading to the Lil' Cup.

She spins the car around in a flash, and I fall into her, realizing I never buckled up. She aggressively pulls into the back of the building and slams the car into park.

"Go and take care of it. Oh, and while you're at it, flush my wallet too."

"It's the only option, Meg," I reply softly. "Listen, I'm going to be there for you—more than I have been. When I saw Mrs. Grant space out, it made me realize how hard it must have been for you when I did the same last night. I should have also been more present these last five years. Maybe I could've—"

"Stop," she interrupts. "I don't need your pity. It was my choice to get involved with all of this. There's nothing you could've done."

I wish I could believe that. It would ease the guilt I feel for yet another person.

"Ok. I'll be right back."

I head to the ancient back door and pull the key from the lockbox. I spin the numbers for the four-digit code. One. Nine. Six. Seven. The lock clicks open, and the silver key clangs as it falls onto the ground. It's the master key. There's a smaller key on the ring too, but I've never used it. I don't even know what it's for.

Sliding it into the lock, I give the door a hard shove, releasing the deadbolt. As I step inside, the door slams behind me because of the weak hinge.

My phone vibrates. Pulling it out, I see the caller ID: *Grimaldis' Office*.

"Hello?" I answer.

"Hey, Kid. Your old pal Gio here," he says casually.

"Yeah, I know. How's it going?"

"I was calling to inform you that everything is taken care of. The sensitive information has been deleted. Oh, and one more thing. Remember when I told you to walk me through everything that happened? Well, you forgot to mention the camera."

"Camera? There weren't any cameras."

"Kid, if I say there was a camera, it's because there was a friggin' camera. The doorbell, moron."

Suddenly, the warning bells trying to alert me ring loudly in my consciousness. *The doorbell camera.* How could I forget?

I freeze and start chewing on the inside of my lip. Blood seeps out, its release slightly calming. I head to the kitchen and spit the blood into the sink. The taste of metal remains in my mouth, along with a new wound.

"Hello, are you there?" says Gio.

"Yes, I am. But I never even used that doorbell. I knocked."

"Are you dense? It's motion activated. The video would have started the moment you pulled up to the house. You got lucky, though," he says, laughing to himself. "The naïve always do. That's why they never learn."

How could I have possibly gotten lucky?

"Hold on, I'm getting another call. Hang tight," he says as the familiar waiting music plays.

I step onto the main shop floor, squinting as the setting sun makes it harder to see. I switch on a light, which illuminates only the coffee bar. I need just enough light to see the bathroom door, but I don't want to signal to customers that we're open.

The waiting music stops abruptly, and the call disconnects.

I open the bathroom door and flip on the light. Lifting the heavy lid on top of the toilet, I find nothing but water and the basic mechanisms that make it flush.

I'm about to set the lid back down and call Meg in to help me look when something catches my eye—a bag taped beneath the lid. Rolling my eyes, I pull it off, and make sure there's no more. I open the bag and dump the powder into the toilet bowl, watching it dissolve. I flush and observe as it swirls away, feeling like the whirlwind of a night is finally coming to an end. With this last major issue taken care of, our tracks should be covered now.

I wonder how Gio's guys managed to hack into Liz's video camera and phone. Flushing the toilet again, I dismiss the thought. I don't care. It's done, and that's all that matters.

At the sink, I scrub my hands with warm water and rinse out the bag. I wonder what they did with my car. Did they take it back to the Grimaldis' office?

Grabbing some paper towels, I dry my hands, ready to leave when I hear the familiar muffled chime of the front door, followed by the sound of footsteps steadily moving through the Lil' Cup.

CHAPTER 46

6:17 PM

I immediately turn off the light and text Meg to move the car.

I'm stuck in the bathroom, I add.

lol, she responds.

I'm serious!

You're stuck somewhere again?

The cruel realization hits me.

I'm glad I warned her because whoever's here is going through the kitchen toward the back door.

My phone has been vibrating with Gio's calls.

Then a text message appears from an unknown number: *Answer the damn phone!* It must be from Gio's cell phone.

I want to. Trust me. But I can't right now, I reply.

I don't want to tell him where I am; he doesn't need to know about the drugs. It's probably for the best that I forgot to mention it earlier—it was easy enough to handle on my own, no hacking or espionage required.

I check my phone and see that I've been stuck here for twenty minutes, hiding from an unknown person. Is it Mr. Grant? A burglar? How much longer will I have to wait?

I hear mumbling, heavy grunts, and what almost sounds like wood being split by an axe. What is happening out there? If they really do have an axe, I'm a goner.

The movement stops. For about three minutes, there's complete silence. The door hasn't chimed, so I know they're still here.

I read Meg's text: *I'm parked across the street out front.*

Do you see who's inside? I text back.

It's dark. No lights on. Want me to look through the glass? she replies.

No. Too dangerous.

I could sprint toward the front and try to outrun whoever's out there. But what if they have a gun? Another twenty minutes pass in silence as I wait with my ear pressed against the door. The time nears 7:00 p.m.

I take a deep breath and slowly open the door.

The shop is almost completely enveloped in darkness. The light I had turned on over the bar is off. But there's a warm glow coming from somewhere, along with the sound of crackling.

I quietly inch out further and peek my head around the corner. The fireplace casts a soft glow across the back corner where the couches sit. The scent of burning wood is soothing, yet the tension inside me refuses to dissipate. My senses battle for control—my eyes and ears urge caution, while my nose tells me that it's safe.

A figure sits on one of the couches, with something in his hand and on his lap. I squeeze my eyes shut, then reopen them, straining to identify him. I stifle a gasp as the older man comes into focus.

CHAPTER 47

7:00 PM

I observe Mr. Grant's aged, worn-out face as he sits with his eyes closed, holding some kind of bourbon on the brink of spilling. His face bears a permanent frown.

I could easily escape through the front door in time. But something about the way he looks makes me freeze. With the stories I heard about him just hours ago, I should hate him. I thought I would have to restrain myself the next time I saw him so that I wouldn't lash out. Yet, here he is, and part of me feels pity for him.

"I bought this years ago when Marge and I toured this distillery in Kentucky," Mr. Grant said to me once, his hands slowly pulling out the bottle from beneath the counter—a secret stash behind a trapdoor.

"I doubt this is your first drink, son, but let's make your first drink as a twenty-one-year-old man a memorable one, shall we?"

He brought out two specialty crystal glasses, designed specifically for this beverage. As he poured from his decanter, the liquid cascaded gracefully like a golden stream, its hue illuminated mesmerizingly by the light.

"Salud," he said, handing me my glass.

I took a large sip, exposing my ignorance about strong alcohol. The liquid burned on its way down my throat, its harshness reminiscent of Mr. Grant when I first met him.

"You need to take small sips. Focus not on the taste, but on the warmth. Focus on the texture and its smooth qualities. Find the depth behind the alcohol. Picture the flavors all melting together as they're marinated in a barrel, soaking in all the aromas over months and years."

Lost in his description, I was suddenly eager for another sip. This time, the deeper, smoky notes and the silky texture overpowered the basic taste of alcohol.

That's how it was with Mr. Grant over the years. Initially, I saw an overbearing, angry, obnoxious man. Although those qualities didn't go away, over time, I became more focused on the depth beneath his tough exterior. I thought that deep down, I might find qualities that made him an honorable man. Mrs. Grant must have experienced this too.

Her words echo in my mind: "He felt like a whirlpool I couldn't escape. I wanted to break free, but he always sucked me back in."

No, *I* won't get sucked in. I'm leaving. I walk slowly and quietly toward the front door, knowing that the moment I open it, the chime will be triggered, forcing me to sprint out. Not that Mr. Grant could catch up anyway. A loud, sudden snore makes me stop in my tracks. I turn toward the elderly man nervously sipping his bourbon from a half-full glass. He looks at the metal box in his hand, then leans his head back on the couch. From his upside-down vantage point, he notices me.

"Mark, my boy. Is that you?"

I freeze, hoping my stillness will make me invisible.

"Where did you come from?" he asks, now changing his position to get a clearer look.

"I . . . I had to, um, use the bathroom, and this was the closest one I could think of," is the only excuse I can come up with.

"Come join me. I just opened a new bottle for this special occasion."

"What occasion is that?" I ask, feeling myself being sucked in as I walk toward him.

"Mark, I've lived a long and successful life," he says, slurring some of his words. "Every occasion is one to celebrate."

I wonder how many glasses he's had while I was stuck in the bathroom.

"What's that?" I ask, pointing to the box in his hand that now appears larger than I originally thought.

As I approach him, I notice wood scattered around the couches and fireplace, evidence of a violently torn-up wall. Cautionary warnings go off in my mind as I take in the scene: a drunk man holding an unknown box he retrieved from behind a ripped wall. If he was desperate enough to harm his own beloved shop, there's no telling what he might do to me.

"I said sit down!" he now orders, his strong, overpowering words echoing through the shop.

I flinch and do as he says. I'm sitting on the leather couch, which is surprisingly comfortable. The warmth from the fireplace has softened the leather, allowing it to mold perfectly to my back as I lean into it.

"Sorry for the demand. It's been a hell of a twenty-four hours," he says, pouring himself more of the drink.

He has no idea what a bad twenty-four hours looks like. I'm certain his night hasn't been worse than mine.

"Never get married, and if you do, promise me it won't be to some ungrateful piece of trash like the old lady I'm stuck with," he says, laughing as he stares into the distance.

His words bite, and any pity I felt for him evaporates. If my glimpse into their personal life has left me stressed, I can't fathom what Mrs. Grant has endured. But even when she spoke about Mr. Grant's—no, Edwin's—secrets, lies, and true nature, she still talked about him with respect. I, however, refuse to call him Mr. Grant anymore; he doesn't deserve the respect.

"What's in the box?" I ask.

"None of your concern!"

I'm now determined to help Mrs. Grant put this monster away for good. If we can't expose him for all the abuse he's inflicted on Mrs. Grant, then I will help uncover other crimes he's no doubt committed. There must be some secrets buried in that box for him to have hidden it in the wall.

But why did he light the fireplace?

"You're going to burn whatever's in there, aren't you?" I

ask, rising from the couch.

He stands unsteadily, then pushes me back down.

"Give me the key!" he demands, holding out his hand.

"What key?" I ask.

Why would I have the key to a box that I'm seeing for the first time?

"Mark, I want you to have something," he says, moving toward the gap in the wall, which is large enough to step through.

I don't move, debating whether I should leave. The promise of learning more, however, makes me want to stay. I text Meg and tell her to call the cops if I don't come out in twenty minutes.

After what seems like an eternity, he finally comes out, carrying a large rectangular object, wrapped in packing paper.

"For you," he says, handing me the object. "One last parting gift before I leave."

Leave? Where to?

As I unwrap it, I discover a painting—unlike anything I've ever seen before. The imagery is disturbing and undeniably dark, with a color palette of deep blacks, muted browns, and cold greys, similar to the painting I noticed the first day I ever stepped into the Lil' Cup. My eyes immediately gravitate to a little girl, standing hesitatingly as she looks up at a larger figure. The horizon is covered with dark storm clouds looming over a desolate wasteland.

If the setting were different, I might have assumed the man beside the girl was a father figure. But he isn't. The fear in the girl's expression makes that clear. She isn't holding his hand, but he's pulling her toward an unknown space. It's far too disquieting for my taste. Why would he give this to me?

"What is this?" I ask, not hiding my dislike.

"You don't know? I'm surprised someone I hold in such esteem couldn't figure out who's behind all the paintings in the shop."

"Mrs. Grant?" I respond with unrestrained shock.

"Pretty talented, that woman. I was always so supportive of her work. I never liked any of them myself. Too dark and disturbing. Yet, I supported her. That's just who I am."

I hate this man. In all his arrogance, he sees himself as the world's greatest husband.

"Why would you hide it if you were so supportive?"

"Because this painting, her first one, proved that she's a liar. The way she portrays the little girl is erroneous."

"Who is the little girl?" I demand.

"Give me the key to the box and I'll show you," he says, downing the rest of his drink.

If he wasn't plastered before, he will be now.

"I don't know what key you're talking about."

"I'm done playing games with you. How did you get in here?"

"The back door. Why?"

"What key did you use?"

"The one from the—" I start, then realize that I put the key in my pocket after I opened the door.

I reach into my pocket and feel the small bronze key attached to the larger silver one.

"This opens that box?" I ask.

"Yes. Was that so hard? Hand it over!" he demands.

The mystery of what lies in that box consumes me as I weigh the possibilities. What if it contains a gun? Or a knife? Liz had wanted me to follow her into the kitchen to get the key to the handcuffs, but that only led to her cutting my arm with a knife.

But what if the box contains answers? What if evidence that could help Mrs. Grant lies just within reach? I owe it to her—after all she's done for me—to find out.

I reach into my pocket and hand him the key.

CHAPTER 48

7:20 PM

The warm glow of the fireplace is all that illuminates the Lil' Cup as I wait eagerly for Edwin to open this box.

"Mark, can I get a little help here?" he says.

My phone vibrates, and I figure it must be Meg or Gio. How long has it been now?

I take the box and slip the key into the tiny lock the same way I did with the handcuffs that locked me to Liz. I twist it slowly, and a satisfying click follows as the lid pops open.

"Ok, hand it over."

I hesitate for a second, wanting to see what lies underneath the metal. He said he would show it to me. But I can't trust him. Can I run out of here with the box? As I deliberate my options, I hear another click. I slowly look up, and my panicked gaze meets the barrel of a small revolver.

"I won't ask again," he says, pointing the weapon with unwavering steadiness.

How is his hand so stable despite the amount of alcohol that must be in his system?

I raise my hands as he snatches the box from my lap.

"That's the smart boy I know. I'm going to show you what's in here. Have a little trust and faith."

His audacity shows me how detached this man is about how he comes across. How can I trust someone who points a gun in my face? How could anyone? Yet, that is what this narcissistic psychopath expects.

He opens the box with the hand that isn't pointing the weapon at me.

"Can I trust you not to do anything stupid?"

I nod my head and force a smile.

"Good."

He lowers the gun and stares at the now open box. Then he pulls out papers of various sizes.

"You're the only person on earth that will know what I'm about to show you."

He hands me an ancient-looking newspaper article. I scan it for the date and my eyes land on *January 2, 1967*. Then my heart sinks when I spot the city: *Medford*. It's the same article that Phillip had in his binder.

I look at him, and he just pours himself another drink.

"What is this?" I ask, my voice suddenly shaky.

"It's how Marge and I met," he says with a disturbing smile.

I look at the familiar article.

The community of Medford remains on high alert following the mysterious disappearance of 12-year-old Virginia Rose McKinley. Last seen at her middle school at 3 p.m. on January 2, Virginia vanished shortly after classes ended for the day.

My hands shake uncontrollably now.

"What in the hell is this?"

"I'm sure Marge has mentioned her sister to you before" he says in a mocking tone.

"Yeah! What does that have to do with this? Why do you have this?" I ask, holding it purposefully high and in his face.

"I keep records of everything. Look at the next paper."

It's a list of names. I read them under my breath.

"Tim Lancaster. Donald Smith. Frank—"

I look up at the man sitting in front of me.

"Garland."

My shaking continues irrepressibly like an excited puppy. But it's not excitement, only pure, undeniable fear.

"Well, keep reading!" he commands.

"Harrison Blackford. Edwin Grant."

My heart pounds in my chest and in my ears. A tremendous pressure grows behind my eyes, and my head splits in pain. Dread encompasses my whole being. Edwin looks confused, no doubt because of my reaction to the name Frank Garland.

"Who are these people?"

He falls into a long, contemplative silence.

Then he finally speaks. "My dearest boy. They are me."

CHAPTER 49

7:30 PM

I've never been afraid of Edwin. Intimidated, yes—but never truly scared. Until now. The gut-wrenching, demoralizing terror that I now experience is unlike anything I've ever felt. But the person sitting in front of me is no longer Edwin. He's Virginia Rose's kidnapper.

But how could that be? Does Mrs. Grant know?

Despite the horror inside of me, I need to play the fool.

"What do you mean?"

"I mean, I was these men at one point in time. They were me. I've had to move around so much, run so often, that I had to make these."

He hands me a stack of IDs, each one bearing a different name, a different life.

"Frank Garland was the first, and at the time, the only name I thought I would need."

If he truly is Frank Garland, that means he's the top suspect in Virginia Rose's disappearance. He was the substitute teacher! Did he really kidnap her? Did he do it to get with Mrs. Grant? Did she agree only if he let Virginia go? Regardless, I'm sitting beside a monster of unknown proportions.

"I had to run from my parents. They were awful, Mark. Abusive drug addicts. I was practically raised in a cult. I had to come up with a fake name so they couldn't track me down."

If that's true, where did he get such a massive inheritance from?

"I started to teach at the local school, and that's when I met Marge. A poor child, neglected by her parents too. I took her in and started to mentor her."

My mind races. If 1967 was the year Virginia Rose went missing at twelve, Marge would have been at least a senior in high school. But Frank Garland was a middle school teacher.

"It says in the paper that you taught middle school. Marge would have been older than that," I say, with absolute bewilderment.

"That's right. If what that crazy woman told you was true."

"What did you do with her sister? Mrs. Grant's sister!" I finally demand.

"Oh yes, Mrs. Grant's sister," he says, once again in that unbearably condescending tone. "You still can't see it, can you?"

God, I hate this man! I loathe him more than anyone or anything. I hate him more than my mother's ALS.

"See what?" I yell.

"My wife is mentally ill, son. Her name is not even Margarine. She made that up years ago. Look. This was her name on our wedding day."

He hands me another paper, but my vision has become too blurry to see clearly now. Anger is radiating from me. I close my eyes and take some deep breaths to control myself, recalling Phillip's exercises with Mrs. Grant. I lift the marriage certificate higher than I need to, dated 1973. The names read:

"E. M. Grant and V. R. McKinley."

I drop the paper and the dizziness returns. I want to puke.

"You . . . No . . . You married Virginia Rose McKinley after you kidnapped her?" I ask, horrified.

"Yes," he says smiling, "Margarine is Virginia Rose McKinley."

CHAPTER 50

Unknown

I don't know how much time passes. My phone's constant vibrating is the only thing that keeps me from slipping into another hallucination. But even my darkest delusion would be better than this.

"You're a monster!" I finally say.

"No, her parents were the monsters. They were so fixated on having another child that they abandoned Virginia. We were the same. I bonded with her. I helped to give her the support she needed at that tender age. I only wished somebody had done for me what I did for that little girl."

"You had no right!"

"I had every right, damn it!" he yells, and I can smell the alcohol on his breath.

"I saved Virginia!"

"You abused her!"

"No, I would never. I treated her like a child and raised her like my own. She was like a friend to me until she was much older and graduated."

"Her parents loved her. Did you even read this paper?" I ask, slamming it on the table, "Look at what they did to try to find her!"

"It was all for appearances. They didn't care, just like my parents didn't care."

"You hid these from her, didn't you? She never knew how much her parents loved her."

"She came to me, Mark. All I did was listen. I wasn't going to lie to her and tell her that her parents loved her when they didn't."

"You were projecting your awful parents onto them. She was a confused little girl, and you took advantage of that. You've taken advantage of her your entire marriage."

"No! No! Shut up! You don't have a damn clue! You're a stupid kid. How dare you tell me what I did and didn't do? She chose to leave with me. She chose to marry me. I never forced her. I gave everything I had to give. We have had a wonderful life. We traveled the world. I never denied her anything."

"You denied her the truth!" I yell.

I can see that any reasoning with this man is futile. He's insane. I can't fathom why Mrs. Grant—no, Virginia—didn't leave him when she was older.

Then realization hits me suddenly, like when a light bulb screws on, completely connecting to power. She had nothing to go back to. Her parents had died, and she had no independence.

"I gave her freedom!" yells Edwin.

"You imprisoned her! You took everything from her. Her innocence! Her independence! Her family! Her life! Why do you think she made up the stories about Virginia? She couldn't bear what had happened to her, so she created a distorted reality to cope."

"No! You're lying! You don't have any damn idea. You stupid, incompetent kid."

He says this, but I can tell the words are breaking through the clouded facade he's created to justify his decisions.

"And then you cheat on her, time and time again. And you make her think she deserves it!"

"No! Shut up! You don't know what you're talking about. She forced me to be with those other women. The crazy woman couldn't give me offspring. I was only trying to have a child to keep my family legacy alive."

"You tell yourself whatever you need to. I know you're an adulterous snake who kidnapped a little girl and did unspeakable things to her. You're going to rot forever in a prison cell, and no one's going to remember your family name, whatever it is."

He shakes his head uncontrollably.

"No! No! I will have a son! You will see."

He slaps his face repeatedly. I move back from the scene unfolding before me.

His life is unraveling like an old cassette tape. He stands up suddenly and snatches all the papers.

"No, don't!" I yell out, reaching toward the pile.

But it's too late. The fireplace eats the papers in an instant.

"There. It's done. That was all the evidence there ever was."

I want to cry. I want to pull my hair out. How did I let that happen?

"How could you?" I ask.

"I'm always one step ahead. How do you think I made it this far in life?"

I play out the act of defeat, savoring every second of him imagining he's getting away—until he raises a revolver to my face.

"You are the only remaining evidence. Sorry you got dragged into this mess. You can thank your beloved Mrs. Grant for this," he says, clicking off the safety.

"You already lost," I say, with a lot of confidence for someone with a gun to my face.

"I will never lose. Can't you see that? I will have a son. I will leave this place with my new family. Virginia will be left with nothing."

"I wouldn't be so sure," I say. "You've been so focused on yourself that you forgot to notice something."

I point to the top of the fireplace, where a hidden camera is quietly recording.

He jumps to his feet, snatching it. "What is this?" he demands, turning it over.

"Don't feel too bad, Edwin. I never noticed them either. I guess we're both one step behind Virginia Rose McKinley. She's already won. You were never a match for her."

He suddenly looks defeated as the realization dawns—he's

just confessed to his crimes on camera. My satisfaction grows alongside his humiliation.

"It's over," I say. "You're going to prison and Virginia will be free."

"No. It can't end this way. I saved her. I protected her. I loved her. No! No! No!"

He paces frantically and starts sobbing.

"You have to help me, Mark," he pleads. "You have to help me. I'm not a bad man. You see that, right? I gave her everything. I want to see my child."

"What child?"

He must be losing his mind after years of keeping up this facade. He bends down to my feet and begs. But his pathetic desperation morphs into hostility and rage.

"Where are the recordings? Tell me damn it!" he demands pointing the gun at me again.

I don't give him a response. He doesn't deserve one.

"I'm not going to prison for this," he says. "I didn't do anything wrong!"

I brace myself, thinking he's going to pull the trigger. His next vile act on this earth will be murder, completing the trifecta of his sins. Hopeless people are capable of anything. At least I will die knowing the truth. My last act will be saving someone. I can take solace in this.

But to my greatest surprise, he doesn't. Instead, he presses the gun to his temple.

"Tell Virginia I'll see her in hell."

Then, a single, deafening gunshot fills the air.

CHAPTER 51

Unknown

I'm lying next to Esther as we stare into each other's eyes. My stab wound doesn't exist, and there's no deadly wound imprinted on her skull.

"I love you, Mark Stratford," she says. "I cannot wait to spend the rest of my life with you."

"I love you. I'm so sorry I told you we couldn't leave this place. We will. I promise. I spoke with my mom, and she—"

Her finger presses against my lips, silencing my words. She pulls me in for a kiss—a long, overdue kiss. I close my eyes and savor this moment of pure bliss. At last, we're going to leave Slidell. And I'm finally going to give her the life she deserves.

Suddenly, my lips are ice cold, and I open my eyes to find Esther no longer beside me. I'm alone on the floor.

"Mark, you need to get up. You've been lying there for hours now. Stop being so dramatic," Meg's voice fills the room.

I roll over to see her walking down the hall from her bedroom.

"Seriously dude, this is pathetic. You're not the only guy in high school to get his heart broken."

"Where . . . Where is . . . Esther?"

"I'm assuming she's long gone by now. She said she was leaving, right?"

A familiar ringtone makes me turn away from Meg and toward the sound. My cell phone sits on the living room coffee table. I look back to where Meg was, and she's no longer there.

I hurry to check my phone. A beautiful girl stares back at me—a picture I took of Esther reading her favorite book under a lone bald cypress tree outside of school.

"Hello, Esther. Where are you, baby? I need to talk to you. I have great news!"

"Mark! Is that you? I need..."

Her voice, filled with panic and terror, trails off.

"Esther! Esther! Where are you? I'm heading there now! Tell me where you are, love!"

The phone disappears from my hand. Esther is now waiting for me by the front door.

"Are you coming, silly? The bags are in the car."

She's wearing the red dress. Her hair falls beautifully past her shoulders.

"I'm sorry. I hadn't noticed you started crying again," she says, walking over and drying my eyes.

"I... I was just talking to you on my phone," I say as I feel the warmth of her palm on my cheek.

"I know. I called to tell you I was coming over. That was over an hour ago. Did you say goodbye to your dad and sister?"

My mom! Where is she?

"Not yet!" I say, running over to my parents' bedroom.

I instantly feel like I'm trudging through quicksand as I walk through her doorway. She's lying in her bed with oxygen tubes in her mouth and nose.

As I slowly approach, I notice her eyes, wide-open and staring back at me. She's as strong and unafraid as ever. She recognizes me.

"Mom! Can you hear me? Mom!"

She blinks twice as her answer.

"Mom. I can't leave you. I can't. I want to be by your side until..."

My words fade, and my throat closes shut as I swallow the tears. If she's going to be strong for me, I'll be strong for her.

She begins shaking vehemently.

"Mom, calm down! Relax! I'm right here!" I say, trying to calm her.

She spits out the tube from her mouth and sits straight up. "Mark, why are you still here? Go! Be with Esther. Free her from this hell!"

I stumble back at her words, and I observe her skin turning to a sickly yellow, then a ghostly pale. She falls back, and her arm drops open. The sound of my phone ringing fills the room. I look over to find it in my mom's limp hand. Esther, reading her book under that cypress tree, looks back at me.

"Esther! Where are you?"

"Mark. Is it really you?"

"Yes, baby! Yes! It's me! Tell me where you are!"

"I'm not sure. I see . . . I see . . . lights. Yeah, there are lights. They're so bright, Mark. They are moving . . . moving . . ."

Her voice fades.

"Moving? What do you mean? Sweetie, please focus! Don't look at them. Focus on my words. Where are you?"

I race out of the room where my dead mother lies. I run outside, and the rain instantly drenches my clothes, while thunder booms in the sky above.

I hop into my car, and the rain suddenly stops.

"What did your family say?"

I look over to the passenger seat to once again find Esther in that stunning red dress.

"You're here? I was just talking to you on the . . ." I look down, expecting to feel my phone in my hand. But nothing is there.

"Mark, I know this is a lot for you. Want me to drive?"

"You don't know how to drive manual," I say, numbly, gazing straight ahead at my childhood home.

"I know. You promised to teach me. Now is a better time than any to learn. It will be a nice, terrifying distraction," she says, giggling.

I glance at her as I shift the car into reverse.

"We will have plenty of time for that. Where are we heading?"

"Anywhere far away from here!" she says while smiling gracefully out the window.

"Oregon?" I suggest, looking at the now empty seat.

The rain is once again beating against the windshield, as the windshield wipers battle against it.

My car drives down the flooding streets as my high beams reflect off the wet asphalt into my eyes. My phone is against my ear, and I can hear Esther crying out in pain.

"Where were you heading last?" I ask, trying to stay calm for my girl.

The gut-wrenching fear is making me want to burst.

"I was driving over the train tracks."

"Which part?" I demand, "Hurry, Esther!"

"Mark, I see the lights again."

"No, baby! Don't look at them. Stay with me. Hear my voice!"

The sky is clear as I drive on the highway, passing a sign that indicates we're leaving Louisiana.

"I'm starving!" Esther says, rubbing her stomach the way she always does when she's hungry.

"Where are you, sweetie? Tell me, please!" I beg.

"I've always been here—with you. What are you talking about?"

"No. This isn't real. This is what I wish had happened if I didn't have that conversation with you at school."

"What conversation? I don't know what you're talking about."

"I broke your heart."

"No, you didn't silly. You would never."

"I did. I told you that I couldn't leave with you. I couldn't tell you why. I couldn't tell you that my mother is dying and that I needed to be with her."

"Mark . . . your mother just passed away." She gently takes my arm and leans her head on my shoulder.

"No, I was just talking to her. I was just . . ."

"Mark, you were saying goodbye to your sister and dad."

This isn't how I envisioned things would have been. It's what I imagined would happen after my mom died.

"How? When did she die?"

"Two weeks ago. We had the funeral this last weekend," she says slowly. "Don't you remember?"

"No, I don't remember any . . ." I look at the rain hitting the windshield.

"Mark. I see a train coming!" Esther shouts in her unbearably weak voice on the phone.

"Get out of the car! Now! Esther, please, baby. Listen to me. Get out of the car!"

"I . . . I . . . can't. My leg—it's pinned."

"I'm almost there. How far off is the train?"

"I love you, Mark. I love you so much. Please find me. Come find me! You will save me!"

"I will! I'm almost there."

Esther goes silent.

"Esther! Esther! Dammit! Answer me, sweetie! Esther!"

I turn the corner as my wheels slide to find traction on the wet street. Finally, I see the tracks straight ahead. I slam on the gas.

"I see you, Esth! I see you! Answer me, baby!"

The car comes to a halt at the end of the road. I hop out and run toward the tracks as the deafening horn of the train warns me against it. I rush to Esther's car and open the driver's side door. Nothing. I pop the trunk open. She's not there either. The passenger door swings open and I spot her phone on the seat. I pick it up and see that it's still connected to the call.

The lights of the train reflect now through the windshield as I dive out of the way. The two vehicles collide, and I turn to see the explosion. Fire engulfs me, but I stand, unharmed, staring into the brilliant orange flames.

The fireplace crackles back at me as it consumes the items Edwin had tossed into the flames. His lifeless body lies on the floor beside me.

The glass entrance door shatters as police officers rush into the Lil' Cup.

CHAPTER 52

Three Days Later.

2:30 PM

"Mr. Stratford, we know this has been a lot for you," says a detective standing across from me in the interrogation room while the other one leans against the door. "But please try to focus. What did Edwin Grant say his plan was, exactly?"

"It's all there in the recordings," I reply.

The one with a thick coffee-stained grey mustache sits down in front of me now. He doesn't speak immediately, allowing the silence to stretch on.

"We're going to need your full statement for our records," he finally says. "We've already received statements from your sister, Phillip Barns, and Margarine Grant. We would love to give you more time, but the circumstances don't allow for that luxury."

"Her name is Virginia Rose Mckinley," I say in protest.

"Yes, we're still looking into that, Mark. However, her legal last name is currently Grant, so for these interviews, we will use that name."

"I went to the Lil' Cup to use the restroom," I start. "Then I heard the front door open and came out to see Edwin siting by the fireplace. I tried to leave, but he called me over. The wall was torn out and he was holding a box. He held me at gunpoint and told me to open it with the key attached to the main key for the shop. I did. That's when he told me everything. He had all these fake names, and he admitted to taking Virginia Rose from her parents because she was unhappy and lonely. He said she went willingly, but I don't believe him. Throughout their marriage, he abused her and cheated on her. That's everything I know."

THE CUSTOMERS

"Thank you, Mark. I know that was difficult for you," the detective says. "There's one more thing that we need to ask. Are you aware of Edwin Grants involvement with Elizabeth Hill?"

The name makes the back of my head hurt. Sympathy pains, perhaps, for the deadly blow to her head.

"Yes. Only because of what Phillip and Virginia told me."

"There's a video recording we've uncovered from her house. Are you up for seeing it?"

It turns out that an anonymous person noticed Liz's disappearance, which led to a welfare check in under forty-eight hours

"I guess so," I say, not knowing what to expect.

The detectives bring in an older TV and press play. At first, there's nothing but a blue screen. As the footage begins, my skin prickles and the hairs on my arms stand. But I manage to hide any facial expressions fairly well, at least I think so. All I see is the burnt orange square—a car that no longer evokes sympathy, but pure revulsion.

"Do you know what this is?" the detective asks.

"I have no idea," I respond.

"This is footage we received from Liz's doorbell camera."

The time shows that it is 7:00 p.m. on the same night Meg and I were there. The screen flashes bright white as headlights appear, and I expect to see my junky car, even though the timing is off. Instead, another familiar vehicle pulls into the gravel driveway: Mr. Grants' car from the early nineties.

I lean forward, suddenly very interested, and the detectives notice.

"You recognize the car?"

"Yes, it looks like . . ."

I don't finish as the answer becomes apparent. Edwin now frantically knocks on the front door. I hear it open, and the audio comes into ear.

Liz opens the door. "Edwin, what are you doing here?"

"I'm going to leave town. I want you and the baby to come with me. Pack up now!"

The baby? I lean in closer, straining to hear.

"I'm not going anywhere with you. We agreed that I would be your surrogate. After that, no interactions. That was the plan."

"The plan changed. Now get your damn things."

"I can't just leave. I have a life here."

"Your life is about to change."

"No, you can't come in."

"What in the hell did you do?" demands Edwin.

The conversation trails off as Edwin goes inside and the door slams.

"That's it?" I ask.

"For the audio portion," the detective replies.

He takes the remote and fast-forwards about thirty minutes into the footage. Edwin races out of the house, his hands raised up like something is on them. He hops in his car and drives away, swerving onto the grass. I realize now that it was him who drove through the fence and busted the sprinklers. I take a long swallow, bracing myself for the next part of the footage—the inevitable clip of Meg and me arriving at the house. Instead, the screen shows a notification that the battery is dying.

The detective fast-forwards to the end, and the screen goes black—only fifteen minutes before Meg and I would have arrived.

"Is that all?" I ask, still unsure if I could have possibly gotten that fortunate.

That must have been what Gio meant when he said I got lucky. I had told Gio the time I was there. Whoever he sent must have seen that the recording ended at 7:36 p.m. Did his goons even see that Edwin, Gio's own client, went to the house right before me?

"Yes, that's it. The autopsy on Liz puts her time of death anywhere between 7:00 and 9:00 p.m. As far as we know, Edwin Grant was the last person to see Liz alive. He's the top suspect for her murder."

I want to leap for joy when he says this. Could it really be this simple? Maybe I finally got dealt a good hand.

"The motive is airtight. Elizabeth Hill was pregnant at the time of her death. She was only four weeks along."

My heart aches at the realization that the innocent child died along with Liz. At the same time, I'm relieved that no offspring from that awful, tyrannical, narcissistic, evil man will ever be in this world. Shame over that thought makes me sick. The child deserved its own chance at life. Maybe he wouldn't have been like Edwin.

"Edwin Grant offered Elizabeth Hill and her husband $10,000 to bear his unborn child. There is just one problem—we can't seem to locate Mike Hill."

This revelation takes me back to the van that Liz had mentioned. I'm sure the detectives searched the house more thoroughly than Meg and me ever could. Where in the heck could Mike's body be?

"When we searched Edwin Grant's car, we found blood everywhere. It was not a match as belonging to Elizabeth Hill. We're left to assume it belonged to Mike Hill. This is an ongoing theory, but at this time, he is still a missing person."

Did Edwin help Liz kill her husband? Did they hide him together in the van? It would have been possible. The van was out of view from the doorbell camera. I want to ask about the sticky substance in the van, but for obvious reasons, cannot. They also haven't explained who I let connect to the Wi-Fi. Some mysteries might have to remain just that.

"So, am I free to go?"

"Yes. Your statement and the footage from inside the Lil' Cup confirm your innocence. Thank you for cooperating with us. You're free to go."

I walk out of the room as the other detective nods in respect and opens the door.

Meg, Phillip, and Virginia wait for me in the lobby of the police station. Meg is the first to embrace me.

"Are you ok?"

I gaze straight ahead at Virginia, then look over at Phillip.

I reach out to shake his hand.

"Mr. Barns, I would love to get your help with something."

"Anything! But I must insist you call me Phillip."

I smile and walk over to Virginia, momentarily seeing the little girl I had imagined so many times. I hug her and when I pull away, the older version looks back at me.

CHAPTER 53

4:00 PM

"So, what can I help you with, Mark?"

This once-mysterious man has now become my closest confidant. We sit at the diner, in the usual booth with the worn-out table, where Esther's initials are inscribed alongside mine.

My finger follows the outline of the crooked heart that Esther had carved out.

"Do you know why I brought you here?" I ask.

"I'm going to guess that this is a special place for you."

"You're right," I say, with less emotion in my voice than in our previous conversations.

I feel numb after my last hallucination. And Phillip is the only one who can help me uncover its meaning.

"I think I have repressed memories."

"What makes you think that?" he asks, pulling out a notebook.

"I keep blacking out and having these weird dreams. Only, I'm not asleep. I think they are memories, but I know some of them are completely distorted realities."

"Close your eyes, Mark."

I slowly close my eyes, savoring the satisfaction and relief that comes with rest. The lack of sleep these past several days has been agonizing.

"Walk me through a hallucination—if you're up for it."

"The first one came when I was . . ." I pause, realizing I can't tell him where I was for most of them, "when I was with my sister at home. I was suddenly enveloped by a familiar scene. I was opening the coffee shop. A customer, a homeless customer, was waiting outside early. I opened the shop for him and let the old man in. This all really happened once. I know it was a memory. But then, when I was serving him hot water, he turned into Edwin and stabbed me. Obviously, that never happened."

"I see. And was this before or after you found out about Edwin?"

"Before. I was completely unaware of who he truly was when I imagined this."

"Do you think maybe your subconscious was signaling you about his nature, perhaps warning you?"

"That must have been it." The realization is so obvious now.

"I had a few more," I continue. "There was one where I was waiting in my room after breaking up with my girlfriend."

"How long ago was this?"

"Shortly after the first one. Maybe a couple of hours."

"Were you in the same place in your house?"

"No," I respond, not wanting to lie to him. "This next one happened right after Edwin—well, you know. I was looking out at a raging rainstorm from my bedroom window, a memory from five years ago. There was tremendous flooding. Suddenly my mom came in and told me that my girlfriend was waiting out in the living room for me. She told me that we should get back together and leave Slidell. This never happened. I broke up with her to stay and take care of my dying mother. When I went out to see her, she turned into my sister and stabbed me. Then she changed back to Esther."

"Esther is your girlfriend's name?"

"Yes. Why?"

"What's her last name?" Phillip asks, glancing up from his notebook.

"Foster."

An expression of shock breaks through his composure.

"What?" I ask.

"Oh, nothing. It's a pretty name."

I know there's something more, but I continue.

"This hallucination turned into one with different layers.

The first one—I was imagining what would have happened if I had left Slidell with Esther five years ago. In the second one, I was imagining what would happen when I left with her after my mom—" I pause, not wanting to say it.

"Go on, I'm following," Phillip says.

"While I was imagining all of them, Esther kept disappearing, and I kept talking to her on the phone. She was trapped somewhere, and I could tell she was hurt. I asked her where she was, and she told me she was stuck on the train tracks with her leg pinned in her car. I drove there as fast as I could. The whole time, she told me she was seeing moving lights. A train was going to hit her. She told me to find her and save her. She then stopped talking. I got to the tracks and saw the train about to hit the car, but I had time to search it before it did. Esther was nowhere to be found. The train hit her car, and the next thing I knew, I was being taken by the Slidell Police. What do you think it means?"

"What do you think it means, Mark?"

"I don't know. It might mean I'm afraid of losing Esther. My plan is still to leave Slidell with her, but I'm afraid she won't want to."

"Mark, you had mentioned that in these hallucinations, some things you see are real memories, and others are not. Do you think that phone call with Esther was real or fake?"

"Fake. That never happened."

"When I was helping Mrs. Grant uncover her past, she had a lot of memories that felt so real, but she was also convinced they were fake."

"Are you trying to tell me that you think that conversation was real?"

"Do you think it was real?" he asks again.

"No! It's not. Esther works for the Grimaldi brothers and comes into the Lil' Cup."

"She does? How often?"

"All the time."

"Mark, when was the last time you saw Esther?"

His tone mirrors the one Meg used when she asked the same question outside of Mike and Liz's shed.

"Why?"

"I'm only curious. That's all," he says, trying to calm me.

"I saw her about a week ago. Mrs. Grant, I mean, Virginia, would have the recordings. I will show you!"

"I'm actually connected to her cameras, so I can go back and watch. But we can do that another time."

"No. I want to prove it to you now."

"Mark, please, that won't be good for you."

"Why? I want to see her."

"Please listen to me, Mark."

"No. I want to watch the recording now. Show me."

Lyda comes to our table when she hears the commotion.

"Mark. Is that you? I didn't hear you come in. I'm sorry. What can I get for you two?"

"Hey Lyda, sorry for yelling. This is Phillip."

"How do you do, honey?" she says, looking him up and down.

"It's nice to meet you, ma'am."

"Ma'am? Who are you calling ma'am? That makes me sound old. Call me Lyda, sugar."

I cannot deal with the fact that Lyda might be flirting with my therapist right now.

"Oh, Ok. Nice to meet you, Lyda."

"Mark, I haven't seen you in here for nearly five years now. How are you dealing?"

"I'm fine. Thanks. I would love a slice of your pie, and one for Phillip too."

"It's pumpkin today," she says.

"No berry?"

"No, sweeties. We haven't had berry pie since you and that precious girl stopped coming."

"Can I get a cup of coffee?" Phillip interrupts.

I can tell he's trying to change the subject away from Esther.

THE CUSTOMERS

"Right away!" Lyda says, heading back through the swinging kitchen doors.

"Phillip, what's going on?"

"Mark, trust me. Be patient and trust me."

"No. I've been patient my entire freaking life. And look where it's gotten me. Tell me now!" I demand, strong emotions now rising from deep within.

He pulls out his phone.

"What time did you say she came in on Friday?"

"First thing. Probably between 7:00 and 7:05 a.m."

I can tell he's watching the recording.

"Come on, show me," I beg.

"Mark, I need you to be prepared. Can you take some deep breaths with me?"

I do the breathing exercises with him, feeling absolutely bored and eager at the same time.

"Ok, here you go." He finally hands me his phone.

I watch myself making drip coffee behind the counter at the Lil' Cup. I start pulling espresso shots, and the door opens. A girl walks in with dark pants, an oversized blazer, and a perfect blonde ponytail. I exhale as the love of my life walks closer to the register.

"Two hot double shot lattes, please," she says. "And a decaf iced latte for me. Thanks, Mark!"

"Would you like some caramel?" I ask.

"Sounds perfect! Thanks."

The voice makes me swallow. My throat dries, and I gasp for oxygen. I look up at Phillip, and he can see my panic.

"Breathe, Mark. Breathe! Lyda, can we get some water?"

I look back down at the recording, and it's no longer Esther I see.

"What is this?" I shout at Phillip!

The girl I was on the phone with days ago looks back at me. Marcy is the one who places the order in the video.

It's always been Marcy.

CHAPTER 54

Unknown

I'm in Esther's uninhabited room. The full moon shines through as I slowly turn in circles, taking in the emptiness. I hear a knock on the door and quickly go to open it. I'm hoping to see Esther on the other side, but a flat, grey wall stares back at me.

"I'm here for you, Mark," says a voice from the corner of the room. I turn to find nothing there. The room is void, and there is nowhere to hide.

"Who said that?"

"Behind you," says the voice in the back of my head.

I turn to once again find nothing. I run over to the window and try to slide it open. It won't budge. I start hitting it with all my might.

I notice a figure standing outside by the line of trees at the edge of the Fosters' backyard. The figure stands still, watching me. I can't make out details of the face. It begins running towards me, like it's running from something, getting closer and closer until finally it comes crashing through the window as I duck for cover.

My hands cover my head as glass shatters around me.

I rise to my feet, wanting to leap out the window. But as I do, a hand grabs onto my leg and yanks me back onto the ground.

"What are you?" I ask, looking down.

"Mark. It's me—Silas."

The bright white illuminates his grotesque features.

"Can you help me?" he asks.

Unlike the first time we met, I'm overcome with pity for

Silas, and I pull his head into my chest. He looks up at me with his wide-set, innocent eyes, welled up with tears. He isn't the man I saw in the shed but a young boy.

"What happened to you?" I ask, the sorrow in my heart growing.

"I was shot."

I raise my hand away from his back, and the crimson on my palm gleams in the moonlight.

"Tell my mom . . . tell my mom that I'm sorry she had me," he says, then falls limp in my arms.

I shake him in a desperate but feeble attempt to bring him back. I sob audibly and uncontrollably as I hold the lifeless boy in my arms. Trembling, I lean over him, struggling to stop my sobs. Then, a hand gently brushes the back of my head. I look up, but it's no longer him.

"Mark, my love. Don't cry," Esther says softly.

"Esther, where are you?"

"I told you already. You have to come find me."

"You were stuck in the car. When I came, you were gone. How did you get out?"

"I know you will find me," she says as she closes her eyes.

Her face is not limp and it's not lifeless like my mother's. She's simply sleeping while she waits.

CHAPTER 55

Unknown

My eyes open, and I look at the old popcorn ceiling in our living room. As I sit up from the couch, I see Meg in the kitchen, stirring something in a pot on the stove.

"Megan? Is it really you?"

"Oh my god! You're awake!" she says, running over to embrace me.

"Are you ok?"

"Yeah. What happened?" I ask, reaching for my forehead.

"You had another panic attack and blacked out at that diner you used to go to. Phillip brought you home."

The memories are all coming back to me now, even the ones I wish wouldn't. I long for the distorted realities I've created over the last few years to be the truth.

"Meg, is Esther . . ." I cannot finish.

My sister closes her eyes and slowly nods. I pull her close, my tears soaking her shoulder.

"How could I forget she was dead?"

She gently pushes me away.

"Mark, we don't know if she's dead or not. They never found her body when they searched."

"Esther's abandoned car by the tracks? It was real?"

"How did you forget? Yeah. It was real. You were there and called the cops to report her abandoned vehicle."

How can I not recollect any of this? My only memory from that night is from my hallucination which is clouded with false information.

"When you told me that you went to Liz's to buy that food truck and leave with Esther, I froze. I didn't know what to think.

It was like you were back in time and, frankly, it freaked me out! I decided to wait until we were with Dad."

"You should have told me!"

"And have what happened to you at the diner happen at," she looks around and whispers, "Liz's?"

Unfortunately, that entire night was real. I stay silent.

"How long have you thought Esther was working for the Grimaldis?"

I ponder the question and a cold realization washes over me.

"I can't remember," I say, pulling her into a hug.

"It's ok. It happens to a lot of people. Phillip told me that when he dropped you off. He also told me that if you woke up remembering what happened, I should show you this."

She holds up a newspaper, dated October 18, 2019.

"It was printed the day after Esther went missing," she says.

I snatch it out of her hand and start reading.

Search for Missing Teen Intensifies

Authorities are urgently searching for 18-year-old Esther Foster following the discovery of her abandoned vehicle.

Surveillance footage shows a girl, believed to be Foster, being led away by hooded figures into the nearby tree line. An initial investigation revealed no victims in the vicinity.

Mark Stratford, a local resident and Foster's boyfriend, says he rushed to the scene to assist Foster after receiving a phone call from her in need of aid. Upon arriving, he found the area eerily deserted, with no signs of Foster.

Local authorities have intensified their efforts, launching a city-wide search and urging the community to provide any information. "We encourage anyone who may have seen anything unusual or has information about Esther Foster's whereabouts to come forward," said a spokesperson for the investigation.

The community remains hopeful that Foster will be found and that those responsible for her disappearance will be brought to justice.

I look up at Meg.

"She's still missing?"

"Investigators are still looking. Those detectives you talked to are assigned to the case. I told them not to mention anything about Esther. They didn't, right?"

"No, I started to remember after Edwin shot himself. I had another hallucination. Turns out most of it were my memories from the night Esther went missing. Phillip had said traumatic events can unlock repressed memories."

"Do you remember that we've never stopped looking for her?"

"Everything else is still a haze. Was there a train crash?"

"No, why?"

Another distortion of the truth.

"All I remember is that she's gone. I still can't recall any other conversations I might have had with people about Esther. I don't even remember talking to authorities."

"If you need to ask questions, ask. I will try to help you remember," she says. "This is why we would listen to those crime podcasts, so that we could learn from other missing person cases."

"See, that's what I'm talking about. I remember the podcasts, but I have no memory of why we listened to them."

A sudden realization comes to me, along with hope, though restrained.

"Meg. I think I might already have all the information I need to find where Esther is buried somewhere in my mind. I just need to unlock it."

EPILOGUE

Six Months Later
7:10 AM

I gaze through spotless glass windows. Gentle rays of sun glisten on the wet asphalt as if drying the tears from the night before. This is my view as I open the new coffee shop in Slidell—The Rosewood. What a perfect name.

This is Virginia's coffee shop, one she could open because Edwin's will left everything—his entire fortune—to Virginia, a detail he apparently forgot to amend before exiting this world forever.

The Rosewood is bustling with laughter and joy. Customers form a line inside. Virginia smiles as she energetically pulls espresso shots and pours coffee art into cups. A few customers observe and admire her paintings, which adorn every wall, as they sip on a variety of creative beverages. Gage, a regular, orders his dry cappuccino and heads to his usual spot by the window.

Stacks of cups sit by the register as I scribble orders and names on them, passing each one to Virginia. She pulls shots at twenty-nine seconds; the extended extraction draws out the coffee bean's deeper notes.

It seems the deeper notes from her past have been surfacing too. Sharing the same afflictions with someone who has become like a grandmother to me, has been lifesaving. She doesn't talk about Edwin. She talks about herself. Memories of who she was before him. I shared with her how he left this world, but the details of his final words will burn with his past in the fire.

She hasn't watched the footage from that night. I hope

she never does. I don't want him to do anymore harm from the grave.

My mother still cannot speak. I don't think she ever will again. Yet, she speaks with me in my memories.

My father has become more disconnected, lost in the inevitability of her death.

I know now that my mother wants me to move forward. She doesn't want me to be trapped by her bedside. She wants me to find Esther.

I also know that I must compartmentalize my discoveries about Esther. I can't slip in and out of delusions at every new revelation.

Memories surface daily, flickering like radio static—fragments of voices, songs, and commercials that fade in and out. Occasionally, something will trigger a memory. The hardest part is knowing what is real.

One thing I do know—I *will* find Esther. I have a strong lead from someone who is set to arrive at the shop any minute now.

Meanwhile, Virginia eagerly covered my debt to the Grimaldis—$15,436.34 for three hours of "consultation." The itemized bill included a $247 charge for "fuel services," apparently for transporting me from Oil Well Road to their office.

"Mark, why do you owe them that much money? What possibly would make you turn to them?" she had asked months ago.

I told her that they helped with my mom's hospital bills. The desperation I showed covered up the truth very well.

I couldn't tell her the real reason, but lying to a woman who has been deceived her entire life felt crushing.

I haven't had the displeasure of hearing from Gio since Virginia paid my debt. I think he enjoyed the irony of getting paid by his former client's wife. It gave him some sort of power trip.

His last words ring eerily in my head: "My boy, you may

think you escaped having to work for me. But I know you. I know who you are and what you're capable of. Mr. Grant was right about you. Our paths will cross again. Until then, Salute!"

What was Edwin right about? I may never know, and I'm certain that's for the best.

I head over to Gage and serve his rosetta art cappuccino.

"Mark, did you hear about the sudden rise of people moving to Slidell?" he asks, holding up his newspaper, sporting his usual cap.

"Does it say why?" I ask, trying to read over his shoulder.

"They say it has to do with the disturbing stories of missing people like Esther Foster and Mike Hill."

Their names jab at me, and a familiar, haunting sensation —one I haven't felt in months—settles in my body.

"I would have never agreed to meet Liz if I knew she was married," he adds.

"You were meeting Liz?" I ask, stunned.

"Yeah, I thought you knew. I was actually supposed to meet her the day she was murdered. She never showed, so I left. I tried reaching out and heard nothing, so I had the police check on her."

I think back to that full, untouched cup of lemon ginger tea that he had left behind. It was Liz's.

"You were the one who called for the welfare check?"

"Yeah, and I'm glad I did. I knew she wouldn't just stand me up. She was a gracious woman. I still feel awful about what happened," he says, taking the first sip of his cappuccino.

The door chimes, and in walks the customer I've been waiting for all morning.

"Hey Marcy," I say, as she elegantly walks to the table without saying anything.

"Oh, this is Gage," I add awkwardly.

"Nice to meet you," she says quickly to Gage before turning back to me. "We should go."

"Yah, lemme clock out. Did you get the . . ."

"Yeah, I have it right here," she says, holding up a manilla folder as her pearl nails dance across it. "Can you make me a caramel iced decaf latte before we leave?"

I nod, stepping behind Virginia to make the drink. I smile as the last bit of caramel drains from the bottle.

Marcy managed to retrieve some files about Brandon Foster. Whatever happened in New Orleans that drove the Fosters to move here—that's where I need to start.

Marcy and I slip through the back door, which glides with ease.

I climb into the front seat of Meg's car, and Marcy slides in the back.

"Who is this?" Meg asks.

"Meg, this is Marcy," I say, slightly embarrassed by Meg's lack of manners. "She's risking a lot to help us out."

"I want to help you find that poor girl," she says. "I know the Grimaldis have something to do with it."

"Ok, ok. Well, where are we going?" Meg says.

Marcy looks through the open folder. "There's someone in New Orleans that may be able to help us learn a little more about Esther."

"Give me an address," Meg demands.

"555 . . ." Marcy starts while Meg and I exchange a look, both feeling the same dread at the familiar number.

"6, Oak Street," she finishes.

We smirk, and Meg shifts the car in reverse.

Virginia Rose McKinley was finally freed from her prison. Liz was freed in a more devastating way—like the Onionhead, or like my mother will be soon. I'm helping my sister to free herself from addictions. And I'm being helped to free myself from my delusions and hallucinations.

I'm finally facing reality.

I need to free Esther. The question is—from *what*?

This single thought frightens me to my very core.

THE CUSTOMERS

ABOUT THE AUTHOR

Talon Hawke Ellus

I am deeply grateful to all who embarked on this journey with me through the pages of my book. The process of writing has been a rewarding exploration of the emotional and psychological facets of human nature. Delving into a diverse range of perspectives has enriched my understanding of the variety of personalities, thoughts,
and feelings that shape our lives.

I would like to extend my heartfelt thanks to my supportive family and friends who stood by me throughout this endeavor.

A very special word of love and praise goes to my unwavering and loving wife, Kim, whose encouragement and belief in me have been my greatest inspiration.

Thank you for sharing in this adventure.

Made in the USA
Las Vegas, NV
01 April 2025

20420873R00169